P9-DTQ-480

YOU
TRULY
ASSUMED

YOU TRULY ASSUMED

LAILA SABREEN

WITHDRAWN

inkyard
PRESS

ISBN-13: 978-1-335-41865-4

You Truly Assumed

This edition published by arrangement with Harlequin Books S.A.

For questions and comments about the quality of this book, please contact us at CustomerService@Harlequin.com.

Inkyard Press
22 Adelaide St. West, 41st Floor
Toronto, Ontario M5H 4E3, Canada
www.InkyardPress.com

Printed in U.S.A.

Recycling programs
for this product may
not exist in your area.

For Mom and our weekly library trips that started it all.

This book contains instances of racism, anti-Muslim hate, and online harassment.

SABRIYA

ABINGTON, VIRGINIA

Whoever told me perfection was overrated straight up lied. All the mistakes I may have already made run through my head as I lower my leg from *arabesque* and transition into a *plié* and my outstretched arms curve into first position. The faint, barely there taps of my pointe shoes grazing across the polished wood floors gets swept up in the music as I set my feet to prepare for the turning combination. My eyes meet Morgan's as I glance at myself in the mirror, and she winks at me quickly. I fight the urge to grin back, trying not to do anything extra to stick out more.

The tempo rises, and I tear my eyes from the mirror and fix them on a fold in the curtain to use to spot. My eyes slide back toward the mirror, seeking my reflection, but the music crescendos before I can pick apart the imperfections staring back at me. I push off the floor and *pirouette*, locating the specific fold in the black curtain with each revolution. A sense of power settles in my bones, and I revel in the feeling of control that determines my movements.

The music dips, and the last notes of the song vibrate through the studio as we hold our final positions. My breathing slows, and the Allah charm on my necklace rises and falls in time with my heartbeats. I fight to hold back my grin. My technique may not have been 100 percent perfect, but I still bodied the combo. If I dance like this at the audition tomorrow, I'll be set.

"That's all for today, dancers," my teacher says, turning off the music. "Morgan, you're still sticking out in the ending." Her eyes dart between Morgan and me as realization slowly dawns on her. "Actually, my apologies, that comment is for Sabriya. Morgan, you're blending in better, but I need you and Sabriya to listen more closely to the music so that you both can get the timing."

I fight not to let my posture loosen, giving a little nod. I glance at Morgan, and she gives me a barely perceptible shrug. Even though it's not surprising anymore that our teacher mixes us up when giving feedback, it still stings. Whenever I think I did well enough to avoid critique, whatever comments Morgan gets dished usually end up on my plate and vice versa.

"Don't forget, auditions for the preprofessional summer intensive are tomorrow!"

"Thank you!" the class says, and I force my wobbly legs to curtsy without collapsing. Then I grab onto the ballet barre and lean down to untie my pointe shoe ribbons and put on my slides before leaving the studio. I flop down on one of the benches in the hallway that connects the studios, grab my water bottle, and chug it. Once my heart doesn't feel like it's still dancing, I take off my wrap-skirt and use it to wipe away the sweat beading on my forehead.

Some of the parents give me sympathetic smiles, but I brush them off. I don't need sympathy. Being this exhausted means I'm doing something right. Even if being one of only two Black dancers in the advanced pointe class means I'm always doing something wrong. I riffle through my dance bag, looking for my MetroCard and a pair of sweats to slip on over my leotard and tights. Aliyah, one of the handful of Black dancers in the pre-pointe class, waves at me from where she sits, and I grin and wave back. Aliyah's been at the studio basically as long as me, so I've seen her grow up here. I like to think that Morgan and I do our best to look out for the younger Black dancers because, as classes advance, the environment becomes more hostile and there are fewer and fewer of us.

"Bri, you were on fire today," Morgan says, sitting down on the bench next to me.

"I could've been better. My turnout could've been greater in that turning combo and—"

Morgan gives me a look, and I roll my eyes, her message clear. Besides being my best friend, Morgan is one of the reasons that I've made it this far in ballet. Being the only Black ballerinas in our level, we always have each other's backs.

"Sure, okay, maybe it was good. But if I want to convince the judges at the audition tomorrow that I deserve a spot in the ABT intensive, I need to be great."

The summer intensive at the American Ballet Theatre has been the dream that I've been trying to reach all year. Last summer, I wasn't selected, so this year I need to prove myself at the audition. I have to.

"And you're going to be great," Morgan says as she throws her sweatpants on over her tights. "But the intensive isn't the end-all be-all. It's summer break now, so you should chill a bit, moe. You've been working hard in and out of the studio all year."

"I'm jih chill," I say.

Even though the beginning of June brings the end of the school year, it also brings the chance to spend more time at the studio. If I'm going to nail the audition and get selected for the ABT intensive, I can't let up just because I'm now homework free. Morgan's right that the intensive isn't the end-all be-all, but if I'm going to pursue ballet professionally, then this is a step I need to take now. It'll help me figure out whether pursuing ballet professionally is something I should even consider, and with college apps coming up I need to figure out by the end of the summer if I want to prioritize ballet and go to a college with a strong dance program.

Someone sits down next to me, and I glance at them out of the corner of my eye before shifting closer to Morgan.

"Besides," I say. "We both know that you'll be here just as much as me during the break."

Everyone seems to stop talking as soon as I finish the sentence, and I look over my shoulder at the rest of the people in the sitting area. I bite the inside of my cheek, unsure if I was too loud. Even though there are a few Black littles and their parents in the sitting area, Morgan and I definitely stick out.

"Can someone please turn on the news?" one of the parents asks the person behind the sign-in desk where the TV is mounted on the wall. Their voice rises at the end of the question, panic tinging their words, and they stand up and move closer to the blank-screen TV as the receptionist tries to find the remote. I look at Morgan, and she raises her eyebrows, silently telling me that she doesn't know what their deal is either.

"Does that TV even work?" Morgan asks me. "I've only seen it on once in all my years of dancing here."

"I honestly thought it was just for decoration." I glance around the studio again, feeling unsettled by the silence. "Why is everyone on their phones?"

"I don't know. The studio is never this quiet." Morgan pulls out her phone, all of the messages that she missed during rehearsal popping up. "Holy—"

A scream interrupts her, filling the studio, and I jerk at the suddenness. The shrill tone makes me tense up, and the person next to me breaks into sobs. One of the dancers in my class, Lydia, runs down the hallway yelling that someone bombed a metro station near the Capitol. Her voice sounds far away, and her words bounce off the shield of disbelief that surrounds me.

I chuckle. "She's joking, right, Morgan?"

Morgan doesn't say anything, her body rigid, and Lydia turns to look at me, her eyes wide. Lydia shakes her head, and I freeze, reality swallowing my laughs.

"You're joking," I repeat in a whisper. "Right?"

Lydia says something, but a burst of frenzied chatter drowns out her words. My heart starts to race as I search through my bag to find my phone so that I can call Dad. Parents grab their children's hands, and people run up and down the hallway, colliding and ricocheting off one another. I can make out someone saying, "It's going to be okay. It's going to be okay. It's going to be okay," and I cling to that as I grab my phone.

"What happened?" a voice behind me shouts.

"There was a terrorist attack at Union Station," Lydia answers.

No no no no no. That's Mom's stop.

Morgan nudges me and holds out her phone, and my stomach lurches as she scrolls through the hashtag that's sprung up, the words hitting me like a bucket of ice-cold water. My hands start to shake, and I take a deep breath, trying not to drown in the rising tide of claustrophobia. I need to find Dad. My phone buzzes every time I type in the wrong password, the numbers spinning together. Goose bumps replace the perspiration on my arms, and a shiver runs through me. One missed call from Dad.

Please pick up. Please pick up. Please, Allah, let him pick up.

"Sabriya?"

"Dad? Where are you? Are you okay?"

"I'm almost at the studio. Everything near the White House and the Capitol is shut down. Constitution Avenue and Independence Avenue are completely blocked off. Stay inside until I tell you to come out, okay?"

"Okay." I pause. "Are we in danger?"

"What did you say, Sabriya? I can't hear you."

"Is the DMV in danger?" I ask over the chaos in the studio.

"I don't know. No one has all the details yet. There's been a bombing, but right now the origins are unconfirmed."

I take a deep breath, forcing out the words. "They haven't said anything about the attacker's religion?"

"Not to my knowledge," Dad says. "Things are still very

much up in the air, and I'm sure more information will be released to the public soon."

I take a deep breath, trying not to throw up. "Right."

"Stay there. Everything is going to be okay."

I hang up, my eyes stinging with tears. People start to leave the studio, speaking in hushed whispers. I wrap my arms around myself and rock back and forth, trying to let the rhythm calm me.

How could this have happened? Why? The questions pinball back and forth, and the tension starts to build into a headache. I curl my fingers into fists and dig my nails into my palms, the pain muting the shakes. I'm safe. Everything's going to be okay. I'm safe. In the furthest corner of my mind, I can see my plans for the summer crumble. They too will be collateral damage of the terrorist attack.

My phone buzzes, and I look down, hoping it's Dad. It's not. It's a news update. I skim the short article, and my stomach drops when I read the name of the person who authorities believe is behind the attack. Hakeem Waters. The first name is a pretty common Arabic name, but that doesn't necessarily mean that they're Muslim. I send a silent plea that they aren't because if it turns out that they are, then the consequences of their actions will be put on Muslims across the country.

I swipe out of the news update and open Twitter, and anger burns my throat as I scroll through the trending hashtag #DCBombing. Besides the suspect's name, no other concrete information has been released, and yet people are already taking opinions as fact, pointing a finger at an entire religion. The Allah charm on my necklace weighs heavily below the hollow of my neck, and I run my finger over the silver like a prayer. "There needs to be a Muslim registry," one comment reads, and I close out of Twitter. I know from experience that reading too many of those comments will make my necklace feel as if it's choking me.

My phone buzzes with a text from Dad, and I grab my bag and turn to Morgan.

"Do you need a ride?" I ask.

She shakes her head. "My ride's right around the corner."

I almost start to say that I'll see her tomorrow, but I nod instead. Who knows the next time we'll have ballet.

The silence grates my ears as I head out of the dance studio. Quiet is the last word I'd ever use to describe Wisconsin Avenue, and even though the studio is half an hour from Union Station, I expected there to be nothing short of full-scale pandemonium. But instead there are just a few police cars, lights on but not making any noise. The air smells like smoke, but the sky is clear and blue, so maybe I'm making that up.

Dad unlocks the car door when he sees me, and I slide into the passenger seat.

"Thanks for picking me up," I say, buckling in.

"As soon as I heard the news, I left work and started making my way over." Dad begins driving. "A lot of the roads were already shut down. I've been trying to call you, but cell service has been down. But I'm here now and you're safe, and that's all that matters."

I hear Dad's words, but they don't sink in. Instead, they stick to the numbness coating my skin. I close my eyes and pray.

"Are Mom and Nuri okay?"

"Nuri's already at home. She got a ride from a classmate's parent." Dad swallows. "I haven't heard from your mom yet."

"What?!"

"Her school is close to the station, and there have been reports that calls and texts aren't going through right now since so many people are trying to reach their loved ones. But I'm sure she'll text us as soon as she can."

My stomach churns, and I clutch the door handle. "I'm going to throw up."

Dad looks at me, my pain reflected in his eyes. "Need me to pull over?"

I nod, and he swerves over to the side of the road. I fling open the door, a dizzying warmth spreading through me. My stomach clenches, and I cough up water. No food since I made sure not to eat before ballet class. Dad rubs my shoulder as I wipe my mouth and close the car door, my stomach still clenching.

I look out the window, at the buildings and cars that seem to pass by in slow motion instead of streaming together in a blur like they usually do. Everything moves in slo-mo. I feel as if I'm looking down on me, like my body's here but my mind is lagging behind, trying to pick up the pieces.

"I never thought something like this would happen here," I whisper.

Downtown DC has always felt untouchable. Officers with guns line the sidewalk blocks past the White House and the Capitol, and people jog and bike past them all the time without batting an eye. Seeing them on the drive to school every day has become normal since I don't find them as unsettling as I did when I first started going to school and taking dance classes in the city.

Dad takes my hand and I anchor myself to him.

"Your mom is going to come home. We'll get through this."

I look out the window as we turn onto Key Bridge and see the Capitol far in the distance, and it hits me that in my ten years of living in this area I've never once had to think about what would happen if that building fell. The Potomac River is devoid of canoers, which never happens during the spring and summer. Traffic inches along even though Virginia is only a jog across the bridge.

I grab a plastic bag from the glove compartment in case I need it. Nuri occasionally gets migraines and sometimes needs them, but I've never had to use one before. I grasp the plastic bag as traffic crawls, the jolt from the constant starting and stopping shaking my stomach.

Once we cross the bridge, the traffic breaks and Dad hits the gas a little harder. Twenty minutes later, we arrive in Abington. The familiarity of the neighborhood is a welcoming sight, but our street is devoid of the children that usually ride their bikes and play at the small park across the street. Even outside of DC, people seem to be hiding. Dad pulls into our assigned parking spot in front of the row of townhomes, and my shoulders drop as a fraction of tension leaves my body.

"Come on, Dad," I say, grabbing my dance bag and running up to the front steps.

Dad unlocks the front door, and as soon as I push it open, Nuri jumps up from the couch. She runs over and throws her arms around me, the waves of her twist-out brushing against my cheek as her chin rests on top of my head. Even though I'm older than her by two years, Nuri inherited both Dad's and Mom's height, leaving none for me. We've recently started being mistaken for twins, and I'm still salty about that.

"Are you okay?" I ask when she pulls away.

"Yeah, I'm fine," she says, biting the inside of her cheek.

"We're going to be okay, Nuri," I say, hoping I sound more confident than I feel.

I wish I had answers to all of the questions she probably has, but those same questions are running through my head. I go over to the living room and turn on the news. Nuri sits down on the couch, her focus locked on the reporter.

"I'm going to go change real quick, but I'll be right back."

Nuri nods, and I head to the kitchen to get some water. A flash of pink catches my eye, and I go over to the counter where Mom's figurine of Black Jesus and Dad's Quran sit to see the somewhat-cheesy daily motivational note she left Nuri and me for today that says: *It doesn't matter what's been written in your story so far, it's how you fill the remainder of the pages that counts.* I choke out a gasp, my eyes suddenly burning with tears fighting to fall.

Please, Allah. Please let her be okay.

I head upstairs to my room, almost tripping over Nuri's lacrosse stick in the middle of the hallway. I gently kick it into her room before heading into mine. I plug in my phone and turn it facedown. That way, I can hear if Mom calls or texts without getting sucked into doomscrolling. I set my ballet bag next to my desk and look up at the poster of Misty Copeland that hangs above my bed, but it doesn't give me the sense of calm that it usually does.

I pace back and forth across the room, adrenaline and anxiety pushing me forward. Mom has to come home. She just has to. I don't want to have to live in a reality where she doesn't come back. I close my eyes and say another prayer. I didn't realize how much I've taken for granted the privilege of simply being able to come home safely.

I open my planner and stare at it blankly, the items on today's to-do list all blending together. Terrible things happen all the time, but I've never once thought that anyone I loved would ever be affected. I guess I've always thought of my family as being in an untouchable bubble. But I guess I now know that no amount of planning or trying to maintain control can keep anyone, including myself and those I love, untouchable.

I close my planner and put it in my drawer. No amount of planning could've prepared me for this, and for once a detailed to-do list can't help me. My eyes travel across my desk and land on a framed photo of Mom and me that was taken at my first ballet recital. All of the panic and fear that's been suppressed so that Nuri can't see it rises to the surface, and my eyes sting with tears. I press my palms to my eyes, but the tears slip down my cheeks. I heave in gulps of air and try to steady myself against the wave of emotions.

"I've got to be strong for Nuri," I say over and over in my head as I change out of my leotard and tights and throw on a T-shirt and some sweats. Grabbing my phone, I head back downstairs. Dad pulls Nuri and me close as I sit down on the couch next to them. My leg bounces and my thoughts pirouette, but I force myself to focus on the news.

"The police believe that the suspect was an individual

named Hakeem Waters who died at the scene," the newscaster reports.

A faint click of the lock sliding cuts through the newscaster's voice, and Nuri and I jump up. We follow Dad to the front of the house, my heart beating so loud I can hear the blood rushing in my ears. *Please, Allah, let it be her.*

"Mom!" I yell, launching myself at her as she closes the door behind her. "You're home!"

I feel Nuri wrap her arms around us and then Dad, and I pull away a bit when I feel tears sliding down my cheeks. I loosen my arms from around her, but I keep one hand on her arm to remind myself that she's here. And she's safe. And she's breathing.

"I'm okay, girls. Everything's fine. It took the police a while to search my building, but it was necessary. I'm sorry that my calls and texts didn't go through. Cellular service is still spotty. But I'm here and I'm safe."

I take deep breaths, my heartbeat slowly steadying. I curl my fingers into fists, my nails digging into my palms. It's okay. She's okay. I repeat that over and over in my head, trying to get my body to stop shaking.

Mom kisses us each on the forehead. "Why don't we all sleep in the living room together tonight?"

She's here. She's here. She's here.

ZAKAT

LULLWOOD, GEORGIA

There's something magical about the way art transforms chaos without apology. On the canvas, there's no room to put anyone else's wants before my own and there's no one to please but myself. I adjust my grip on the short stick of charcoal, the tips of my fingers stained black. Light classical music floats in the background, filling the art studio with airiness. No one is ever up in this part of the school this late in the afternoon while school is in, and I loosen my shoulders and focus on the strip of charcoal paper. Next week, when afternoon and evening summer classes start up, people will start to stream into the building. But for now, as people celebrate the end of the school year, I have the art studio all to myself.

I take in the silence of the first few days of summer. During the school year, chatter and laughter would be bouncing off the walls. Lullwood Islamic School for Girls is a haven that I've had the privilege of attending since kindergarten. But as a rising senior, it's beginning to dawn on me that staying in a haven for too long can turn it into a bubble.

I turn my easel a bit so that it fits exactly in the circle that marks my spot. During the art class that ran on the weekends during the school year, the art teacher let us trace a circle around the bottom of the legs of the easel and write our name on the smooth floor to mark our spots in order to make sure each individual's view toward an object didn't change during a project. I remember how thrilling it was to write in Sharpie on the floor, to make a mark, even in such a small way. Though the mark will fade once the floors are scrubbed before school restarts.

My phone buzzes, and I jump, causing the charcoal to streak the paper. I wipe my fingers on my jeans, leaving gray smudges on my thighs, and see five missed calls from Mama. Shoot.

"Mama?" I ask, answering.

"Zakat, you need to come to the masjid now," Mama says through the phone.

"Alright. Is everything okay?"

Mama pauses. "I'll tell you when you get here. Please hurry. Love you."

"Love you too, Mama. I'm on my way now."

She hangs up, and I unclip the charcoal paper from the easel and slip it into the tan art portfolio that's inside of my tote bag. I wash my hands, most of the charcoal coming off my fingers, and slide my tote bag over my shoulder. The weirdness of the conversation sticks to me like the residue of the charcoal stick, and I try to shake it off. Mama's one of those people who loves texting and adding the perfect GIF to a message. She only calls me if she's worried or it's an emergency, and I can't imagine what would be so big that she could only say it in person.

I slip my phone into my pocket and sprint down the hall, my feet sinking into the soft blue carpet. Quranic verses are painted in Arabic and translated into English across the walls in metallic colors. Quotes from powerful Muslim women are taped to every classroom door. The hall smells of lemon, and I wave at one of the cleaning staff members.

A gust of warm air ruffles the ends of my hijab as I step outside. Hopping onto my bike, I pedal in the direction of the masjid. The sun shines bright overhead, wispy cotton-candy-pink clouds lining the sky as it slowly sets. I ride down the smooth gravel path that winds through the woods that give the city its name. Thick, tall pine trees line the sides of the path, and I swerve around fallen pine cones. The air smells like a newly lit scented holiday candle. This ride has been committed to memory better than my times tables. I love Lullwood with all my heart; it's helped to mold who I am and shape who I want to be. The town has been a shoulder to cry on and the giver of the best hugs. But I'm excited to graduate and expand my horizons. Still, being able to feel completely safe biking through the Atlanta suburbs as a Black hijabi is something that Lullwood has given me and something that I'll always treasure.

The masjid comes into view, and I skid to a stop. A chain-link fence is wrapped around its perimeter, and it reminds me of the kind of barrier that I've seen at playgrounds. The posts of the fence are connected to portable stands held down with sandbags, which gives me a little relief. If the posts aren't drilled into the ground, then the barrier is probably temporary. The silver fence contrasts against the smooth, marble stone that shines under the sunlight. In all my years living in Lullwood, there's never been a fence around the masjid before. I ride through the open gate that's connected to the front of the fence, and I can't help but wonder why the railing has been put up.

I park my bike and enter through the common door. The masjid used to have two separate entrances, as many masjids do. But a few years ago, high school students told the imam that the two entrances, and the two labels for gender attached to them, didn't allow everyone to come into the masjid as they identified and alienated some Muslims from attending prayers. After the discussion, it was decided that the masjid would only have one common entrance and that a nonlabeled prayer room would also be added inside in addition to the men's and women's prayer rooms. That was one of the many moments when I'd felt so proud of my community.

I walk inside the masjid and pause, taking a moment to appreciate its beauty. The masjid is pretty much my second home. The patterns of the tall archway and the golden accents on the red carpets are as familiar as the woods. I remove my sneakers, place them on the overflowing shoe rack, and start to head over to the common area that leads to the prayer hall, inhaling the familiar warm and sharp scent of incense. I squeeze my way through the crowd, dodging babies and bent elbows. The crowd moves slower this evening, and everyone seems more somber than usual.

"Zakat!" Mama cries out when she sees me in the prayer hall. "I'm so glad you're safe."

I let her pull me into a hug. "Why wouldn't I be, Mama?"

"There was a terrible attack in Washington, DC. Someone blew up a metro station. I know you're here and Washington, DC, seems so far away, but I got worried."

I gasp as my panic spikes and a lump rises in my throat. I force myself to swallow and place a hand on Mama's arm.

"Well, I'm here, Mama. I'm okay."

While I try to calm her down, my thoughts start to spin and my stomach sinks. DC is a ways away from the Atlanta area, and Mama worries easily, but attacks like that bring trouble no matter the distance. Is this somehow connected to the gate that's up?

"Was the terrorist Muslim?" I ask, the sourness of the question stinging my tongue.

Mama's shoulders drop. "America is believing that he is. It's his name."

I nod, unsurprised. My jaw clenches, and my palms start to sweat. Anger makes my heart beat faster, as if it's preparing to outrun some source of danger. This isn't the first time my community has been scathed when the nation is clutching at straws—almost always race and religion—desperate for an answer. It isn't right, but it's so common now I no longer feel sorrow. I only feel anger at the unfairness of it all. When I was little, I used to be hopeful that the world would change. That places with the qualities of Lullwood would become the norm. Now, I'm not sure if that'll ever happen. I'm not even sure if that *can* happen.

"What's the news saying about us?"

"Nothing that hasn't been said before," Mama says. "Why don't you go make wudu. Prayers are going to start soon."

I press a quick kiss to her cheek. "Okay, I'll meet you in the prayer room."

It's okay, Mama, I want to add but I don't. Baba says that after 9/11 and the ensuing rise of Islamophobia, Mama lost some of the brightness that she used to have. When these things happen, it's like a shadow comes out from the closet and hangs over her. But if it's easier for her to pretend like the shadow isn't there, then I'll pretend too.

I head toward the ablution room, the voices around me low and solemn. The masjid usually feels full of warmth and light, but today sadness seems to haunt the spaces where joy usually resides. I can feel its weight pressing into me. Sometimes I wish I could wrap Lullwood in a bunch of Bubble Wrap and hide it from the rest of the world, and sometimes I wish I could pop all of the bubbles and hear the sound echo. Most times I wish for both at once. It's a constant push and pull between wanting to stay protected by the haven that Lullwood provides and wanting to explore what lies beyond it.

The sunlight streams in through the bulletproof windows, and some of the heaviness in my chest loosens as I step into the room. A small fountain sits in the middle of the room, with a small tublike ring around its base. Faucets are attached to the fountain, in front of each seat. Taking a seat at the fountain, I turn on the faucet in front of me and dip my feet into the water.

"Bismillah."

I rub the water over my hands and face, splash water onto my arms and neck, and clean behind my ears. I rinse my mouth out last, and then I slip my socks back on. Even though this is a routine that I've done more times than I can count,

I always try to use the steps as a way of re-centering. Almost like my own version of meditation.

Heading out of the ablution room, I follow everyone down to the prayer hall. Usually everyone's laughing and chatting and gossiping, but today I can only hear a few whispers as I move with everyone. It hurts to see Lullwood without its usual brightness, and I can't help but wonder if everywhere else feels as dull as it feels here in this moment. If other places are hurting, yet preparing for the inevitable, like we are.

I wave quickly at Baba before he enters the men's prayer room. He's easy to spot because he's one of only five Black Muslims in Lullwood, one of them being myself. Because I've grown up here, I've never had to experience living in a place where I'm the religious minority. Most days I don't notice that I'm the only Black student in class because I've always been in the religious majority, and that's what's always been the main source of connection in Lullwood. But sometimes that comes at the expense of erasing or minimizing my Blackness because Black Muslims are often overlooked, not only in Lullwood but also the Ummah.

I congregate with the rest of the teens toward the back of the room, all other female-identifying members in front of us. The comforting feeling of home wraps around me as I lay out my prayer rug.

"Make the rows straight and do not differ, lest your hearts differ," the imam says, beginning the prayer service.

Calmness and peace wash over me, and before I know it, voices begin to float through the room signaling that the prayers are over. I fold up my prayer rug and head out to find Baba and Mama. Unease creeps back in at the relative quiet of the hall, and no one bumps into me and starts to chat like usual. It's like we're all stuck in our own bubbles created by our worries about the aftermath of an action none of us are involved in but we're all connected to because of our faith.

It's terrifying.

I pull my jean jacket tighter around me as I walk through the parking lot over to where Mama and Auntie Sara, a family friend, are talking. I squint, trying to see a few stars among the hazy clouds.

"I know her heart is set on going there, but safety should be the number one—" Auntie Sara pauses as I wrap an arm around Mama.

"Zakat, my darling, how's your summer been going?" Auntie Sara asks.

I give her a warm smile. "Well, we got out a few days ago."

"And you're thinking about college, yes?"

"Yes."

"Well, then I should also tell you what I was about to share with your mother. Safety should be a top priority in any decision, especially one about where you're going to spend the next four years of your life." She pauses. "I know your heart is set on Howard University, but I think you should give Spelman College another chance. My daughter loves it there. You could talk to her about it. I know you're very into art, but I hope you're considering more solid career options as well."

"Thank you, I'll keep it in mind."

I'll keep it mind. I'll keep it in mind. I'll keep it in mind. I've already said those words so much, and I feel like I'm going to be saying them a lot more this summer so I should go ahead and make it the tagline of the next three months. I can't risk disappointing Baba and Mama, not when my only job is to make them proud. Plus, I know we're all worried about the financial aspect of college, and the last thing I want to do is send them into debt. I want nothing more than to make them happy, but I really want to be happy too.

"Ready to go?" Baba asks Mama and me, and we both nod.

"I've already put your bike in the trunk, so don't worry about it."

"Thanks, Baba."

When I was five, Baba purchased a shiny new minivan. I think it was because they planned for me to have siblings, but Mama had a difficult childbirth with me and I don't think she wanted to go through that pain again. I know she loves me, but sometimes I wonder if maybe I slowed down and spent more time with her like I used to when I was little, then maybe the minivan wouldn't feel as big. And maybe I wouldn't feel the pressure to fill up the entire minivan.

"Auntie is right," Mama says, breaking the silence as Baba drives. "I can't stop thinking about the attack and how easily you could've been hurt if you went to college in DC."

I don't say anything because any response I give will only be adding gasoline to an already blazing fire, and Baba and Mama don't deserve to get burned. I look out the windows trying to make out the tops of the trees in the dark.

"Hate and Islamophobia are continually on the rise, Zakat, and yet you want to go to college in the very city that was attacked. It's unwise and unsafe."

"Your mother is right," Baba adds. "Spelman is around the corner, has stellar research and academics, and is very prestigious. If you don't want to go to Spelman, there's still Emory,

Clark Atlanta, or Georgia Tech. There's no need for you to go so far away when there are so many options nearby. And we both agree that while it's great that you are passionate about art, passion doesn't always pay the bills. A more stable and concrete subject, like biology or computer science, should be your main focus. You need to look at the larger picture if you wish to be successful, my dear."

"Yes, exactly. Maybe you should look into engineering like your baba and me. It requires some creativity, so you might like it, and it pays well. Even follow in your parents' footsteps," Mama says.

It's not what I want.

I want Baba and Mama to understand that art is important enough to major in. Hopefully I can go into animation and help put more Black hijabis on the page and on the screen. And sure, a business degree could help me navigate the art industry, but business isn't my passion. I can't get lost in it for hours on end. It doesn't stain my clothes or make me lose my breath. As much as I love both of my parents, they don't understand the joy and frustration of being in the same place for almost eighteen years. I can't stay in Lullwood or the state of Georgia forever. As much as I love it here, I don't want to. I almost know Lullwood better than I know either of them. Better than I know myself.

"I want to go somewhere different."

I'm tired of existing. I want to live.

"But different doesn't have to mean unsafe, Zakat."

I roll down the window, letting out some of the hot air trapped in the car. Baba believes turning on the AC, even in the summer, wastes too much gas.

I'm terrified of leaving Lullwood, but I *want* to leave. If I don't, I'll never be able to come back. I'll never be able to see Lullwood from a new perspective. I'll never be able to miss it. If I don't say no to Baba and Mama, if I don't say no to letting their fear keep me in Georgia, then I won't be living for myself. It's two to one, and I've never been the one who tips the scales.

All I have to do is figure out how.

FARAH

INGLETHORNE, CALIFORNIA

The beginning of summer break is a lot like scrambled code. The days blend together like a string of random letters and symbols. But unlike in compsci class, there's no hurry to figure out how to crack it because right now I have bigger things to worry about. Like how my boyfriend is leaving for college at the end of the summer, and I'm pretty sure that means I should break up with him.

The screech of shoes against pavement and the rhythmic dribble of a basketball snap me out of my thoughts, and I look over to see a group of people from the neighborhood playing 4-on-4. A few of them give me nods as I was walk past the block and turn down the street toward the apartment complex. The difference on this street is astounding. Restaurants that have been a part of the community are shuttered, and a parked bulldozer sits at the other end of the street where construction is already underway. South LA has been rapidly gentrifying, and parts of Inglethorne have already been chewed up and spit back out with sleeker high-rises and more expensive boutiques and places to eat.

Mom and some of our neighbors have started worrying that the rent has been slowly going up as a way to force us to leave so that the building can be torn down to make way for something else. The idea of that happening hangs over all of us like June Gloom. I make my way up the steps of the apartment complex and grasp the handles on the paper grocery bag, internally cursing as it tears. My fingers, stained red from the juice that leaked from the carton of strawberries and through the bottom of the bag, stick to the house key as I fumble it into the lock. This is what I get for splurging on strawberries instead of going with apples, which are always cheaper.

The silence hits me as I step into the apartment. Hot stickiness settles on my skin, and I groan, locking the door behind me. Mom must've left for class already. I kick off my shoes and head past the living room and the bedroom that Mom and I share to the kitchen. Once there, I turn on the fans and set the groceries down. As I go into our room to double-check that Mom isn't here, I see piles of folded laundry on my bed that Mom must've done before she left. My side of the room is almost bare besides a poster of the greatest Lakers players on the wall, the college guidebook that's five years out of date, and a few books on programming that I got from the used bookstore. Mom's side of the room is a bit more personable with her nightstand full of my baby photos and photos of us with my grandparents. Two empty frames that have Congrats next to a little graduation cap also sit on her nightstand, and every time I see them my heart warms a little. The room is a bit of a squeeze, but it works for the two of us.

I go to the kitchen, rinse off the strawberries, and pop one into my mouth, savoring the summery sweetness. I unload the rest of the groceries and slide a single-serving pizza into the oven, leaning into the silence. With Mom taking evening classes to finish her college degree, I've gotten used to being on my own. I've even learned to find comfort in having to share space with my thoughts. Still, there's something sad about a pizza that's only meant for one person.

I sit down in one of the white plastic chairs at the table that Mom got at a garage sale a few weeks ago and pull out my laptop. Mom bought it for me during one of those Black Friday sales, and she stood in line for hours to get it. My laptop is definitely one of my most prized possessions. I pull up all of my code, feeling myself get sucked back into the strings of letters and numbers. Since I'm not doing much this summer besides working at the grocery store and hanging out with Riley, my boyfriend, I thought that learning about app design could be cool. My app is focused on partnering local restaurants with food banks to increase food access and move toward greater food equity. Mom and I struggled with being able to afford healthy produce while she was looking for her current job, so it'd be cool to help others who are going through what we did. I'm hoping I'll be able to finish building it by the end of the summer, but I'll see.

My fingers fly across the keyboard, the soothing sound of me tapping the keys filling the silence. I did a summer coding boot camp at the city recreation center last summer, and for the first time ever I felt a spark. The boot camp was something I signed up for completely on a whim, since it was being offered for free and was a good way to fill the time when I wasn't working at the store. I wasn't expecting to like it so much or feel like it may be my thing. This past school year I took AP computer science and an elective on game theory to see if the spark was fleeting, and I really liked both classes. Not only that, but I was good at them. I don't know where the spark is going to take me, but I'm determined to follow it.

The front door slams shut, and I jump up, clutching my laptop to my chest. I look across the hall, and my shoulders drop.

"Mom, what are you doing home? Don't you have class?"

Mom turns on the TV, still in her uniform and slacks. "The professor canceled at the last minute because something bad happened in DC. Maybe another riot? I think it was near the Capitol, but I didn't really read the email past 'canceled' because I wanted to get home."

I get up and go over to the sofa. "I haven't heard about anything happening in DC."

My mouth drops open at the sight on the TV, the footage making the reality of what Mom said actually sink in.

Terrorist Attack in Washington, DC, appears on loop at the bottom of the screen, and my mouth goes dry. Footage from what looks like a train station is playing on the screen. The news anchor explains how DC, and other major cities in the nation, are shutting down to make sure that nothing else is planned. The sirens and rubble look like a scene out of a movie instead of reality, but the news anchor's somber tone makes me realize that this is actually happening.

"When did this happen?" I ask.

Mom grabs the remote that's on the couch between us and

turns up the volume on the TV. "It must've been earlier today. I hope there weren't any casualties."

"Yeah, me too." The oven beeps, and I get up from the couch, forcing myself to look away from the screen. "Do you want me to toss something in the microwave for you?"

"No, no. I'm fine. But there's something that I want to talk to you about after you grab your food."

I give her a questioning look, but she waves me along to the kitchen. Usually I can read Mom like the back of my hand, but it's hard to tell from her tone if what she wants to talk to me about is good or bad. I glance at the scene on the TV again, and all of the yelling sets my nerves a little on edge. It really sucks that the attack happened. I don't know what I'd do if something like that happened out here. I grab my pizza from the oven, slide it onto a plate, and sit back down on the couch.

Mom searches my face, her dark brown eyes mirroring mine. "Tommy called today."

I throw my hands up. "Wow, Mom, you're really the deliverer of bad news today."

Not that her telling me about what happened in DC and her telling me that Tommy called are on the same level, but Tommy calling definitely hits closer to home.

She frowns as she sits across from me on the couch.

"Why have you even been talking to him?"

Tommy was Mom's high school boyfriend, and their relationship ended up with me. Now he lives up in Massachusetts with his wife and stepkids and their daughter. When he moved to the East Coast for college after deferring for a year and then got married a couple of years after he got his degree, it became pretty clear that he had moved on from Inglethorne—and Mom and me as an extension. Birthday cards, money, and occasional visits from him didn't really fix that. Grandpa and Nana stepped in after he left, and Mom and I haven't ever really had a relationship with Tommy's parents. But Mom follows them on Facebook, so I know that they spend time with Tommy's new family, which is another strike against him. Tommy's always been open to having a relationship, and he pays child support, which always goes toward bills. That doesn't erase the fact that he chose to leave though.

"Well, he's been wanting you to come up and visit for a while now, and I think it'd be good for you to take some time away before school starts back up. Plus, next summer is going to be our girls' summer since we'll be celebrating you going off to college, so you'll be busy then. So now is the best time to see him."

Mom and I have been planning our postgraduation trip to New York since the beginning of high school. Both of us have always wanted to go to the Big Apple, so it seemed like a fitting destination for my graduation gift. But I didn't know that planning that trip meant that there was a certain way that I'd have to spend this summer.

My mouth drops open. "You want me to do what?"

"It'll only be for the rest of June. That's just three weeks! I really think it'll be good for you to be somewhere that isn't Inglethorne at least once this year. This will be an opportunity to travel and explore somewhere new."

"This was Tommy's idea, wasn't it? He isn't in a position to make deals with me. Who does he think he is?"

"Well, he's your father for starters, and I really do think

this will be good for you. Next year, you'll be off and away, and it'll make me feel better knowing that there'll be someone who you can turn to who's in Massachusetts."

"I'm not even going to be in Massachusetts for college. Not when I could go to Berkeley or UCLA or UC Davis. I'm going to be in California."

Mom raises an eyebrow. "I'd absolutely love that, but I also did see that you left your college guidebook open on the page for MIT, so you know."

I sigh, knowing she's got me. "Fine, that's a fair point. But this is Riley's last summer before he leaves for Vanderbilt, and I want to spend time with him and figure out whether or not I want to do long-distance."

"Then consider this visit to be a trial run for long-distance! You'll still have July and August to spend as much time together as you want."

I groan, knowing again that she's got a fair point. The idea of viewing the trip as a tester isn't half-bad. I'd much rather stay here and spend the summer with Riley instead of going to visit Tommy. But deep down, I'm not sure Riley and I are cut out for long-distance, and maybe this trip could change my mind.

Mom gives me a small smile. "I want you and Tommy to both to give each other a chance. If you don't like your time there, I won't bring up anything like this again."

"Fine," I say. "I can spend three weeks in a guest room so that we can go to New York next summer without you bothering me about seeing Tommy."

Mom laughs and pulls me into a hug, and I rest my head on her shoulder.

"I'm proud of you, Farah. I really do think this trip will be a good thing." She glances down at her watch. "We'll talk about this more tomorrow. I have to hit the road since I managed to snag an extra shift at the coffee shop. It's until closing, which is probably why I was able to get it, so I won't be home until late. I love you."

"Love you more."

She gives me a small smile, grabs the keys, and leaves. I stuff the rest of my pizza in my mouth and try not to think about how in a couple of days I'll be on a plane to spend time with someone I don't really want to get to know. Though maybe if I go on this trip, then Tommy will finally be out of my hair for good. He can't keep asking me to visit if I already have. I have to text Riley; he's going to get a laugh out of this. And hopefully me texting will take away from the small argument we had yesterday.

My phone rings, and I look down to see Tommy's name flashing across the screen. "You've got to be kidding me."

I tighten my grip around the phone so I don't chuck it across the room and crack the screen. There's no wiggle room in the budget to account for a broken phone. I take a deep breath, mentally preparing myself, before I answer the call.

"Hello," I say.

"Farah! It's so good to hear your voice."

I hope he isn't expecting me to say the same, because then I'd be lying. I know he and Mom stay in contact, but I don't really talk to him besides my birthday, and Christmas since he celebrates. Though to be fair, sometimes he does remember Ramadan and sends me Eidi and gets Mom a present. But that's pretty much the extent of our interactions.

"You're going to love Massachusetts. I live in a town called Kirby that's right outside Boston, and there's a lot to do in the area. I also arranged for you to be able to take a two-week computer science course at the local community college since your mom mentioned that you're interested in the subject. The course will be a good way to have other people to spend time with besides just the family and me. Plus, I've already started getting the guest room ready."

A compsci course? He's really trying to pull out all the stops.

"I'm glad to hear it."

"I'm so excited to finally see you, and Jess and the rest of the family can't wait to meet you."

"Yeah."

There's a small prick in my heart, but I brush it off. I remember how when I called him to wish him a happy Father's Day when I was nine, his wife, Jess, had picked up the phone. I had hung up, not sure who was talking to me, and eventually Mom called him back hours later so I could speak to him. Even though it was a misunderstanding, it stuck with me that Tommy probably didn't answer because he was spending the day with his new family.

I grimace at the silence that connects us.

"Do you have any particular food preferences?" Tommy asks, breaking the silence. "Jess likes to plan out meals two weeks in advance."

Wow, that's impressive. I can't even plan my life that far in advance. If I had, maybe it wouldn't have been so easy for me to get sent to see him.

"I'm vegetarian. That's all." I don't add that I technically eat fish too. The less I share the better.

"Ooh, environmentally conscious. I wish I could be a vegetarian, but I love a good burger." He pauses. "Farah, I have to wrap up this convo because Jess needs my help with Emma, who I'm sure you'll get to spend time with when you're out here. We'll talk again soon about the details of the trip."

"Yeah, sure."

I hang up before I have to feel the awkwardness of fake goodbyes. There's no way that I'm not being recruited for babysitting duty for a month. Though Emma's probably two or three by now, so maybe his stepkids are old enough to watch her. Or maybe I'll have to entertain all three of them.

I've officially been thrown into an ocean full of sharks that are out for blood. But I don't know how many sharks there are, and I don't even know if I'll sink or swim. All I know is that if I want to get through this trip and the rest of this month, I can't show any weakness. I have to keep it together.

SABRIYA

ABINGTON, VIRGINIA

It's been almost a week since the attack on Union Station, and everything still feels like someone pressed Pause. I crank the music box on my desk, the Black ballerina in the center twirling in *arabesque* as light twinkly music surrounds me. If glitter had a sound, it'd be the cheery music that the music box emits. I click from tab to tab on my laptop, drumming my fingers against my sunshine-yellow desk. It sticks out like a sore thumb from the rest of my room because of its brightness, but right now I appreciate the light it brings to the room. The words *canceled* or *postponed* appear in bold lettering on each website, each word poking a hole in my summer ballet audition plans. As much as I wish I was packing, traveling, pinning on an audition number to my leotard, or meeting new dancers at a summer intensive, I can't figure out how to press Play on my own life. I need to do something, anything, really, besides sitting at my desk waiting for things to feel normal again.

I pull open my audition spreadsheet, the color-coded text jumping off the screen. Red for canceled, yellow for postponed, and green for scheduled. Then there's a column for the date that I signed up for the audition, a column for the date of the audition itself, and then a column for the result of the audition. I type "canceled" in the box for the DC audition for the ABT intensive, and the red text creates more than a hole in my audition plans—it turns my original plan for this summer to dust.

Mom peeks her head into my room, and the sunlight streaming through the windows reflects off the dainty silver cross around her neck. "Good morning, Bri."

Relief floods through me when I see her. Even though I know she's here and okay, my brain is still taking some time to process that. Hopefully the remaining worry will fade, but it feels like that might take a while.

She comes over and stands next to me, looking around my room. "You cleaned already?"

"And did the laundry," I add.

I know it's not an opinion shared by many, but I love cleaning. Clutter stresses me out, and an organized space creates an environment for a focused mind. Right now, I need the focus in order to figure out how to piece my summer plans back together.

"Looking at all the audition schedules?" Mom asks.

I nod, closing my planner.

"That's actually what I wanted to talk to you about," Mom says.

I turn around in my chair, already knowing what she's going to say. "Just because there aren't any auditions being held in DC, Maryland, or Virginia because of the attack doesn't mean anything. We can drive to North Carolina or New York and audition there."

Despite the fact that the person who bombed Union Station has been identified, the DMV is still on edge. Auditions, and even classes at the studio, probably won't resume until more information has been released about the whole situation and people feel like there is no imminent danger—even though the government said that in a statement a couple days ago. I get that the area needs some time to work through the after-shocks of what happened, but trying to move forward and pick up the pieces feels less stressful than getting stuck in the endless loop of questions and fear.

"Your dad and I think it may be wiser for you to recon-sider your summer plans," Mom says.

"Why would I do that? Why should I have to change my summer plans because of the attack?"

"Sabriya, we're not asking you to give up dancing for the entire summer. Your studio is planning on resuming summer classes by the end of next week. With Nuri's lacrosse tourna-ment dates already rescheduled and the current state of our community, we're all needed here. You can still dance, but we'll all be staying here in DC. You can audition for the ABT summer intensive next year."

"Mom, my plans have been in place since last year. I can't change them now. The only part of the plan that's really changed is the location. There are tons of auditions in other cities, we'll just have to drive."

"That may be true, but you can change your plans, honey. You don't want to. And I understand why, but right now, it's safer if we all stay here together. Hate crimes are on the rise, and it's not safe for you to be off in a city without any family or friends to lean on. We're also going to be needed here to help with relief efforts and do whatever else we can so that our community can heal."

"Am I really needed here though? Because it doesn't seem like Muslims are feeling particularly needed right about now. Did you hear all of the assumptions that people made when they heard the guy's name? But maybe you don't get that."

It's a low blow, I know, and Mom flattens her lips into a straight line. I didn't mean for it to be that sharp. Being Muslim and growing up in an interfaith household isn't super uncommon, but sometimes it doesn't feel like Mom can fully connect to everything that I go through. Non-Black Muslims do a double take when they hear my full name as if they're lowkey shocked that Black Muslims actually exist, and when Black people who aren't Muslim find out that I am, their go-to response is usually, "Well, you don't look Muslim." Sometimes it's exhausting living at the intersection where people in both communities don't see me, and I don't always have the energy to explain that to Mom if she doesn't get it.

"Morgan's mom was injured in the terrorist attack," Mom says.

I uncross my arms, all of the fight leaving my body. Sweet Morgan, who always brings extra bobby pins, hairnets in all shades, and hair gels for all hair types? The Morgan who always bakes us healthy muffins before shows? If I looked up *nice* in the dictionary, her picture would be the definition. My heart plummets, bile rising in my throat.

"Oh," I choke out.

"For the first month of summer, our family is helping out with the relief efforts to support the families of the injured and the deceased. A lot of the families affected need help with things like grocery shopping, cooking, walking their pets. In addition, the boss at your dad's new job is asking all of the employees and their families to donate some of their time to volunteer with the relief efforts that are being held at my school. His children go there, and I actually taught one of them last year, so he is familiar with the administrators and teachers."

My shoulders drop as it hits me that getting out of this isn't going to be feasible. Dad's new at his job, one that he worked hard to get, and us all volunteering will keep up appearances. If I dip to go do ballet right after a disaster, that might reflect poorly on him and maybe even put his job in jeopardy, which is the last thing I'd want to do. Maybe if Dad's boss wasn't pressing this so much, then Mom would be more willing to let me travel to audition. But rule number one in the Siddiq family is that we always show up for each other, and that's what it seems like Mom is asking me to do.

"Alright. I understand."

Dad worked for years to get the position he has now at a big-name federal government agency. I've seen the late nights and brewed pots of coffee, and I'll be the last one to throw his hard work down the drain.

"Come down for breakfast when you're ready. Your dad's making his pepper jack grits."

My stomach grumbles at her last three words. "Okay."

Mom leaves my room, cracking the door behind her, and I turn on my inspiration playlist. Pop gospel fills the room, and I feel myself start to relax. I used to feel like I wasn't "Muslim enough" because I blast gospel music when I need motivation or calm. Mom always played the same mix of pop gospel songs on the way to elementary school, and now, going into my senior year, they remind me of simplicity.

For a while I thought that being "Muslim enough" meant that I had to prove myself to people when they couldn't tell. I thought that listening to gospel music or getting presents during Christmas as well as Ramadan meant that I was doing something wrong. I used to wear my Allah necklace in hopes that people would be able to recognize the Arabic charm and instantly know that I was Muslim. But with time, I realized that I don't have to prove myself to anyone and that there isn't one way to "be Muslim." Because I am Muslim and that's really all there is to it. Point-blank period. Now, I only wear my Allah necklace for me.

I open up a new notes page, nodding my head to the familiar beat. With every key I press, every sentence I form, and every thought I dump out, energy starts to seep back into me. Writing has always been something that's just for me. There's no pressure to make my sentences perfect or for my thoughts to be contained. There isn't room for messiness in the studio like there is on the page. I pour and pour until everything that was weighing me down is on the screen in front of me. Even though journaling on my laptop isn't the same as journaling in a notebook, it'll have to do for now. Picking out the perfect notebook is like picking out the perfect leotard. Both have to be cute, practical, and make me excited to actually do the thing. I ran out of pages in my old one and wanted to find the perfect one in New York after I got into the intensive. But since that won't be happening, I guess I can get a new one whenever I want now.

I rub my forehead and sigh. I can't believe my summer plans melted. I can't believe I had to worry about whether or not Mom was alive. I can't believe Morgan's mom got injured in the attack. I can't believe there even was an attack. This is all too much.

There's a knock on the door connecting my room to the bathroom that Nuri and I share, and I pause my music. "Come in, Nuri."

She opens the door and walks in, with her satin bonnet still on and blanket draped around her shoulders.

"What's up? How are you feeling?"

"A lot better now that Mom's home." She sits down on the armrest to my right and wraps an arm around my shoulders so that she doesn't fall. "Did you see what happened in California?"

"Yeah, I saw clips of the hate rally on Twitter earlier. And a group of Muslim girls who were just out walking were harassed in Southern Virginia. It's a lot."

"And the guy who attacked Union Station wasn't even Muslim, but I guess people just heard his name and ran with it. It's kinda scary how quick people are to point fingers."

"You're right, it really is."

Nuri nudges my shoulder. "Anyway, let's talk about something less depressing. What are you writing?"

"Nothing much. I'm doing a bit of freewriting. I ran out of pages in my journal."

"Can I read it?"

Normally I'd say no, but I'll do anything to put a smile on Nuri's face right now.

I shrug. "Yeah, sure. It's just me rambling, so none of it is any good."

Nuri looks at the laptop screen, her eyes narrowed. "Why aren't there any paragraphs? You need to do some formatting." She slides off the armrest and squishes into the chair next to me.

"But that's the thing about freewriting, you just write. You don't worry about indenting or capitalization or adding commas."

"I like these two lines," she says, pointing. "*'The sadness fades fast because I'm no longer capable of being truly shocked. The only residue left behind is anger, quietly simmering because if it boils and spills out of me I'm afraid of what will happen.'*"

I give her a small smile. "Thanks."

"You know what you should do?"

"What?"

Nuri reaches over and opens up the web browser. "I think you should start keeping an online journal, at least until you get a new physical one. That way everything will be more organized than having a bunch of notes saved to your desktop. Then you'll be able to stop complaining about the storage notifications that are always popping up."

I shrug. "I've never considered using an online journal before, but if creating one for me will make you happy, then why not. Just make sure it's private."

Public online journals—and posting stuff online in general—seems so out there. So permanent. I don't think the world cares enough to have my innermost thoughts on display. But if I'm still shaken up by the attack and what happened with Mom, I'm sure Nuri is too, and if setting up an online journal is going to take her mind off all that for a few minutes, then it's fine. I probably won't use it once I get a new journal anyway.

Nuri goes to the blogging platform. "You can make one for free. I think the website is called *Bloggingly*."

"Yep," I say, logging in.

She copies and pastes my words from the note into the empty blog post document and starts formatting. I crank the music box again, letting the sound whisk away my worries. I shouldn't even be worrying. There's nothing to worry about. Everything is private. What's the worst that could happen? Absolutely nothing. Right? Right.

Nuri picks up my laptop and crosses the room to sit on my bed, stepping on piles of old assessments and printed-out stretching routines. I plop down next to her on the bed, the swivel chair creaking when I get up.

"What should the hashtags be?" Nuri asks.

"Why do we even need them? It's not like anyone's going to be able to use them to search for this post."

"Because," she says, her voice rising at the end. "They're fun to make."

"Fine, I'll humor you. What about #TerrorismHasNo-Religion, or #BlackMuslimTeen, or just #Islam?"

"You're boring. I wanted something with some oomph, but okay." She types. "Title? Unless you don't want one since it's just a journal."

My favorite lines from my entry pop into my head.

"You truly assumed that the world would heal and stay healed

while spinning constantly. A spinning driven in part by accepted half-truths and rumors that get taken as facts."

"Let's call the collection of journal entries 'You Truly Assumed.'"

"You truly assumed" is a sarcastic way of telling someone they should've seen something coming. It's the perfect title for the post because I should've seen the reaction to the attack coming from miles away.

"Ooh, that's cool."

"I guess, I feel like it's honest. And it has that extra oomph that you wanted."

Nuri nods and makes a final click. "There you have it, your very first post in your private online journal. I think you have to go into your settings in order to make it public, so you should be fine."

"That makes sense." I pause, the weight of what we just did catching up with me. "I can't believe my words are online."

Seeing my words reflected back at me on an actual website is...different. On the notes app, my thoughts get lost in the shuffle of everything else, so there's no reason for anything to look good. But the template that Nuri picked out makes my words look fancy, as if my thoughts are actually put-together and important. It's like looking at myself through a mirror in a fun house. Still me, but not the reflection that I'm used to seeing. The words stand out against the white background, tempting me to read them and allow all that negativity back in. But the whole point of journaling for me is to get any-thing and everything that weighs me down off my chest, so I tear my eyes away from the screen.

"It's the same thing that you usually do, but online for

now." She turns to me, squishing against my side. "I like what you wrote."

"Really?"

"Really. I don't feel as alone as I did yesterday. Even though I expected the reaction and all of the hate after the terrorist attack, I didn't think it would be to this level. It's super overwhelming, and I didn't know that's how I was feeling until I read your post."

My heart swells at her words, and I bounce a little on the bed, excitement surging through me. The warmth thaws away some of the lingering numbness. Nuri's the first person to ever read my words. I never thought they were much good, so I've always kept my journals tucked away. I put my dancing out there for others to view, but I never knew that doing the same with my writing could also feel great. It's nice to know that my life-raft scribbles can help someone else keep their head above water. Letting Nuri read my writing is alright because I know her, and I don't have to worry about what she'll think about me. But letting other people read my writing would give people the chance to see the parts of me that aren't perfect and judge them, and I don't think I'll ever be ready for that.

"Bri and Nuri, breakfast!" Dad yells.

"Coming!" we yell back.

And as we race down the stairs, it almost feels like it's another normal summer-break day.

You truly assumed that the world would heal and stay healed while spinning constantly. A spinning driven in part by accepted half-truths and rumors that get taken as facts.

Everything seems to happen in DC, but nothing ever seems to happen to it. But maybe I only feel that way because I've been living here for so long. It hits me how easily it could've been me on that platform waiting for the metro. Maybe that's all life boils down to: just a series of fortunate or unfortunate circumstances. But then what differentiates the circumstances that you can control from the ones you can't, the ones that only Allah can control? Maybe they overlap or maybe one circumstance is a mixture of both. I'm sure that those killed or injured in the attack were there in part because that's where they wanted to be. Maybe they were trying to get home from work or heading downtown for a concert. Whatever it was, they controlled that part of the circumstance. But then there's the other part of the circumstance, the wrong place at the wrong time part. That part, the attack, was beyond any of their control. But the attack was in the control of the terrorist, so what role did Allah play in this circumstance? Maybe only the terrorist will ever know the answer to that one.

Circumstance. Coincidence. Chance. All these words to try to make us feel like we're in control of the unknown. In all honesty, that's what I'm most terrified of. Not knowing what I can't control.

The news has been running nonstop, mostly talking about the terrorist and his assumed religious background. Before any photo could even be broadcasted, the country already had its own perception of who this person was just because of his name. But now he's dead and everyone is left to figure out how to move forward from his actions.

I don't think I can have sympathy for the terrorist, regardless of religious background. But when I saw the news in the dance studio, the first thing that crossed my mind was, "Please don't be Muslim." What does that say about me?

It's scary that names can speak for someone before they're given the chance to even open their mouth. Names can decide between who lives and dies. Between who can live in peace and who has to live in fear. Between those who can tell their own story and those whose stories are assumed before they can even pick up a pen.

Some people already have preconceived notions of who they think I am or who I should be, just because I'm a young Black Muslim woman. Maybe that's why I journal. I want to write my own story.

ZAKAT

LULLWOOD, GEORGIA

I pick my sketchbook up from my desk, which shines and smells like pines from me cleaning it last night. Calling it a sketchbook is a bit of a stretch; it's more of a leftover blank notepad from back-to-school shopping last year that I doodle in. I slide into the window nook seat bench that Baba built for me when I was younger and look out at the woods. There's a knock on my door, and I slam my sketchbook shut so neither of my parents can launch into their lecture on why I shouldn't be spending so much time on my art.

"Come in!"

Mama walks in, already dressed with a cup of coffee in one hand. "Good morning."

"Morning, Mama." I sit up straighter. "Is everything okay?"

"Yes, yes, everything is fine, but I did want to tell you something." She takes a seat next to me at the window nook. "I got off the phone with Aafreen's mother, and she told me that Lucy is going to be joining you and Aafreen in the bookstore this summer. I know that the two of you had your issues when you were younger, but I believe that enough time has passed for the both of you to move forward."

I swallow, my mouth going dry. "Lucy? Why is she back?"

The last time I saw Lucy, I was in the fourth grade and she was here from DC visiting family during the summer. She took a pottery class at the community center with Aafreen, and one day, while I was walking with them to class, she told me that if I covered my hair, then that meant it must be ugly and I was trying to hide it. Aafreen, who wears the hijab whenever she's at school or the masjid, defended me, but I still remember how loud my gasp was and how sharp my eyes stung. Lucy gave me my first experience with Islamophobia, and I haven't seen her since.

"Her sister was injured in the terrorist attack, so she's coming to stay with Asher and his family for the summer. They're worried that she won't have any supervision since they're always at the hospital, and they want her to have a chance at getting a somewhat normal summer break."

My stomach drops further, but I fight to keep my expression neutral. Asher Anderson is one of the most popular students and one of the biggest pranksters at Lullwood High, our rival high school on the other side of town. Everything about him screams entitled butthole, from the parties he throws to the fancy sports car he drives. He's also a well-known—and admittedly pretty good—graffiti artist, and we've been in a handful of summer art classes together at the community center. But whatever talent he has fell to the wayside when he joked last year that tagging the Islamic schools would make a good prank. Back when we took art classes together, he used to make a big deal whenever the bell in the minaret of the masjid rang to signal prayer times or whenever the teacher in our art classes only ordered cheese pizza during the last class celebrations. On top of all that, he constantly likes and sometimes retweets content from a well-known alt-right site called *Free the Right*. That alone tells me all I need to know about him.

"I can't believe Aafreen didn't tell me about this," I say.

Mama's eyebrows rise. "That's a bit strange. Aafreen's mom said that it was Aafreen's idea for Lucy to join you two and work at the bookstore for the summer."

Of course she did. Because she's nice to anyone and everyone.

"Will that be okay?" Mama asks.

"Yes, it's fine," I say quickly. "But I thought it was going to be Aafreen and me all summer. You know, like it normally is."

Aafreen and I have been inseparable since we were three. I know her like I know Lullwood, though it hasn't always felt like that recently. She's ready to graduate next year and leave Lullwood behind, and as much as I am ready to branch out, I'm also sad about having to prepare to let go. This summer feels as though it marks the start of everything changing, and I was looking forward to it being only us for the next three months. A to Z, like it's always been.

Mama nods and leaves the room, closing the door behind her. I look at the Islamic wall calendar above my bed and sigh when I notice the date. This is going to be a long summer.

★ ★ ★ ★ ★

The bell attached to the door of Tiny Treasure Trove, Lull-wood's most popular indie bookstore, rings, and I look up from where I'm stacking books. Aafreen waves me over, and the person next to her, who must be Lucy, follows her gaze. When Lucy spots me, she gives me a small smile, and I force myself to smile back. My thoughts start to spin into a headache, and I take a deep breath. I'll be cordial to Lucy because I care about Aafreen and because Lucy's been through a lot with her sister being injured in the terrorist attack. But I don't see Aaf-reen, Lucy, and I becoming the Three Musketeers this sum-mer. My feet feel as if they're stuck in hardened clay as I make my way over to them.

"Lucy, I'm not sure if you remember from your last visit, but this is Zakat. She's pretty great, and she'll be working at the bookstore with us," Aafreen says.

Lucy grins. "It's nice to meet you again."

I nod. "You too."

If Lucy remembers what she said to me all those years ago, she doesn't show it. I know it's unlikely that she does, even though her words have been as hard to remove as glitter. It's gross that people get to have racist, Islamophobic, or homopho-bic or any of the other countless "phases" that get written off as them simply being children. Especially without any regard as to how what they said or did during their "phase" hurt others.

"Well, I'm going to get back to work now." I start to walk away, but my manners kick in and force me to be civil. "And, Lucy, I hope that your sister and the rest of your family are doing alright."

"Thank you," Lucy says.

I nod and make my way back over to the storage room. I dust my hands off, surveying the progress in front of me. The books that were unorganized before are now separated into bins for different charities. Aafreen's mom donates books to various charities in the Atlanta metro area every month, and part of my job this summer is to get everything organized for the drop-off at the end of June. I twirl around the room with my arms out, taking up the space. Earlier this morning, before Lucy got here, if I took one wrong step piles of books would've come raining down. When Aafreen's mom asked if any of us wanted to help out in the storage room as one of our responsibilities, I volunteered. It made more sense to let Lucy take turns working the lone cash register with Aafreen so she could learn the ropes. Plus, the sharp smell of new books is heavier back here in the storage room. And working back here gives me an excuse to avoid Lucy.

A knock vibrates throughout the small space, and I jump at the sound.

"Hey," Aafreen says, stepping inside. "Want to grab lunch?"

"Yeah, I—"

"Is this where the 'Book of Secrets' is kept?" Lucy asks, her voice floating into the storage room.

"Um, no, definitely not," Aafreen says.

"How does she know about the book?" I whisper.

The "Book of Secrets" is an extremely old journal. Every person who's attended Lullwood Islamic School for Girls since the 1990s has written a secret in it. Most of us wrote ours at the beginning of freshman year, our first ceremonial mark. Since there are only about fifty students in each grade, it's a big bonding experience. It always stays with the student body president, which is why Aafreen has it in her basement storage closet at her house.

Before Aafreen can respond, Lucy walks in. She meets my eyes and gives me a small smile, but I don't return it. The memory of her comment and my reaction of hurt and shame barrels into me, and I clear my throat.

"Actually, I brought lunch, and I was planning on eating in here."

"Great, we can join you," Aafreen says. "I brought my lunch too."

I hesitate, part of me not wanting to upset Aafreen and the other part not wanting to spend more time with Lucy than what's absolutely necessary.

Lucy's eyes narrow as she picks up on my hesitation. "Is there a problem?"

"There's no problem, right, Zakat?" Aafreen asks, her eyes flitting between the two of us. "Can we please just eat together?"

My cheeks flush, annoyance warming them. "Nope, not a problem."

Aafreen leans over and whispers to Lucy, and my stomach drops. I've already painted a picture in my head of how this summer is supposed to go, and Lucy isn't in it. This is supposed to be our summer together, A to Z.

"Can I talk to you for a second, Zakat?" Aafreen asks, her voice rising at the end.

"Uh, sure," I say, getting up from the tiny circular table that sits in the corner of the storage room.

Lucy sits down at the table and pulls out her lunch, and Aafreen cracks the door behind us.

"What's up?" Aafreen asks. "You're acting strange. Are you still upset about what Lucy said back when we were kids?"

"You remember?"

"Your mom reminded mine, who then reminded me. What she said back then was really out of pocket, but I also think that a lot of time has passed. Maybe it's time to start fresh? If she says something like that again, then I won't really want anything to do with her, but I don't know. I don't think she'll do that."

So, Aafreen forgot. I guess that isn't that surprising. The comment wasn't directed at her, so it's easier for her to give Lucy another chance.

"I would've appreciated more of a heads-up," I say.

"And I'm sorry about that. Lucy literally found out that she would be spending the month here three days ago, and I found out the day after that. We should both be trying to make her feel at home," Aafreen says. "I know it was only supposed to be us two this summer, and we're still going to spend a lot of time together. So don't worry, we're still A to Z!"

"Yeah, A to Z," I mutter.

The words that usually mean so much feel cheap now.

"Now, let's go eat and move forward. This is going to be a good summer. I can feel it."

I nod and follow her back into the storage room. I still don't understand why Lucy can't hang out with Asher since that's her cousin, but I guess that's none of my business. As long as she doesn't say anything out of pocket while she's here, I can do my best to move forward.

Lucy stands up when the two of us walk back in. "You two don't have to talk about me like I'm not here. If you don't want to eat lunch with me, Zakat, then don't. It's fine."

She turns and leaves, slamming the door behind her.

Aafreen turns to me. "I'm going to go check and make sure that she's okay. I'll be right back."

"Yeah. Sure."

I take a deep breath, my heartbeat the only sound against the silence. Tears rush to my eyes, and I press my palms to them until I can feel the pressure. Here it goes again, feeling too much. Sometimes it's such a heavy weight because one word can land the wrong way and throw me off. Feelings are exhausting, and getting them out on the canvas stops them from overflowing. I reach for my sketchbook and doodle myself among the trees because the Lullwood woods are so soothing. And I scribble stars in the corners of the page because it's nice to be reminded that even though my feelings are large, in the grand scheme of the universe they're actually really small.

I open my container of chili and cringe after taking a bite. It's cold, but there's no way I'm leaving the storage room to go use the microwave. The silence in the room makes me realize that Aafreen is probably going to eat lunch with Lucy outside, and my shoulders drop. That's the difference between Aafreen and me. She's outgoing and loves meeting new people, and she always sees the best in everything and everyone. I try to see the glass as half-full when I can, but I also know that I'm a half-empty kind of person. I don't think Aafreen fully realizes how big the difference between the two of us really is. We work well together, but sometimes I wonder if

Aafreen would be better off if she wasn't connected to me by over a decade of friendship.

I sigh, finishing my chili, and walk back out into the store to help out on the floor. Aafreen waves at me as she and Lucy walk in. A few people come in, grab a book off a shelf, and sit in the plush armchairs strewn across the store. Reading is the definition of adventure in my mind. Who knows what worlds those readers are going to get sucked into, and who knows who they'll be after they turn the final page. Reading is its own form of magic.

The sound of laughter travels through the space between the bookshelves, and I peek over to see Aafreen and Lucy talking like old friends and eating in the storage room. I settle between the bookshelves, made out of wood from fallen Lullwood trees, and rearrange the books so that it doesn't look like I'm completely eavesdropping.

"—you wanted to come over to my place to get ready with me for the party celebrating the start of the summer this weekend?" Aafreen asks Lucy.

"That's so nice! Thank you! But I actually already have plans to get ready with my friends from L-High. It's funny—that's what we call my school, Erwell Lakes High, back home. Anyway, I'm sure I'll see you later. It's nice that the host, Bella, is opening the party up to you all too."

I hold in a snort, inhaling a puff of dust. I start coughing, and Lucy looks over at me, disgust etched into her features.

L-High? No one calls Lullwood High L-High. That has to be one of the most non-Lullwood things I've ever heard. But I guess I shouldn't be too surprised that Lucy's already getting invited to parties, especially when Asher is royalty at

Lullwood High. Parties aren't horrible, but I prefer smaller get-togethers. Those are usually way less sweaty, less loud, and less boozy, which makes them more enjoyable. Lullwood High parties are chaotic, and I only go to them if Aafreen doesn't have anyone else to go with. But I guess she has Lucy now.

I know Aafreen is only being nice because that's who she is, but I feel awful. Some small part of me is afraid that Lucy will somehow replace me because she's more fun, more cool, and more not-Lullwood, and I wish I didn't think that but I do. I sigh, hurt weighing down my shoulders. I should ask to join them. Or maybe not, since then Lucy might make a big deal of telling me no. I step out from behind the bookshelves, and Aafreen's mom smiles from behind the cash register.

"You and the girls have done such wonderful work today, so you all are free to head out early if you'd like to," Aafreen's mom says. "I can cover the afternoon shift. And feel free to take a book with you. Workers' perks. And you and Aafreen are still meeting tomorrow about debate prep for next year, yes?"

"Yes." I paste on a smile. "Thank you. I'll see you tomorrow!"

And then before she can ask me any more questions, I walk out of the store. I hop on my bike and start pedaling back toward the neighborhood. It's fine. Everything's fine. I had no idea that Lucy and Aafreen were this close, but it's probably because Aafreen can make Lullwood feel like home to anyone.

My phone buzzes, snapping me out of my thoughts, and I pull over to the side of the path. I take a deep breath, inhaling the woodsy air. The sun filters through the treetops, casting kaleidoscopes of shadows on the gravel path. I love this path that holds the masjid, the Islamic schools, and the neighborhood together with so much history, protection, and love.

Even when I leave for college, this path will always be tattooed on my heart. I soak in the soft bird chirps, the laughter of the children as they walk in little huddles, and the whispers of the middle schoolers as they exchange secrets that only they and the trees can hear. High schoolers walk along the path with their earbuds in or while scrolling on their phones, and it all feels so magical. This small slice of community going about their lives is what makes Lullwood so beautiful. I'm so lucky to be able to call this place home.

In between the trees, I can see the masjid and the gate around it, and a pit forms in my stomach. Even though it hurts to see it up, I understand why it is. As much as I wish I could bury all the hateful rhetoric that's been spewing around, the gate is an ever-present reminder that things right now aren't the same as usual.

I wish I could do something about the attack, about the Islamophobia, about the fact that my community has to be on the defensive. But I don't know what to do. I'm not good at public speaking like Mama and Aafreen, and I'm an even worse writer. I have no idea what to say or even who I should be saying it to. I try to quiet the whisper in my head, but it grows louder and louder, ringing in my ears. Maybe it's because in all my time in Lullwood, I've never seen the gate up.

Do something. Do something. Do something.

I shake my head, trying to silence the voice.

Lullwood will be fine. We always are.

But the voice doesn't fade, and I sit down on one of the benches that line the trail. I rub my forehead as if that'll get rid of my headache and sigh. Today has felt like a week or even a month. But it's still only the first week of June, which means there's a long way until the end of the summer.

I pull out my phone and accidentally click on my blogging app while trying to swipe out of Instagram. A piece of art catches my eye, and I start scrolling. I've never clicked on the write tab, where people draft and upload their work, but the main feed is full of amazing sketches, paintings, and comics. I keep scrolling, the same voice in my head from earlier nagging at me. A hashtag catches my eye, and I end up on a blog called *You Truly Assumed*. Surprise catches me when I read that the writer is not only Muslim, but also Black. I read the first post and I almost gasp at how relatable one of the lines is: *"But when I saw the news, the first thing that crossed my mind was, 'Please don't be Muslim.'"* I finish reading, and a feeling of connection washes over me.

How did this writer manage to capture so much of what I think and feel with only a couple hundred words? I copy and paste the blog's URL into my notes app so that I can quickly find it again tomorrow and put my phone away, hop back on my bike, and continue on. I think I just found my way toward action.

FARAH

INGLETHORNE, CALIFORNIA

"Hello, baby girl," Nana says as soon as Mom and I step inside.

Grandpa comes out of the kitchen, wearing an apron that has World's Best Grandpa embroidered onto it. "Hello hello, breakfast is almost done."

Nana and Grandpa's house is painted a warm yellowish orange that matches their bright personalities. Nana's parents bought the house after they moved to Inglethorne from Texas during the Second Great Migration, and the house has been in the family ever since. The house smells like fresh biscuits, the earthy incense that Nana always burns, and a lot of love. Music plays from the TV, which is set to a channel that plays R & B songs that they call oldies but goodies.

Mom and I follow Nana to the couch, and we sit down on either side of her. Even though the house has gone through a few renovations, the floral-patterned couch that I learned to crawl over and I sat on while watching my first Lakers games with Grandpa back when Mom and I lived here with them has never changed.

"How have you been doing, Nana?" I ask.

Nana takes my hand and holds it in hers, like she used to do when I was little. "I've been doing good. Your grandfather keeps making me take those nasty pills for my blood pressure, but he doesn't know that I'm secretly tossing them."

"I can hear you, Hazel," Grandpa says.

Nana laughs, and Mom and I both give her a stern look.

"I'm kidding, girls, relax," Nana says. "I can assure you that my doctor says my numbers are much better."

"Good," Mom says. "Keep taking them."

"Don't worry, I'm going to be sticking around for a long time so that I can keep an eye on the both of you."

My phone buzzes, and a news notification pops up on the screen. I start to ignore it, but the name of a city in the valley catches my eye and I click on the notification. My mouth drops open at the images on the screen.

"Oh, my," I whisper, holding my phone out when Nana and Mom lean in so that they can see.

News footage of a ton of masked people chanting slurs and disgusting rhetoric plays out for thirty seconds before a news anchor pops up and explains that it's a rally in response to the attack in DC. Even though the valley isn't that far from South LA, cities there are rich and white, and some of them used to be sundown towns. A hate rally isn't surprising, but the vileness in the clip is still hard to swallow.

Nana sighs. "Some things don't change, girls."

I think about all of the things that Nana has lived through and instantly feel bad for showing her the video.

"Sorry, Nana," I say. "I shouldn't have brought the video up."

She squeezes my hand. "There's nothing to apologize for. Change does happen, but unfortunately things like racism and Islamophobia don't go away. They morph."

Mom and I nod, and it hurts to think how many times Nana's probably had to have a conversation like this one.

"Come on, let's go eat," Nana says, patting Mom and me on our knees. "I'm not going to let anyone ruin our Sunday brunch."

It hits me that today's brunch is going to be the last one I'll have for the rest of the month. Even though that's only three weekend brunches, it's still kinda sad. I don't miss them unless I absolutely have to, like when I had to go out of town for a school programming competition over spring break. I'm going to miss Nana and Grandpa as much as I miss Mom. They'll always be my home, and I don't know if visiting Tommy is going to change that.

★ ★ ★ ★ ★

Riley laces his fingers through mine as we walk across the parking lot toward Tate's. A rare light breeze cuts through the heat and ruffles my hair, brushing my curls against his cheek. I smile up at the peeling letters on the diner's sign, stepping in a few turquoise paint chips on the ground. Tate's is one of the few places that hasn't been forced to close because of gentrification. The diner has been around since my mom was my age, so it's a community fixture that no one wants to see replaced. Tate's feels like the town's collective grandparent. Tate's is home.

Last year, some big company tried to raise the monthly

lease of the property as a way to try to force Tate's to close because someone else was willing to pay the more expensive lease. We could all tell something was up with Tate Jr., but everything was kept hush-hush until the news broke. Once the words *Tate's* and *gone* were put in the same sentence, everyone was enraged and came together to give a collective "hell, no," to the company. We all pitched in to help Tate Jr. meet the more expensive lease and pay off the remainder of the loan that his father took out to start the business. Now the business is officially within his family, and Tate Jr. can't be forced to sell the diner unless he wants to. So for the foreseeable future, Tate's continues to serve greasy fries and overpriced milkshakes.

This is where Riley and I had our first date, after we met during the programming competition that I went to in the spring. Even though we had been in AP compsci together, it wasn't until the competition that I really got to know him. But even though these past three months have been amazing, I'm not sure if they're enough to sustain a long-distance relationship.

I pull open the door, and classic '80s music greets Riley and me as we walk inside. I let go of his hand as we slide into our favorite booth, close to the jukebox but not too close. The booths are turquoise and light pink with silver accents, like something straight out of an old rom-com, and the walls are full of photos of people eating here over the years. There's even a picture of Mom and me hanging up, but it's crooked and sticks out as much as we do in this town.

Clark, the waiter, points at us from behind the counter. "The usual?"

"You know it," I say.

"Thank you!" Riley adds.

Clark nods and bustles off, powdered sugar sticking out against his black apron.

"I'm going to miss this place," Riley says, linking his fingers through mine across the table. "It's so cool how Tate's feels like the past, present, and future all wrapped into one."

I roll my eyes. "Aren't you the one who's always telling me that you're going to be here for another three months?"

"Well, yes, but the nostalgia is already starting to kick in."

I squeeze his hand and take in his tortoiseshell glasses and his curly taper fade. Even though things are going to be different when Riley leaves for Vanderbilt, when he comes back for breaks Tate's is still going to be our go-to hangout spot.

"Speaking of the future," Riley says, his dark brown eyes shining under the disco lights. "Have you thought about what I said earlier?"

Before I can say anything, the waiter sets two milkshakes down on the table and hands us two jumbo straws.

I pull the large Oreo mint milkshake over to my side, and Riley takes his chocolate peanut butter cup one.

"To answer your question, I did. A little."

Riley raises his eyebrows. "And?"

"I haven't really changed my mind. You're going to be basically halfway across the country, and I don't want to hold you back from the college experience," I say, putting air quotes around the last two words.

His shoulders drop, and I look down at the table. It makes more sense to end things now rather than at the end of the summer, when it'll only hurt more. Or when he inevitably meets someone else in college and decides he wants to break things off then. It's better to avoid the hurt before it can happen.

"But why not? You're happy. I'm happy. We're happy."

I know he thinks it's just my insecurities talking, and he's not entirely wrong. A large part of me is still scared to rely on him, even though he hasn't given me any reason to be concerned since we've started dating. But once we aren't in the same place at the same time anymore, I'll be worried about him deciding he doesn't want me or us anymore. Like Tommy did. So I have to be the one to decide first.

"I think you're scared of taking a risk and I get that, but there's no way to know whether or not we'll end up making it long-distance if we end things now. Don't you want to find out the answer?"

I really do want to find out, but the words stay on the tip of my tongue.

"First of all, I am not risk-averse," I say.

Riley raises his eyebrows, and I falter.

"I do. I'm sorry. It's just—" I sigh, stirring the straw in my milkshake. "Can we talk about something else? I actually have an idea that might work as a compromise of sorts."

"Sure, of course, but this convo isn't finished yet." He takes a sip of his shake. "But yeah, what is it?"

"I'm being shipped off to Boston for the rest of the month."

Riley's eyes widen, and he starts to fiddle with the cross dangling from the gold chain around his neck. "Wait, when? Why?"

"I leave on Tuesday." I sigh. "My mom wants me to spend some time getting to know Tommy, and they both think now is the right time. It's important to her and it's only for this month, so I'm just gonna deal with it. But my mom did say that the trip could be a test run for doing long-distance, and I think that's actually a solid idea."

"I'm down if you're down," Riley says seriously. "And I know you're not the biggest fan of Tommy, but I don't think the trip will suck completely. You'll be able to convince him to take you on a tour of MIT."

"You and your optimism," I say, pinching his cheek lightly. But Riley's optimism is one of the things that I like most about him. Our personalities balance each other out, which is why I think we work well. Plus, he's really cute, has great taste in music, and is also a Lakers fan.

"Besides, with the rally and stuff ramping up toward the midterm elections, I'm starting to think that maybe getting a bit of a break from Inglethorne may be a good thing."

Riley tilts his head. "Did you feel like that before the attack in Washington?"

It's a valid question, and I pause. Even though growing up, Inglethorne was mostly just Black and Latinx, with gentrification happening now, more and more white people are buying up the property and putting up Black Lives Matter signs on their lawns without realizing the irony of the fact that Black and Latinx people were forced out because they couldn't pay the rent anymore. Now, I get weird stares when I'm walking home from work, or people cross the street to avoid me, or police approach me when I step outside the grocery store when I'm on my break because they think I'm loitering. It's not the first time any of those things have happened—it's that they're happening much more. It's weird both wanting to be seen and unseen at the same time, and I wish I could exist without even a wisp of concern. It'd be nice to just be.

"I guess all the stuff that usually happens started to happen more when the talk about midterm elections started."

"It's only June, Farah. Midterms are still like five months away."

"I know." I rub my arms, surprised that there are goose bumps despite the heat. "But I don't like the fact that Mark Johnson is running to stir the pot."

Even though no one really expects Mark Johnson to get very far, the fact that he's even running shows that Inglethorne is changing. His rhetoric and potential policies—like his support for the increase in gentrification—make it seem like he doesn't realize that he's running in a city that's mostly people of color.

"Yeah, he sucks. I'm sorry. Is there anything I can do to make you feel better?"

I smile, his gentle tone warming me. "Keep being you."

"Maybe being away for a month could be a good thing. It could be a way to get away from the stress of midterms and Inglethorne for a bit." He pauses. "Plus, like you said, using the trip as a short test run for a long-distance relationship could help show you that we could do this."

His voice rises at the end, hope lifting his words.

"Maybe." I take another sip of my milkshake. "How's your software development internship been going?"

"So great! Yesterday we started working on a project for a new client."

His hands move as he talks, punctuating his words, and his eyes are brighter than the disco lights hanging above us. It's hard to put into words exactly what Riley makes me feel, but being around him feels as natural as programming. Both of them grew on me unexpectedly, but now it's kinda hard to imagine my life without them. I don't know if I get butterflies when I'm around him, but I do know that whenever I hear a love song, I think of him. Riley makes me feel warm, and when I'm around him things just feel good. It's a feeling that I don't want to lose but that I'm also scared might get taken away.

He pauses. "Wait, do you want to hear the story? I don't want to bore you."

"I want to hear anything that you want to share."

He beams, and I can feel the passion radiating out from him. It's hard not to be excited because he's so excited. I tap my feet against the black-and-white-checkered tiles as I listen to him and breathe in the air that always smells like funnel cake and French fries.

He takes a deep breath. "So, yeah, it was amazing."

"It really sounds like it was. I'm happy that you're happy."

"Thank you, you cornball." He takes out his phone and holds it out to me. "Before I forget to mention it, I stumbled onto a blog that I think you might like. It's called *You Truly Assumed.*"

"*You Truly Assumed?* What kind of name is that?" I mutter.

I scroll down the page. The site feels like a bad PowerPoint presentation with too much text and no pictures. My first instinct is to click out of the tab, but somehow the sentences flow together. The writing is actually engaging, but the formatting is a bit of a turnoff.

I click on another post. It's good. I like the writing, but the blog's aesthetic—or lack thereof—makes me cringe. It's basically black text against a white background. The contrast is jarring, but with a little bit of HTML manipulation the blog could look much more spruced up and appealing to the eye.

There are more comments than I expected, and an extremely hateful one catches my eye. I would've deleted the comment, since it's only someone trying to act all tough by hiding behind a screen. But maybe there's some small amount of merit to letting it stay up. It's kinda like saying, "You really thought you could mess with me, but can you really? You truly assumed you could."

"What do you think?" Riley asks as I hand him back his phone.

"The writing is good, but the aesthetic sucks."

"I agree. Which is why I think you could help."

"Me?"

"I know you weren't sure what you wanted to do this summer, prior to the whole visiting Tommy thing, so I thought that maybe you could reach out and see if they wanted help with web design or graphics."

I don't really have enough experience to be working on something that has a message of that kind of magnitude. Plus, if I did offer to help, I might be expected to open up about my experiences and that's not what I want to do. But maybe reaching out would prove to myself that I can take chances and put myself out there. That I'm not entirely risk-averse. I tap my fingers against the tabletop, ideas for the design of the blog already popping into my head. I don't know why, but some part of me feels a connection to it. Maybe because the writing is so relatable that it feels like the author understands some of what I'm going through. The idea of joining the blog doesn't necessarily feel like a risk, but I've never worked on a project of this nature with someone before. A blog is something for everyone to see. It's not contained like the work that's done at a programming competition.

I squeeze his hand. "Thank you for thinking of me. I'll think about it."

"Totally your call," Riley says, squeezing my hand back and looking down at his watch. "Ready?"

I nod, pulling out a couple of bills from my pocket for our tip. Riley puts the bills to cover our milkshakes down on top of that, and we slide out of the booth. Once I get to the door, I look over my shoulder, checking to make sure that Riley's behind me and didn't get caught up in a conversation like he usually does. My eyes lock on the shirt of one of the diners, which reads Don't Kneel, Stand Up for Your Country, and I scoff, slightly surprised. I haven't seen a shirt like that here before, but I guess even Tate's clientele is changing.

We step outside, the hot muggy air sticking to my skin. Even though it's way too hot out, the sky is gorgeous and June Gloom has receded for the day. Bright and blue and clear. If the sky had a taste, I think it'd be crisp, like a slightly tart Granny Smith apple. I slide into the passenger seat of Riley's blue '80s Mustang, his pride and joy. Riley's dad collects, refurbishes, and resells old cars. His love of cars has rubbed off so much on Riley that whenever he's stressed, he watches an episode of *MotorWeek* to calm down. I buckle in, careful not to track any dirt onto the white leather interior. Riley pops in one of his mixtapes and rolls down all the windows, even though the air is too thick to create much of a breeze.

We ride with music filling up the space between us until

Riley pulls into the driveway. I lean over the gearshift to kiss him, and I shiver when he runs his fingers up my arm to cradle my cheek. When he breaks away and kisses my forehead, I swear my heart melts.

"See you later, alligator," I say.

"In a while, crocodile," he says, grinning as he drives off. I stare at the outside of the apartment complex, and it hits me that in two days I'll be walking into a completely different place. The last time I traveled outside California was to go to Texas for a family reunion with Mom, Nana, and Grandpa when I was like five, but it was so long ago that I don't remember anything from the trip. It's weird that after tomorrow, the key that always hangs on the chain around my neck won't unlock the front door that I step into. I have no idea what I'm going to be walking into, and that alone is almost enough for me to beg Riley to figure out a way to come on this trip with me so that he can act as a buffer.

I've worked so hard not to fail at anything my whole life, so that I could never give anyone a reason to count me out. To not mess up so that nothing would be taken away from me or Mom, and now I'm forced into the unknown. With tons of opportunities for me to mess up. For me to fail. My fingers itch to call Tommy and tell him that he can back off because I'm not coming. But I can't put any more stress on Mom than she already carries, so I grit my teeth and head to the room so I can pretend to pack.

SABRIYA

ABINGTON, VIRGINIA

I press my hands flat against my yoga mat and take deep breaths as I bend forward to rest my chest against my knee and parallel to the bedroom floor. It's been a week since the attack at Union Station, and things are beginning to feel like they're in motion, rather than paused. Maybe that's because I know that I'm volunteering for the rest of this month, so I have a plan again. My phone buzzes, and I reach forward to grab it, sinking farther into my center split. The familiar ache buzzes up my legs and to my inner thighs, and I embrace the feeling and breathe through it. If I don't feel the stretch, I'm not stretching well enough. I rest my forearms on the floor, deepening the stretch, and scroll through my notifications. My eyes widen when an email notification pops up from the platform that Nuri used to create my online journal, and I sit up.

Hello! This is a really cool blog idea!

"No, no, no," I say.

Someone liked the journal entry that I wrote a couple of days ago. And commented. I scroll further, and my panic rises as more email notifications from the blog blur together. Multiple people liked the post and commented on it too. How in the world could that have happened? I click on the blog post and groan at my huge mistake. I thought all the posts were automatically set to private, not the other way around. Don't you have to publish a post or a website before it goes live and turns public? I should've dug deeper and poked around on the site more to make sure that nothing like this could happen, but I didn't think I needed to. Damn it. This is why I should've gotten a journal. I should've made a plan and stuck to it. Thoughts start to bounce around in my head, crashing into one another, and I can feel a stress headache coming on.

My phone pings with another email notification from the blogging platform, and I flop onto my bed and resist the urge to scream into the unicorn backrest pillow next to my regular pillows. Restlessness and worry wash over me, and I grab the remote from my desk and turn on the LED wall vine lights above my bed. Something about the soft white lights and cute aesthetic of the green fake leaves soothes me a bit. I click on one of the emails and a comment pops up.

Hi! I'm also a young Muslim woman of color, and I wanted to say that I felt so seen by your post. Your writing was so soothing and open, and I hope you post more in the future.

Warmth tinges some of the panic that threatens to fill up my lungs. That might've been one of the kindest things someone's ever said to me, albeit virtually. More times than not, I don't see myself fully represented within the mainstream Muslim community. If I want to embrace the community, my Blackness is rarely taken into account, and those two identities are so tangled that I can't separate them. I tried for years to separate both identities in order to feel like I fully fit into each group. Eventually, I realized that it wasn't worth it to break off different parts of myself and try to stick them into different puzzles when both pieces belonged to the same one. The fact that a young Muslim woman of color saw herself reflected in my words gives me the same rush as nailing the landing to a difficult turn sequence.

But still. Making *You Truly Assumed* public was never part of the plan, and it still isn't. But it's weird, though also kind of cool, that people are able to connect to that part of me, and to my writing in general. If I'm not going to be spending as much time on ballet this summer, then maybe I can shift my plan a bit and spend some time blogging. Uploading posts can't really be more draining than spending hours at the studio every day. Making the online journal into a blog would be low-commitment and low-stress and maybe even fun. Plus, I need to spend this summer figuring out if I want to apply to colleges with the goal of doing ballet professionally, and maybe trying out something new could help.

The comment runs through my head, and I stand and shake out my legs, which are cramping from me tensing up. I need to talk to Nuri. She always knows what to do.

I walk through the attached bathroom and cringe at the

scene Nuri left behind from doing her hair. Leave-in conditioner, a tub of hair gel, and a ton of other products are scattered around both sinks, and the bathroom smells like vanilla and sweet almond oil. I grab the edge of the sink, almost slipping on the soft-bristled toothbrush that she uses to lay down her edges. The joys of sharing a bathroom.

I tap my knuckles against the connecting door to Nuri's bedroom.

"You can come in, Bri!"

I open the door and almost trip over one of her lacrosse sticks. In addition to the messiness of her room, our rooms are basically opposites. Her walls are a bright purple, her desk is overflowing with assignments that were probably never turned in, and trying to get through her room is like playing hopscotch. I could go on and on, but I like the oppositeness. It creates a balance between us that I've grown used to having to steady me.

"Nuri, I need advice."

She looks over at me from the ground, crunching to the beat of the music. "Yeah, what's up?"

I sit down on the edge of her unmade bed. "So, I thought you set the blog to private, but it turns out that you didn't." I take a deep breath, forcing myself to get my idea out before I can overthink it. "Now I have people commenting on my post and giving it likes. And now I think I want to turn the online journal into a blog."

"Really? That's awesome. You should totally do it!"

"I think I'm going to go for it." My voice rises with excitement. "But also what about the plan? I'm supposed to be focusing on ballet, so that next summer when I audition for the ABT intensive I'll be as close to perfect as I can possibly be."

Nuri flips over and starts doing push-ups. If I wasn't a dancer, I'd be exhausted just by looking at her.

"Bri, you came up with that plan a few days ago. It isn't set in stone. You can think about the future and blog at the same time." She starts doing those weird clap push-ups, the sound reverberating over her music. "People like your words! And you sound really excited about starting the blog. You could even bring other young Muslim women's voices to the blog."

I shiver, her suggestion sending a spark up my spine. That would be pretty cool. Maybe *You Truly Assumed* could be a platform geared toward any young Muslim woman. Maybe *YTA* could be for others in my communities besides only me.

"That's not a half-bad idea. You might be onto something." She switches to mountain climbers. "So you're not going to go back to your room and delete the blog?"

"Nope. I'm going to do this! I'm going to start a blog!"

"Good, that was my sisterly deed for the day. Actually, for the summer."

I stick my tongue out at her and head back through the bathroom to my room. Sliding into my desk chair, I open up my laptop. I turn the knob on my ballerina music box and let the glittery music wash over me. My finger hovers over the email app, and I sigh. Is it worth it to let people see my innermost thoughts? Journaling is my safe space, and it's only safe because it's mine. If people start reading the posts, then they'll no longer be mine. At least not fully. But something in my gut is telling me to do this, and I'll still have control over what I choose to share in the end.

Plus, if this ends up being an absolute disaster, I can always just delete the site and pretend this never happened. I pull up a tutorial on how to add pages on *Bloggingly* and manage to whip together a decent contact page and an about me page that says, *"Just a Black Muslim girl trying not to get caught up in the mix."* Right now, the background image of the blog is a warm peachy-pink color, which is better than the plain white background that I originally had. I survey my work as I scroll through the site and click on the three different pages, and for someone who knows nothing about blogging it's honestly not half-bad.

I stop at today's post and go to the comment from earlier. "Okay." I set my shoulders back. "Here I go."

I click on the reply button and start typing a quick response.

> Hi! I really appreciate your comment, and I'm so glad you were able to connect with my words. I'm looking for a few young Muslim women (preferably in high school) to join me in writing posts for You Truly Assumed. If you're interested, please let me know! Best, Bri.

I press Send and then go to my closet and pull out a pair of faded jeans and an old T-shirt. The clothes should work for relief work, though I still don't know the exact details of what I'm going to be doing. The uncertainty is a bit unsettling, but I'm sure that'll pass once I get started. I look at all of my leotards and tights, perfectly folded and ready to be packed, that are on one of the shelves and sigh. My laptop pings, and I lean away from the closet before I can start wallowing and click on the response from the commenter. Anticipation buzzes as I wait for the message to load. I didn't think I'd get a response so quickly.

Hi, Bri! As much as I appreciate the offer, I'm not much
of a writer, so I'm going to have to politely decline. I
wish you all the best with You Truly Assumed, Mashallah.

I reread the response and the rejection stings, despite having tough skin from years of ballet. I shouldn't have assumed
that a couple of likes and comments meant that I should actually try to start a blog with other people. Maybe the comment
wasn't a sign after all, and even if it was, the idea isn't practical. An ache pinches my heart sharp and fast, even though I
know it wasn't personal. Another example of why sticking to
the plan is my favorite route. I glance at the clock and then
at the poster of Misty Copeland that hangs above my bed,
and I sigh as I leave my room. Time to put my new summer
plan into action.

★ ★ ★ ★ ★

I look out the window as Mom pulls into the parking lot.
It's as packed as it is when school is in session, which means
a lot of people must've shown up for the first day of volunteering. A rush of memories attached to the average redbrick
middle school floods through me, and it hits me that until five
years ago this building was like a second home to me. This
is one site in DC where the relief efforts are being held since
the principal offered up the school to be used to help. At this
particular location, a lot of the efforts are going to be centered
around assisting people who were affected by the bombing
with any errands they may need to get done and collecting
donations to help support them and their families. Since this
is my old middle school and Mom works here, it makes sense

that she wanted me to help volunteer at this location. But since Dad's boss, Mr. Smith, is apparently on the school board and his kids go here, that also adds a bit of pressure.

Nuri and I hop out of the car. Even though she won't be volunteering for as long as I am because of her lacrosse tournament, it's nice to be starting off together. Since I get Friday and the weekends off, Dad is going to join Mom on those days. Most federal government employees are already back at work, so it's harder for him to take off time during the week.

The smell of Lysol and cardboard boxes hits me as I head inside the middle school. The lights seem dimmer than they used to be, and the motivational posters hang halfway off the wall. The lockers are all open, wearing another year of dents and scrawled Sharpie messages. I peer into a classroom and see that the chairs and desks are stacked, the space stripped bare. Like its students, the building has entered summer hibernation before starting fresh in the fall. But even though it looks bare, voices echo down the hallways as people move through them. There's a collective buzz in the air, and maybe that's because there are a lot of people here.

"Hello, Ms. Siddiq. It's so great to see you and the girls," Ms. Chandler, one of the teachers who works with Mom, says from behind the sign-in table as she checks us in.

"It's great to see you as well," Mom says. "Though admittedly I wish it was under better circumstances."

"I certainly agree." She nods. "You all can head to the gym."

We walk in, and Mom and Nuri both instantly split off to go talk with their friends. Chatter and laughs bounce across the gym, and it still smells like prepubescent sweat and rubber dodgeballs. I head toward the folded bleachers and the edge of the crowd, scanning the space and spotting a few people from my grade. But there's no one I dislike enough to avoid or like enough to go talk to, so I lean against one of the walls away from the center of the gym and hope that I don't look as out of place as I feel. Despite the occasion, the tone in the gym is more positive than I thought it was going to be. I expected to feel some type of heaviness walking in. Maybe it'll come later once we start working, or maybe we're all still in shock.

"Hello, everyone," Principal Barry says, not a strand out of place in her sleek press and curl. "On behalf of the greater DC metropolitan area, I'd like to thank each and every one of you for choosing to be here today. Your time and energy are greatly needed, and we have an important month of healing ahead of us. I will now let Ms. Carmen, head of our school board, explain how today is going to work."

Everyone nods, the gym now silent and somber, as Ms. Carmen takes the microphone.

"We have separated you all into groups at random. Each group will have a group leader and will be partnered with two to four families of those directly impacted by the terrorist attack. Our goal as volunteers is to help ease the burden on the families by assisting them with meal prep and delivery and running any errands that the families may need so that they can focus on healing. Each group will be tasked with setting up a rotating schedule so that at least two people will always be available when the group's assigned families need assistance. The group leaders are standing behind me, and I'll now read the names of the members in each group. Please listen up."

I look at all of the group leaders, Mom being one of them, and my stomach flips when I spot an unfortunately familiar face in my peripheral vision. Hayat Price. If I'm in the same group as him, I'm going to scream. I already had to endure seeing him first thing every Tuesday and Thursday mornings in English 11 during the school year. He's my school's star lacrosse player—which makes him high school royalty since we don't have a football team—a class clown, and a master of distracting our teacher from staying on track in class when I actually wanted to talk about Toni Morrison. On top of the fact that he's deemed the cutest guy in our grade, and he soaks up the attention that comes from that. Hayat isn't horrible, but he's way too self-centered for my liking.

If he took things seriously and wasn't always so annoying, then maybe we could get along. Dad and Mom used to want us to be family friends and for Hayat and me, along with Nuri and Hayat's younger siblings, to be super close. Being Black Muslims with interfaith parents who attend a primarily white elite prep school, I must admit, did have a lot of bonding potential. But after Nuri and Amir, Hayat's younger brother, decided to break up after dating for a good chunk of their freshman year, that potential evaporated, and I'm still beyond fine with that. Out of sisterly solidarity, both Price brothers are now on the Siddiq Sister No List. Though Hayat's younger sister, Aliyah, who's a rising junior and goes to my studio, is one of the sweetest people.

"Up next is Jonathan Smith's group, which will be partnered with the Clark family, the Seed family, and the Taylor family."

I perk up a little at hearing the last name Clark. I'm not sure if Morgan's family signed up for assistance, and I've been running errands to help her and her family before this, but getting partnered up with them would be great. An extra excuse to hang out and check on her couldn't hurt.

"The group's members are Hayat Price, Sabriya Siddiq…"

I groan internally. Nuri gives me a sympathetic smile from across the gym where she is with her group. I spot one of her friends who also plays lacrosse with her, so at least she has someone that she knows. Her group lead is Ms. Carmen, who seems nice.

"Feel free to join your group and make your way to each group's designated room. I'll be bouncing around and checking in," Principal Barry says once all of the names have been read.

I sigh, making my way to where Mr. Smith stands holding up a sign with his name on it. I push my way toward my assigned group, elbowing a few people in the sides.

"Hey," Hayat says.

Ignore and don't engage. Ignore and don't engage.

Hayat grins, as if he knows that he's getting on my nerves. Because he does. He opens his mouth, and I hold out my hand.

"Nope, not today. I don't want to hear any of your knock-knock jokes."

"Suit yourself." His shoulders drop. "So, how's lacrosse going for Nuri?"

"Why are you even here? Isn't there like a lacrosse off-season or something?"

He takes a small step back, wincing. "My mom was one of the first responders during the attack, and she thought it was important that my family help the victims and their families. So I'm here to do that."

My stomach drops, and I instantly regret being too harsh.

"I'm really sorry to hear that. If you can, please tell her that the community thanks her for her service. Myself included."

He nods. "Thank you. I will."

We follow Mr. Smith down the hall to the faculty kitchen, and he looks like any other average white dude so I don't have much to go on. His hair is gelled back, and his business shirt and pants are smooth with not a wrinkle in sight. I don't know why he's dressed like he's going to work, but hey, whatever works. He looks like he could be between my parents' and grandparents' ages, and he smiles at us as he leads my group down the hallway.

"Here we are, group," Mr. Smith says, holding the door open for us. "I can't wait to work with you all."

I walk into the faculty kitchen. "Thanks!"

"Of course. Also, are you Ansar Siddiq's daughter by any chance? He said that his family would be volunteering, and I recognized the last name since it's not that common."

Oh, shit. I forgot that Mr. Smith is Dad's new boss. I thought being put in a group with Hayat was bad, but this is so much worse. I'll have to keep my feet pointed and my back straight at all times. I can't afford to slouch and mess up at all.

I nod. "I am."

"How wonderful, he recently joined our office!" He glances at my necklace. "What's your necklace say?"

I touch my neck, and my eyes widen with realization. Sometimes, I forget that I wear the necklace because it feels like an extension of myself. Putting it on every morning has become a habit, a ritual of sorts.

"It says Allah in Arabic."

Mr. Smith raises his eyebrows. "Oh, I didn't realize that you and your father are Muslim."

"Uh, yep, we are."

Mr. Smith opens his mouth, but shakes his head and keeps walking over to the rest of the group. That was weird and lowkey a microaggression. But he's Dad's new boss, so I'm sure he's mostly decent. Besides, I'm not here to rock the boat.

"Now I see why they never let us in here," a voice says from behind me.

I jump, and Hayat grins, knowing he scared me. But he's right. The faculty kitchen and the cafeteria are on separate sides of the school, and as a middle school student I was always told that going into the faculty kitchen would result in detention. Now I understand why. The kitchen looks like something out of a home magazine. Stainless steel appliances, two stoves, and even a kitchen island. I'm impressed.

Mr. Smith walks to the front of the kitchen standing before all of us. "Hi, everyone! My name is Jonathan Smith, and I want to start off by saying that I'm very excited to be leading this group. We'll be working closely with our assigned families to make and deliver meals, as well as to run other errands for them such as picking up prescriptions, walking pets, or doing other everyday tasks. All I want is for our community, our city, to be safe. None of us should have to live in fear."

He looks at all of us, and his eyes land on me as I nod along with the rest of the group. He's right, and that's why the resulting Islamophobia in the news has been so awful. I don't feel as safe in my identity as I did a week ago, and that's terrifying.

"Alright. That's all I have to say. Hands in, team on three!"

We all crowd in close, the air buzzing with energy.

"One!"

"Two!"

"Three!"

"TEAM!"

I'm pulled into the moment as I throw my hand up with everyone else, and I almost forget that I wish I was away auditioning for summer intensives. Almost.

I GUESS WE'RE DOING THE DAMN THING

This week I started getting involved in the relief work. I'm part of a group that's dedicating the rest of the month to helping the families impacted by the terrorist attack. I was wondering if any of you have gotten involved in taking any sort of action since the aftermath of the attack? If so, I'd love to hear how you all are engaging in your respective communities, so feel free to share your experiences in the comments!

So, speaking of doing new things, I've been convinced by my younger sister to keep *You Truly Assumed* public. I had no idea that my first post was public until you all started leaving comments. I'm honestly surprised that people actually a) read it and b) enjoyed it. That post was just me dumping everything on the page. It was a hot mess, honestly, and I can't guarantee that the rest of the posts on this journal/blog/some combo of both aren't going to be the same. So if you're here, you can get ready to read some hopefully relatable garbage.

I was both surprised and humbled at the fact that so many of you commented. The first post got around 100 comments, which I was definitely not expecting at all, so thank you to everyone who took the time to leave one. I know what it's like to feel unseen and unheard. To read books or watch shows and not see yourselves represented, or to see yourselves misrepresented, in them. So, if *You Truly Assumed* can provide any of you with a mirror and a clear, true, unblemished reflection, then I want to do my best to make this site the best it can be.

Okay. That got kinda deep, though it's 10000% true. Everyone deserves to see themselves represented as the protagonist. If these ramblings help take steps toward reaching that goal, then yay.

I've added an about me page and a contact page, and I'm going to do my best to upload new posts every Monday and Thursday. Also, if any of you are familiar with website design and would be interested in helping me spruce up *YTA*, then definitely let me know. And feel free to leave any feedback either in the comments or send it via my contact page. I've never run a blog before, so I'm open to any suggestions. That's pretty much it for now!

Until next post (this is a cute sign-off, isn't it?),
~Bri

ZAKAT

LULLWOOD, GEORGIA

I slide the last book onto the shelf and head toward the lone register at the front of the store. The bell above the door rings, and my mouth goes dry when Asher walks in. His camouflage pants and dark brown shirt rub me the wrong way, and he shakes the can of spray paint in his hand as he walks closer to the register as if in warning.

"Can you please put that away?" I ask.

"Lighten up, Zakat," he says, mispronouncing my name even though we've crossed paths enough times for him to know how to say it. "I haven't been in this part of town for a while because it's boring and nothing ever happens here. I still don't understand why Lucy even agreed to work here."

"Why don't you ask her. I'm getting back to work."

I turn away from the register, and Asher laughs.

"I didn't realize that you were sassy. You seem so quiet, especially since you wear that," he says, gesturing to his head.

I bite my tongue so that I don't say anything to instigate and spur him on more. If there's one thing that Asher loves more than anything else it's attention, and I'm not going to give it to him.

"Lucy," I yell. "Asher's here."

I don't know if he actually came here to see her or if he's using her being here as a guise to come over and be annoying. Asher will venture over to the community center for the art classes, but he's never set foot inside Tiny Treasure Trove as far as I know. If I had it my way, he never would again.

Lucy looks up from where she's shelving books and gives me a small smile. "Thanks for letting me know."

I nod, making sure to hide my surprise. Aafreen must've said something to Lucy in order for the water to be under the bridge so quickly. Aafreen steps out of the storage room, her brows furrowed.

"Asher's here? That's gotta be cap," she says, crossing her arms.

"It's not."

"There's something about the guy that screams bad vibes."

"You mean besides the fact that he follows *FTR* and reposts their content on social media?" I glance back over at where him and Lucy are talking. "I don't understand how she hangs around him."

Aafreen shrugs. "That's her family."

I start to say something about how maybe she hangs out with him because she shares some of his views, but stop myself. Lucy's going through a lot right now, and maybe being around family, even Asher, is helping her.

I turn back to Aafreen. "Are we still on to do some debate prep for next year over at your place this afternoon?"

She pauses. "About that, I actually made plans with Lucy to grab a bite to eat at Waffle House and go shopping in Midtown this afternoon. I'm so sorry. I totally forgot about the prep for debate."

"Oh, wow. Okay."

"I'm sorry. I really did forget. Do you want to join Lucy and me? You're more than welcome to."

My annoyance subsides a little at the eagerness in her voice.

"It's okay, we'll reschedule," I say, starting to walk away. "You and Lucy have fun."

"Zakat?"

I spin around. "Hmm?"

"I know you don't trust Lucy and you don't have to, but I think she's changed since then, as we all have, and she's going through a lot right now."

"I still don't know how you can welcome her so easily."

"Because she's given me no reason not to."

I sigh. She has a point there. Lucy hasn't said anything remotely close to Islamophobic since she's gotten here. Maybe Aafreen's right and she has changed.

She shrugs. "I actually think you'd like her, if you'd give her a chance."

"I'll see."

As much as I want Aafreen to be happy and for everyone to get along, I'm not going to let Lucy catch me off guard again.

"If you keep only holding on to the past, how are you going to move forward?"

That's a fair point, but I'm not sure it outweighs the chance of getting hurt again by Lucy. Her old insult is buried in my childhood, but that doesn't mean the impact of it is too. But I also trust Aafreen and her judgment.

"Fine. I'll give her one chance. One."

"Yay, thank you! I don't like it when we aren't on the same page." She hugs me. "I have to go, but we'll catch up soon."

She disappears around the corner, and I sigh. Sure, Lucy needs a friend. I need my best friend too. But if giving Lucy a chance means making Aafreen happy, then I'll make that choice any day.

I pull out my phone to text Baba and Mama that I'm about to leave work and accidentally click on the notes app instead of my messages. The note with the link to the blog from yesterday reminds me that I need to ask them if I can join. I hop on my bike and begin to ride down the path. The sharp scent of the leaves energizes me for the conversation that I'm about to have. Baba and Mama have always been a bit wary of the internet, so I didn't get my first phone or start to use any form of social media until my freshman year. It didn't bother me because I had Lullwood, but now that I'm older I want to expand. Hopefully my parents will understand.

I spot Mama looking out the window, waiting and watching out for me, and when she sees me she unlocks the front door.

"Zakat, I'm glad you're home! How was work?"

"Work was good. Thank you for asking." I wash my hands and take off my shoes, the two rules for entering the house, and turn back to Mama. "Ma, there's something that I want to talk to you and Ba about."

The words feel clunky leaving my mouth, but I don't reel them back in. Being a part of *You Truly Assumed* is something that I want to do, and it feels like a controlled way to start to expand beyond Lullwood.

"Is everything okay?" Baba asks as Mama and I sit on the couch next to him.

"Yes, yes. Everything is totally fine."

Mama lets out a sigh of relief. "Okay, Zakat, what is it?"

"Can I join a blog called *You Truly Assumed*? It's a space for young Muslim women, run by young Muslim women. I think it'd be really great to work with them and share my art and support my Muslim sisters. This is something that I really want to do."

"No," Mama says.

My throat tightens, even though a large part of me expected this response. I take a deep breath and set my shoulders back, determined to press on.

"May I ask why, Mama?" I turn to Baba. "This could make my college applications stand out! Not many teens blog. It's unique."

"That's a good point, but will you be able to focus on college applications, applying for scholarships, and working if you're also contributing to a blog? You're already spending a lot of time on art, and soon you'll be starting your business classes," Baba says. "We want you to make this summer count, especially in terms of college, and blogging may be adding too much."

"I'll be able to handle it!"

Baba and Mama exchange a look before they both turn to face me.

"Once you put something on the internet, it is there forever," Mama says. "I don't think it's safe. What if people steal your work?"

"Then I'll copyright them. Every piece I have is signed. Please, Mama? This is something that I really want to do, and I don't think I've ever given you a reason to not trust me."

Baba and Mama carry on the conversation with their eyes, and I look between the two of them, trying to pick up what I can.

Mama turns to me. "I'm sorry, Zakat, but the answer is no. The online world isn't as safe as Lullwood is."

"But, Mama, *You Truly Assumed* is safe."

"It sounds like a good idea, but the answer is still no. Lullwood is the closest thing to safe that we can give you, and it is far safer than the online world will ever be. What if some horrible people find the blog and start harassing you? Out there, things like that happen so much most people don't notice anymore. Or don't care. Do you understand?"

I press my lips into a thin line. "Yes, Mama, I understand."

"I get that you want to share your art," Baba says. "Maybe you can put up some of your newer pieces at the community center."

"Thanks, Ba, I'll think about it."

I know they're both doing their best to look out for me. Maybe Baba is right and there are other ways to share my art. *You Truly Assumed* seemed similar to Lullwood because it came across as a space that was bigger than me. But perhaps I'm reaching out too far too fast. If I'm going to convince Baba and Mama to get more comfortable with the idea of me going out of state for college, then I can't do anything to jeopardize that.

★ ★ ★ ★ ★

I hum, bopping my head to the beat of the music flowing through my earbuds. A shiver runs down my spine, even though sunlight streams through the windows behind me. Wiping away a few stray eraser shavings, I look down at my drawing in satisfaction.

It's of a girl covering her ears in the middle of an explosion. Whether the debris descending around me represents my dreams, my parents' dreams, or Lullwood's dreams I'm not really sure. The debris is a bunch of falling leaves amid speech bubbles filled with headlines like *Rise in anti-Muslim hate crimes thought to be correlated to the DC Metro terror attack* or *Mayor under investigation after saying that Muslims should've prevented the DC Metro Attack*. Even my subconscious is a wreck.

I turn and look at the trees through the bedroom window that's above the nook. Even though it's only the second week of June, I'm already looking forward to when the leaves start to change to bright shades of red and orange. Aafreen and I used to climb them, whispering secrets to each other among the leaves, but we stopped after she fell and fractured her arm in the fourth grade. I flip the page in my sketchbook and start drawing, letting the music decide my strokes. I turn the volume down and let myself get lost in the soft scratch of the pencil lead against the rough paper. In the way my feelings move and take form until it feels like they're capable of flying away, leaving me lighter.

"Zakat!" Mama yells, storming into my room. "Something's happened at the school. The Islamic School for Boys!"

I jolt, my pencil streaking across the page. "What's wrong?"

"Eggs were thrown at it! And someone drew on it." Her brows furrow as she searches for words. "What is that called?"

"Graffiti," I whisper. "Someone graffitied the school."

My stomach plummets as my heart races. I start to shiver as the reality of Mama's words pours over me like an icy bucket of water.

Mama nods. "Yes, that's the word. There's going to be an emergency meeting at the masjid after Jummah prayers. Aafreen's mama called and said that whoever did it left slurs and graphic drawings on the walls. Nothing like this has ever happened before. That's why the board members at the masjid voted to put up that fence. A lot of people thought something might happen after the attack in DC, but I hoped we would be alright because this is Lullwood. But I was wrong, Zakat, and we need to leave right now."

She places a hand on my shoulder, and the touch breaks the rest of my shock. The tears come flooding. They burn, tracking anger down my face as I wipe them away. Whoever graffitied the school committed a hate crime, even if graffitiing a building is juvenile. Part of me also believed that Lullwood would be protected from the ripples of the attack in DC, but even Bubble Wrap doesn't keep everything from breaking.

"Who did it?"

"We don't know."

It's got to be Asher. He's one of the few graffiti artists in Lullwood, and he's joked about doing something like this before. But I have no way to prove that, and the realization makes my tears flow faster. Lullwood needs my help, and I can't do anything. The pain and the anger and the fear can't be buried anymore. Hateful things do happen here, and that was never a possibility to me. Anywhere beyond these woods, sure, but never within.

I used to think that there was something powerful, magical even, about Lullwood's woods. But they're nothing more than a bunch of trees.

Mama pulls me into her, and I cry into her shoulder, my heart breaking for my sanctuary.

★ ★ ★ ★ ★

Everyone crowds into the large auditorium-like room that's been filled with lines of foldable plastic chairs in preparation for today's meeting. Our collective dismay, anger, and alarm forms a tangible energy that fills the room. Baba, Mama, and I find spots in the middle of the room, and I spot Aafreen and her parents sitting a couple of rows in front of us.

"Hello, everyone," Ms. Aden says from the stage. "Thank you all for coming today, though I wish we were gathering together under different circumstances. This meeting will be an open forum, and anyone is welcome to speak. My fellow board member, Mr. Amal, will make sure that the microphone gets passed along efficiently. Our goal today is to figure out how to best move forward as a community following the targeting of the Boys' Islamic School."

I fidget in my chair. Finding out who was behind the graffiti wouldn't necessarily address the root of the problem and end Islamophobia, but it would give me part of my sense of safety back. Maybe it'd take us all back to before the terrorist attack when everything felt alright. Could we move backward instead of forward?

Suggestions fly as the meeting carries on: check the footage from the security camera on the school, put a fence around both Islamic schools, update our school IDs so that students have to swipe or scan to get through that fence. All the suggestions are focused on how to keep others out, and even though that makes sense, it's also sad that we have to hunker down and stifle ourselves. Fear makes people small, and even finding out who was behind the vandalism won't completely erase the fear that something like this will happen again.

As the meeting starts to come to a close, Mama raises her hand.

"Okay, this will be the last comment," Ms. Aden says as Mr. Amal hands the microphone to Mama.

My heart swells with pride as Mama stands up.

"Hello, everyone. I wanted to take the time to say that while ramping up security is essential to take into account, we must also make sure that all of us, especially our youth, still feel like this is their home. Perhaps that means holding more community events at the community center, but no matter how we move forward, I don't want us to lose sight of what makes Lullwood special while we're trying to protect it."

People murmur their approval, and a few even clap. Ms. Aden says her parting words, and then people begin to get up and mingle or leave. Even though a concrete plan wasn't decided on, the energy in the room is lighter and less charged. This meeting made me realize that, for better or for worse, Lullwood is going to change. It can't stay stagnant, and neither can I. But though Lullwood is going to contract, I'm going to expand. Even if that means pushing against what Baba and Mama want me to do.

As both of them chat, I slip outside so that I can use my phone. I take a seat on one of the benches in the garden behind the masjid, which is one of the prettiest and most calming places in Lullwood. The colors of the flowers mirror the pastel shades of my favorite set of brush pens, and the faint splashing sound from the small fountain that sits in the middle of the garden is as soothing as falling rain. I pull up the blog *You Truly Assumed*, and see that there's a new post. I skim over it, and a nervous energy starts to buzz in my chest as an idea begins to form. Ideas for a piece inspired by the new post swirl in my head, a wave of blended hues flowing from a laptop screen. The title of the blog would be written over the color either in a typewriter or cursive font. Or maybe the title could be written on the back of the laptop screen, like a sticker. So it'd be a sticker within a sticker, which would be a bit meta.

Bri's post said she's looking for someone to help with website design, so maybe I can offer to help contribute as well. Before I can talk myself out of it, I go to the new contact page on the blog and start to type.

> Hi, Bri!
> I wanted to say how relatable your content is. I connected to it so deeply, and I can't wait to read more of your work in the future. If you ever need any contributions or any help with the blog, I'd love the opportunity to be considered.
> Best,
> Kat

Before I can come up with a million reasons why this is a bad idea, I press Send. My stomach drops a little when it hits me that I can't unsend the message, though I could technically ignore a response if I get one. Being brave doesn't always feel so good, especially when I'm going against Baba and Mama's wishes. I'm pretty sure that this is the first time I've ever done something that neither of them has recommended, but a part of growing up is forging my own path, even if that means deviating from the one that my parents set out for me. *You Truly Assumed* looks like a good way to start creating that path.

My phone buzzes. I pick it up to see an email notification, and I click on it.

From: ballerinabri@xmail.com
To: katr54@xmail.com

Hi, Kat!
Thank you so much for taking the time to read, and I really appreciate your message. I'm looking to bring a few young Muslim women on to the admin team with me to write content. If you're interested in writing for You Truly Assumed, as you indicated in your email, then I look forward to hearing from you!
Best,
Bri

I grin down at my phone, rereading the email over and over to make sure that I'm not making this up and getting excited over nothing. My excitement wanes a little bit each time my eyes lock on the word *write*. I can't write like she does, and it hits me that I didn't specify what I want to do. Besides designing a logo, maybe I can also doodle for *You Truly Assumed*. Or I could submit a comic strip or two. Aafreen's always telling me that I need to work on opening up more, and this could be the push I didn't even know I needed. This could be a way of stepping out of my comfort zone, without having a big risk attached to taking the chance. Except for people I don't know saying that they don't like my work. My excitement drops.

But if I don't know them, then I can overlook those comments. And I could help other Muslims feel seen, like the way Bri's writing does for me. I could make a difference. I could do something.

This could be perfect.

From: katr54@xmail.com
To: ballerinabri@xmail.com

Hi, Bri!
I'm still interested; however, I don't write. I draw, so maybe I could illustrate your posts. Or my drawings can stand on their own. I could also submit a comic strip or two. I've attached photos of a few pieces of my work. Most are done in pencil and pen, but I also work with charcoal. I realize that a lot of my doodles are related to nature and a lot of my charcoal sketches are of faces, but I can definitely do other stuff. Thank you for the opportunity!
Best,
Kat

I go through my camera roll, and I click on two photos of my art. The first is a true-to-life drawing of Aafreen that I did for her last minute, and the second is a sketch of the Lullwood trees. That way Bri can see that I'm able to draw both people and landscapes and get a sense of my range. A spur-of-the-moment idea pops into my head, and I attach the

photo that I drew earlier of the girl covering her ears surrounded by fallen debris comprised of headlines. Hopefully
that'll show her that I get the experiences that she's blogging
about on *You Truly Assumed*. Bri responds quickly, letting me
know that she's excited to see what I come up with for the
blog and that I can text her with any questions or concerns
since it'll probably be more convenient than emailing back
and forth. Excitement churns through me instead of dread.

This is the summer of tipping the scales, and I can't do that
without changing things up. As long as I go by Kat and not my
real name, I'll be fine. And maybe the blog will take off and
I can use it to show Mama and Baba what art can do. What I
can do.

FARAH

INGLETHORNE, CALIFORNIA

I push one of my box braids behind my ear as a gust of wind ruffles the bright red patio umbrella. The sun beats down on us, but today I don't mind the warmth because it helps to block out the chill from the wind. Voices and elevator music float on another strong gust, and I take a sip of my hot chocolate, savoring its sweetness and the sweetness of this moment. Hot chocolate is a year-round drink, and that's a debate I'm always willing to have.

Mom decided that today was worth a tiny splurge since I'm leaving tomorrow, and we ended up at Bailey's Cozy Corner after I finished getting my hair done earlier. True to its name, the small outside eating area feels homey with the little seat pillows, plastic cups, and tiny planters hanging from each tabletop.

"We should come here more often," Mom says, munching on her tortilla salad bowl.

I take a bite of my tomato, basil, and mozzarella sandwich. "Yeah, we should."

"How are you feeling about leaving for Kirby tomorrow?"

"I'm fine, I guess." I shrug. "I did some shopping yesterday, so there's a ton of microwavable meals and quick snacks for you. I also organized the bills that need to be paid while I'm away. I know you won't forget, but just in case."

Mom reaches across the table and squeezes my hand. "Thank you, Farah. I'm definitely going to miss your organization. I still can't believe you're going to be away for three weeks. That's almost a full month."

"You're the one who's sending me away!"

Mom rolls her eyes at my joking tone. "You'll end up thanking me someday, just wait."

But I understand what she means. Mom and I have never been apart for longer than three days, and that's only because of the occasional school trip. I've never stepped foot out of California. I'm not scared to leave, but I'm worried about leaving Mom and her being on her own. Even though I know she can take care of herself, I'm worried she'll forget to eat before her evening class since I always pack her a to-go dinner. I'm worried she'll misplace her glasses and I won't be here to help her find them. I wish I didn't have to go, but I wish even more that I could take Mom with me.

I fight to keep my expression neutral so she can't see how scared I really am.

"I'll be home before you know it."

She leans back in her chair, her stare as heavy as the whipped cream that floats on top of my hot chocolate.

"What, is there something on my face?"

"No, nothing's wrong. I'm thinking about how much you're going to change and grow over the rest of the month."

I sigh. "Mom."

"I mean, think about it. You're setting out to go explore the world. You deserve that." She takes off her sunglasses, looking me in the eyes. "You're in a much better place than I was when I was your age, and that lets me know that I'm doing something right."

"You do everything right."

"Oh, honey. Thank you. I do try."

I reach over and wipe away the tears on her cheeks, almost knocking our food off the table. A bit of nervousness surges through me as I catch more of her tears. We're both so strong from having to carry so much that sometimes it catches me off guard when either of us sets down some of that weight. I remember the weeks when I walked to school and she walked to work after our car got taken away in the middle of the night because we couldn't afford the monthly payments anymore. So many things are buried deep, and I like to keep them there.

"You've been such a rock for me," Mom says.

I fan my face with my folded napkin. "Mom, you're going to make me cry. And if we're both crying, everyone's going to think we're weird."

"Let them stare. We're having a moment."

I laugh and wipe my eyes.

"I'm so proud of you, Farah Rose. I want you to go out to Boston and live the experience to the fullest because I'm going to be living vicariously through you."

"You make it sound like I'm going to party on the beach for three weeks, but okay."

Every negative thought and fear seems to disappear as I down more of my hot chocolate. Mom thinking that I'm going to go up to Boston and live my best life makes me think that maybe I can. She'll be fine and so will I. She'll always be with me, no matter if I'm traveling alone or with her.

"Don't worry, Mom. I'll live big enough for the both of us."

Mom squeezes my hand. "I want you to be on your best behavior. No acting out of line or being disrespectful. And please don't bully the two-year-old."

I roll my eyes. "Okay, Mom."

"I'm being serious, Farah. I need to know that while you're away you won't break our trust."

The weight of her words hits me. We've been able to get through everything together because of the strength of the trust between us. I can't break it.

"I promise."

Mom relaxes, her shoulders dropping. "As long as you carry yourself out there the way you do around me, with hopefully fewer sarcastic comments, I know you'll be fine. I believe your promise as much as I believe in you."

Tears rush to my eyes again, and I dab them away with a napkin. I can't break my promise. I won't.

"I know this trip is outside your comfort zone, but I'm proud of you for taking a chance," Mom says.

First Riley talking about risks and now Mom talking about chances. The website that Riley showed me pops into my head, some part of me still drawn to it.

"I'll be right back," Mom says, taking our empty plates and heading inside the café.

I pull out my phone and click on the tab where the website

You Truly Assumed is still up. The page refreshes, and a new post appears at the top along with a recently added about me page and a contact page. The background of the site is now a solid shade of orange, which is a bit better than the original paper-white one.

I start to read the new post, and my eyes stop at the lines: *Also, if any of you are familiar with website design and would be interested in helping me spruce up* YTA*, then definitely let me know.* The owner of the blog, Bri, is looking for someone to do web design, and if that isn't a sign, then I don't know what is. Everything is changing this month anyway, so potentially helping on a whim would just be another change. Plus, I want to prove to Riley, Mom, and myself that I can handle change and take chances, even if I often try not to mess with either.

I go to the contact page on the site and type out a quick message.

> Hello,
> I've really enjoyed your posts on YTA, and I saw that you're looking for someone to help with the design of the blog and its overall aesthetic. I'd be more than happy to do it.
> All the best,
> Farah

I swap the period at the end of the last sentence for an exclamation mark to hopefully come across as friendly and then click on the submit button. A spike of nervousness shoots through me, and I take a sip of my now-lukewarm hot chocolate to calm down. If I get a response back, then great, but if not that's fine too. Offering to help definitely isn't a super big risk in the grand scheme of things, but it's one that I took and for now that's enough.

Mom comes back over to the table. "Ready to head back home?"

I stand up and slip my phone back in my pocket. "Yep, I'm ready."

★ ★ ★ ★ ★

I grab some of the clothes from off the floor and toss them onto my bed. Besides one of the programming books that I stuffed into my backpack so that I can read it on the plane, the room looks the exact same as it did yesterday. Knowing Mom, I'll probably come back to aesthetic wall decor that she found at Marshalls and Ross or a bunch of plants because she's always saying that they'll help us study and increase our productivity. But for now, my side of the room looks like I'm just leaving for a regular day instead of almost a month. At least Mom won't be able to say my room isn't clean anymore once I finish dumping everything into a suitcase. I mean, packing.

"I hope this one will work," Riley says, stopping the suitcase in front of my bed.

"Thank you, Ry. It's great."

Neither Mom nor I actually own a suitcase, and I didn't realize that until an hour ago. We've never needed one. It's the small things like that which are making me realize how big me leaving really is. But I'm trying not to think about that part.

I dump some of the clothes on my bed into the square purple suitcase. There's no need to roll anything up to save space. I'm sure everything will fit—and with room to spare. I basically wear the same thing every day anyway.

"Have you given any thought to our convo yesterday?" he asks.

"A little. I'm still trying to figure everything out."

As much as I like Riley's kind eyes and his uncanny ability to make me feel content whenever I'm around him, part of me is wondering if what we have now is still going to be around come the end of the year and his first semester in college. Mathematically, I know that there's a fifty-fifty chance, but realistically I don't like those odds. One part of me is saying to let go now because the hurt that could come from losing our relationship would be terrible. Then the other part of me is saying to hold on tighter despite everything changing because Riley gets me and I get him and that's enough.

Riley makes the face that he does when he's tasted something sour or when he knows he's about to say something that I'm not going to like.

"I was actually going to tell you that I got accepted into a STEM preorientation program that's for first-gen students and students from minority backgrounds."

I smile, throwing my arms around his shoulders and pulling him into a hug. "That's amazing news." I pull back a little so that I can see his face. "But why'd you make that face?"

He tightens his arms around my waist. "I have to leave a week earlier for the program."

"Oh," I say. "So instead of the fifteenth, you're leaving on the eighth?"

He nods and gives me a small smile.

"Okay, so we'll have one week in August instead of two. That's fine. Totally fine."

He gives me an amused look. "You seem like you're convincing yourself."

"Just a little, but I'm also the one who's leaving for the rest of this month so I can't hold this against you. Especially when it'll be a good way for you to meet people and get to know the campus. I'm proud of you."

He leans down and presses a soft kiss to my forehead. "Thank you."

My heart melts, and I rest my head on his chest. Even though a one-week program isn't a big deal at all, it's just another reminder of how much things are changing between us. If I want to make our relationship work, then I have to accept that things will be different, even though I have no control over what will change. I've always seen myself as an all-or-nothing type of person, but if Riley and I do end up doing long-distance I have to give it my all or it won't work. Right now, I feel like I'm close enough that if he breaks my heart I can catch it before it completely cracks into smithereens. When he's halfway across the country, I won't be able to protect myself like that anymore.

"I'm still going to think about things," I say, sitting down on the bed. "But your pre-orientation program doesn't change anything at all."

"I understand." He pauses. "I brought something else with me, but it can wait."

I blink. "What? Riley, you didn't need to get me anything."

"I know, I know," he says, scooting over a pile of folded shirts and sitting down next to me, his side pressing against mine. "I know I didn't need to, but I wanted to, and I needed something to do on my lunch break at the mall."

I give him a look, and he grins at me sheepishly.

"While I was on break, I found something that I thought you'd really like, so I got it. Open it!"

He pulls a small red box out from his drawstring bag and hands it to me.

"And don't worry, it was less than twenty-five," he says quickly.

At the very beginning, when we first started going out, Riley and I agreed to a twenty-five-dollar budget for gifts and treating the other to dates. It relieved a lot pressure for me and put us on equal footing.

"Open it!"

"I'm going, I'm going."

I open the box to see a bright red rose charm attached to a choker. "It's a rose!"

He grins. "Yep!"

Roses are my favorite flower—and also my middle name, of course—which Riley obviously remembered because he's Riley.

I kiss him, and my heart races when he pulls me closer.

"This is so corny," I say into his chest.

"I know."

"I love it. Thank you." I pull back. "Can you put it on for me?"

He nods and clasps the choker around my neck, his touch sending sparks up my spine.

I touch the rose that rests in the hollow of my throat. "Riley Alexander Chesterton, you're amazing."

"And you, Farah Rose Rafiq, are equally as amazing, if not

more. Definitely more." He laces his fingers through mine. "I know you still don't really want to go, but I think you're going to end up enjoying yourself. I'll be here when you get back."

His words make my heart soar, and I want to grab them and never let them go. But it hits me that when he leaves in August, I'm going to be the one who has to say those words and trust that they're enough.

I hold our linked hands up to my cheek. "If you fit into the suitcase, I'd take you with me. But I still think that the time away will help us figure out what we want."

"You mean what you want," he says with a soft smile. "I know what I want, and that is you."

The words stun me and send my emotions scrambling to come together in a way that makes sense. Sometimes he manages to throw me so off-kilter with his heart and his words, and it can be a little scary because I like to be grounded.

My phone buzzes, pulling my attention away from my scattering thoughts.

"Let me check this real quick," I say, grabbing my phone off the bed. "It may be good news."

Riley raises his eyebrows. "What kind of good news?"

"I was thinking about what you said about how I may be a teeny bit risk-averse, and it turns out that the person who runs the site that you showed me is looking for someone to help with web design. So, I sent a little message through the contact page saying I could help. You know, for practice and to add something to my résumé, and also because I still have all of these ideas running around in my head and nowhere to put them."

"That's so awesome, Farah," Riley says. "You think she responded?"

I look down at the notification to see the answer to his question and nod. "Yeah."

"Well, what are you waiting for! I'm sure she was super stoked to get your message."

The spike of nervousness from earlier shoots through me again, and I take a deep breath as I click on Bri's response. I can feel Riley watching me as I read her message, waiting for me to react before he does.

"She said, and I quote, 'Hi, Farah, it was so great to get your message. I'd love some help with making *You Truly Assumed* more engaging, and I look forward to hearing your ideas. Best, Bri.'"

"Farah, that's amazing. I'm so proud of you!"

He hugs me and swings me around, and I laugh as my feet leave the ground.

"Thanks for giving me the push I needed," I say once I'm steady again.

"That's what I'm here for." He taps the rose charm that hangs from the choker. "And I think this long-distance test run is going to go well."

"You do? What makes you so sure?" I ask, looking up at him.

"Because I think what we have is pretty special."

I look at Riley, at this guy standing next to me that believes in me so much and nudges me gently out of my comfort zone. Who makes me feel safe and seen.

Reaching out to the blog was just one small step toward putting myself out there and taking a chance, and maybe I need to do the same with Riley. He makes me feel like I'm flying, but I'm still really afraid to fall.

SABRIYA

ABINGTON, VIRGINIA

A knock sounds through the door that connects my bedroom to the bathroom, and I groan, putting my pillow over my head. "Go away, Nuri."

I hear footsteps rushing closer, and before I know it the bed dips as Nuri lands on me.

I look at the time on my phone while pushing her away. "Okay, okay, okay, I'm up."

Nuri hops back off the bed. "Now, that's what I thought."

"Brat."

She sticks her tongue out at me and leaves my room. I groan again, kicking off my covers to get ready for day two of volunteering. Sunlight streams in through the blinds, and I take my phone off the nightstand. The posters of Michaela DePrince and Debbie Allen on the other side of my room make me realize how much I should be working right now. I should be getting ready for ballet practice right now. I should be getting better at my craft. I should be going to auditions and keeping up with everyone else. The relief work is important, and I enjoy being able to sleep in instead of waking up for morning rehearsal, but I feel like I'm falling further behind. Like my dream—and everything I've worked for— is escaping me, the way water falls through cupped hands.

I pull up the email for *YTA* to see if there are any new comments, and the number of messages in the deleted items folder catches my eye. I click on the email at the top of the folder, and a comment pops up.

> **MisterX:** Muslims are terrorists. Should've kicked you all out years ago.

A sour taste fills my mouth, and I'm sure it's not only my bad breath. That's the second negative comment that's appeared. The unexpectedness stings more than the hate. I thought the first comment was a one-off, but I guess not. I take the comment out of the trash and press Approve. Kat must've put the comment in the trash, but if this person wants to hide their face behind a screen, then the whole world is going to see what they do show: their hate.

Swinging my legs over the side of my bed, I shiver at the chill from the air-conditioning. My phone buzzes as I start making up my bed, and I pick it up from the bedside drawer. I jump, dropping my phone as it starts ringing.

"FaceTime?" I mutter, clicking Answer.

The top half of Kat's face fills my screen, and I realize I'm looking up her nose.

"Kat?"

"Hey, sorry, that's an awful angle." She shifts on my screen until I can see her full face. "Is this weird? I hope this isn't weird. I started texting, but the message got too long, and then I started to overthink, and now here I am. I was about to cancel, but you picked up. So sorry if it's weird. Also, you can call me Zakat. I just go by Kat on the blog for privacy reasons."

"Gotcha. My name is Sabriya, but I go by Bri, so I totally understand. And no need to apologize, it's not a problem at all," I say, sitting down at my desk. "It's nice to meet you! Or see you, I guess."

She laughs. "True. So, uh, I don't want to be awkward, but I was wondering why you approved the comment from earlier this morning after I deleted it? I get a notification every time a comment is approved since I'm signed into the account for *YTA*. I was going to text you, but it seemed too confrontational and I didn't want you to read it the wrong way."

"So you FaceTimed me at 9:47 in the morning instead?"

"Uh, yes?"

"I approved it because I don't want whoever sent it to think that they're going to get away with their hate. If we trash it, then we're letting them off the hook."

"I see where you're coming from," she says, nodding. "But depending on who sees which comment, we can each make the decision to approve or trash a comment for ourselves, yes? And that decision is final."

"Yes, it should definitely be that way. I'm sorry, I didn't mean to go behind your back by approving it. I'll go back and delete it again."

Her shoulders drop a little. "It's okay, you don't have to. I just wanted to make sure we were on the same page."

"Yeah, of course, that makes sense. Next time, can we each deal with the comments in our own way and then whoever sees the comment first gets to decide how to handle it? We're not going to react to all comments the same, so I guess it's fine if we do it differently. But we could also have one person go through the comments."

"We could, but don't we both enjoy reading them?" Zakat asks.

"Everyone can still read them, but maybe just one of us can respond."

"Yeah, sure!"

"Okay, great," I say. "Oh, one last thing. Someone reached out about helping to spruce up *You Truly Assumed*! Her name is Farah, but she'll go by Rose on the blog. We've been emailing back and forth, and she knows a lot about coding. The three of us make up the admin team for *You Truly Assumed*, so we'll have to find a time for us all to meet. But once I get her number, I'm going to make a group chat with the three of us."

"That sounds great," Zakat says. "Have a great rest of your day!"

"Thanks! You too!"

Zakat waves, and then my phone goes to the home screen, the call ended. Usually I schedule FaceTime calls, but I appreciate the randomness. Plus, it's nice to be able to put a face to a name and know who I'm working with a bit more.

I open my laptop, click on my audition spreadsheet, and go to the yellow highlighted section full of possible reschedules. I go to all of the websites that I've organized into my spreadsheet, checking all of the dates, but with every click each audition remains a canceled one. That's not surprising. Most summer intensives outside of this area didn't change their start dates, so it was unlikely that they were going to reschedule their canceled auditions out here when there were others that people could still go to. Most summer intensives at companies in DC haven't updated yet, but it doesn't make sense to do one out here when I can still go to summer classes at my own studio. Plus, the goal was always to audition for the ABT intensive that's in New York, so even though I have to push back that goal to next summer I don't really want to change it.

Auditions wait for no one; you either keep up or you fall behind. Most dancers in the DMV are probably traveling to North Carolina or New York where other auditions are being held, and I'm stuck here. Still, it sucks. I was hoping that at least one audition in the DMV would've been rescheduled by now, but I guess it's too late. It's like a big red X has been drawn through the few remaining scraps of my summer plan.

I throw on a cropped hoodie, a pair of athletic shorts, and my Allah necklace and head downstairs.

"Morning, everyone," I say.

The light from the fridge hits me as I push around some of the items, trying to find the last slice of bean pie from yesterday. I put a note with my name on it and attached it to the carton that had the slice of pie because, in this household, all nameless food is fair game even if it means something gets eaten by only one person. Namely Nuri. I peer from behind the open fridge door when I don't hear a snarky response.

"Where's Nuri? And where's my slice of bean pie?" I push aside the milk carton and lemonade jug. "All of the Minute Maid fruit punch is gone too? I didn't even get any."

"You know that juice goes fast around here, Bri. And Nuri

had a rescheduled lacrosse practice this morning, so your dad had to take her," Mom says, sipping on her coffee. "I think the note with your name on it didn't stick to the pie, so she ate it not knowing it was yours. Ready to head out?"

"She would." I let out a long dramatic sigh. "I just need five minutes to grab something to eat."

I pull out some leftover take-out fried rice and pop it into the microwave. Once it's warm, I drizzle on some mumbo sauce and grab a spoon. Mom raises an eyebrow, and I grab an apple from the fruit bowl.

"Okay, now I'm ready," I say. "I can eat in the car."

"Alright, let's roll out. We're running a bit behind, and I want to talk to you on the way." I must make a face because she adds, "You're not in trouble, Bri. Relax."

We get in the car, and once she's backed out of the drive-way, I turn to her expectantly.

"I wanted to check and make sure that you're okay with going back to your dance studio before you go to ballet class today."

"Yeah," I say slowly. "Why wouldn't I be?"

"Because that's where you were when you found out about the attack, and I wanted to warn you that going back so soon might cause those memories to reemerge."

I nod. "I have hip-hop class today, Mom, but you don't have to worry about me. I don't feel nervous about going back to my ballet studio. I just miss dancing."

"I know you do, dear."

The rest of the ride passes in a comfortable silence, and I work on creating a Twitter account for *You Truly Assumed*. I'm not sure I'll do much with it besides tweet links to the blog posts and retweet to boost similar blogs, but making a Twitter for the blog makes everything feel more official. Admin team. Check. Twitter. Check.

Mom pulls into the school parking lot and puts the car in Park, and I step outside. I take out my bun, the waves from my twist-out brushing my shoulders, since the air feels light and cool instead of muggy and humid. The weather could be a sign that it'll be a good day, because any day where my hair doesn't poof up from the heat is usually at least a decent one. I stretch my arms and tilt my face toward the sky. Sunlight washes over me, and I try to let the brightness seep into me and make me excited to be here.

Mom presses a quick kiss to my cheek as we enter the school.

"Have a good day, Bri-Bri," Mom says as she heads toward the cafeteria.

"You too, Mommy."

I crack my knuckles, roll my neck, and shake out my arms and legs like I'm about to go out onstage.

"Good morning everyone," I say, walking into the faculty kitchen.

I hear the sizzle of pancakes being cooked and smell the sweet scent of freshly cut pineapples. Megan, who goes to school with me, and Mr. Henry, a parent volunteer, say hello but Mr. Smith stays silent. A few other people in our group of eight trickle in behind me, and for some reason I notice that Hayat isn't here yet. Light rock music plays in the background, but the people who are already working are quiet. The kitchen has been divided into stations: prepping, cooking, and packaging, and I start to head over to the one that has the fewest people. Mr. Smith looks over his shoulder at me, his gray eyes hardening, and it seems like both his lips and white mustache curve into a frown. I'm not sure what's up with him. He seemed nice yesterday.

I give him a small nod and take my place at the packaging station.

Mr. Smith tucks his clipboard underneath his arm and slides his pen behind his ear. "I didn't know that you were part of a blog. How's that been going?"

I blink, shock pausing my steps. How does Mr. Smith know about *You Truly Assumed*? I don't even go by my full name on the blog, so there's no way that he could know it was me unless he read some of the blog posts and made the connection between me blogging about being in DC and volunteering. But there's no way he could be interested in *You Truly Assumed*. Or maybe he could. He did make a passionate speech about making sure everyone in the community feels safe.

"How did you find my blog?"

"Some of your fellow classmates in the group were talking about it, and I must admit I was intrigued by the concept."

My shoulders drop. "Well, it's going fine! It's still relatively new and getting off the ground, but I'm glad that you're enjoying it so far."

"Good to hear. It seems very professional."

"Uh, thank you," I say, not sure what to do with that compliment or where it's coming from. I see Hayat, who must've just come in, and he gives me a tiny shrug, mirroring my thoughts exactly. I'm surprised that Mr. Smith likes *YTA* this much, but I'll take his reaction compared to the comment from earlier about how Muslims are all terrorists.

"Can you work at the cooking station instead of the packaging station? We need more people there."

"Sure." I pause. "But Megan's already cutting the fruit and Mr. Henry is already on pancake duty, so there's only bacon left."

"Yes, exactly. Is that a problem?"

I bite the inside of my cheek to keep my expression neutral. "I don't know how to cook it."

A weird tension seeps into the room. I almost start to add that I have never touched bacon because of my religion and that the smell of it cooking makes me nauseous, but I don't. Mr. Smith is still Dad's boss, and even though I'm not being difficult, I don't want to come across that way.

"It's really not that hard. Are you sure you can't do it?"

I dig my nails into my palms, annoyance rising. "Yep, I'm sure."

What does he mean am I sure? I just said I can't do it. I lift my chin higher, waiting for his response. Everyone else continues to work, and I don't understand why I'm the only one being singled out right now.

He throws his hands up. "Fine, since you can't do what I need you to do and everyone else is busy with their assigned roles, you can start prepping the dinner meals. Everyone else is working, you should be too."

I bite my tongue, holding in my retort as Mr. Smith walks away. I look at Hayat, confused, and he shrugs again. Mr. Smith's change in attitude came out of nowhere. It's not that hard to understand where I'm coming from. I get sticking to the plan and assigned roles, but I'm not cooking bacon. Maybe he's having a rough morning or needs another cup of coffee, but whatever it is he needs to get it together.

Heading to the station farthest back in the room, I stop by the fridge and grab the various ingredients that are listed in the binder of recipes on the counter and make my way past the breakfast and lunch prep stations. My hand twitches with the urge to grab my phone, but I can't text Dad. Usually we'd joke dryly about a situation like this, but we can't joke about his boss.

One of my classmates catches my eyes as I open the basket and she mouths, "Do you want any help?"

I shake my head and mouth back, "I'm fine."

I see Hayat making his way over, and despite my hard stare he keeps approaching.

"What's up, moe." He rests his arms on the tabletop. "Knock knock."

"Seriously? Who's there?"

"Orange."

I roll my eyes. "Orange who?"

"Orange you glad I'm here?"

"That's the best one you could come up with? I don't understand how people always think you be jonin."

"It was the first food-related knock-knock joke that popped into my head. And it's not my fault people think I'm funny." He laughs. "But really, they're about to cook the bacon and I hate the smell, so do you need any help?"

"I've got this all under control. But you can sit silently on that stool, if you want."

He rolls his eyes at my tone but sits down. "Fine, but I have a quick question."

"What?"

"Are you alright? Mr. Smith was being weird."

"I'm fine, but I'm glad I'm not the only one who thought his reaction was uncalled-for. He's my dad's new boss though, so I can't exactly be pressed."

"Yeah, that definitely sucks."

I shrug. "It is what it is. Now, since you're still here, make yourself useful and wash off the veggies."

"No bacon-induced headaches?" His eyes light up, and I almost laugh at his excitement. Almost.

I give him a small smile. "I'll be nice and spare you today. Only." I shake the spoon at him before he can respond. "Today only."

Then it's back to no more Hayat for the rest of the summer. As planned.

* * * * *

I gulp down water, my shoulders heaving and my heart racing to the fast beat of the hip-hop song that the routine is choreographed to. The lyrics loop in my head as I wipe away the sweat that trickles down my face. Volunteering seems like it was hours ago, even though the hip-hop class was only forty-five minutes. But time also goes by differently in the studio.

Three times a week, I trade my pointe shoes for street shoes and take a hip-hop class after my conditioning class for ballet. Hip-hop became my safe haven after I took a month away from ballet in fifth grade, when I was told again at an audition for the part of Snow White that there was nothing wrong technically with my dancing but that I didn't fit the role well enough to get the part. I was told that my body type fit jazz or hip-hop more than ballet, and even though hearing that led me to my love of hip-hop and the impact of the comment has faded, I haven't completely forgotten it either.

"Hey, Bri?"

I look up from where I'm sitting on the bench at the front of the studio to see Hayat, his skin glistening with perspiration. My breath hitches, and I try not to focus on his arms, which look really good in his muscle tank. I write off the observation on my surprise because Hayat's the last person I'd expect to see at a hip-hop studio. I know his younger sister, Aliyah, is amazingly talented at both ballet and hip-hop, and I always see her around since we go to the same studios. But I've never seen Hayat here. I look away from his biceps, which are on full display, before he can catch me staring.

"Hey, what are you doing here?" I ask as Hayat takes a seat on the bench next to me.

"I've been coming here ever since I recovered from the hamstring injury I got during lacrosse season last spring. Aliyah convinced me that taking a class would be a good way to stay in shape until I was officially cleared by my doctor to be back on the field. And I've been taking classes ever since."

"You've been dancing for a year?" I ask. "I didn't know that."

That knowledge is surprising, but in a good way.

"Did someone mention my name?" Aliyah asks.

She navigates around all the bags and shoes and comes over to where Hayat and I are sitting at the front of the studio.

Aliyah plops down on the bench next to me. "He's actually not that bad."

Hayat grimaces. "I am."

"So, you know the dance showcase that the studio is hosting as a fundraiser for relief efforts?" Aliyah asks me.

"Yeah. I think I'm going to be in two or three numbers."

"Well, this year I'm choreographing a hip-hop number."

"Oh my goodness, that's awesome! Congrats!"

"Thank you! It's a beginning-level duet. I've roped Hayat into doing it, which means he needs a partner. It's my first time ever choreographing, and I'm a little intimidated to ask someone in my class, so I thought I'd ask you since you already know both of us."

"Please say no," Hayat begs jokingly, and Aliyah elbows him in the side.

I look between the two of them, and it's almost like seeing double. The only noticeable difference is the scar that Hayat has under his eye from a nasty lacrosse play. It was during the championship game, which Morgan made me go to since we were playing against her school.

"What's in it for me?" I ask.

"Fame. Glory. Power," Aliyah answers.

Hayat shakes his head. "Absolutely nothing."

As much as I thought I wasn't a big fan of Hayat, he's so far proven to not be that bad. And even though Aliyah's dance probably wouldn't take up that much time, I'm supposed to be focusing on ballet this summer, on top of prepping for college apps and running *You Truly Assumed*. But I don't want to say no to Aliyah, and honestly, the duet sounds fun. Plus, a very small part of me wants to dance with Hayat.

"I think I'll be able to," I say. "I need to check my planner to make sure, so I'll text you this evening and let you know."

"That sounds like a yes, Bri," Hayat says, feigning worry.

"Thank you, thank you, thank you." Aliyah hugs me. "This is going to be so much fun."

I didn't expect this at all, but I don't think I can say no to Aliyah when she's so excited. Hayat and I share a glance, and I look away before I can start laughing. Maybe spending more time with Hayat won't be the end of the world.

Still, I'm not a fan of spur-of-the-moment decisions, especially when they come with adding another new thing to my plate. That would completely throw my summer plan out the window, not that I have much of one right now. But I'm working on that, and I'm not sure if I need another thing with that much potential to spiral out of my control.

UPDATES AND INTRODUCTIONS!!

I was watching the news today, and it hit me that the terrorist attack has already fallen out of the news cycle. There were a few vigils held last week, but it almost feels like the attack never happened. I'm not sure if that's because DC moves so fast, or what. But it doesn't seem like anyone was given time to grieve or pay respects before it was on to the next news bombshell. Have any of you noticed that too, or is it just me? Maybe the news moves fast everywhere?

And last but not least, I have some really exciting news to share! Drumroll! *insert drumroll here*

I'd like to introduce you all to Kat and Rose. Kat's the artist behind the comics and doodles you'll be seeing more often going forward. She helps add some color and brightness to the blog (and she brings a unique perspective!), so hopefully you all won't get bored and skim over the posts. Just kidding. Mostly. Anyway, please give her a warm welcome in the comments if you want to! She's super excited to be here, and I'm pumped to start working alongside her.

Next week, the blog is going to look completely different, and that'll all be thanks to Rose. She's working on redesigning *You Truly Assumed* so that it's more interactive and engaging. I'm super excited to work with her to bring you all *YTA* 2.0. Please give Rose a warm welcome as well. The three of us will be the admin team for the blog going forward, and as always if you have any feedback or questions for us, feel free to drop a comment or reach out via the contact page.

Until next post,
~Bri

ZAKAT

LULLWOOD, GEORGIA

I wipe the pen ink on my thumb, smudging it further. After six hours, I managed to finish coming up with the rest of the summer programming for the "lil tots reading nights," which is a story-time event for toddlers and kids at Tiny Treasure Trove. Lots of selecting books, finalizing times, and ordering food. Even though the storage room is mostly full of books and boxes, with the circular table it's actually the perfect office space. There are a lot of memories and secrets seeped into these walls, and the door frame has markings in the corner in different colors from when Aafreen and I tracked our heights up until middle school.

I pull out my phone and sign into the blog's email account. Checking the comments is probably one of the aspects of blogging that I enjoy most, and I need to distract myself.

There's something so beautiful about the fact that my doodles of trees and stars and Bri's words can travel to places that

I've yet to go. I've only been outside of Georgia for a handful of debate tournaments, which is how I fell in love with
Howard, and yet my drawings have already made it halfway
across the globe.

I click on an email notification for a new comment, even
though it looks like Bri has already opened it.

jr987: Every Muslim needs to die.

I almost drop my phone, all the air whooshing out of me.
Simmering anger fills up the gap left in my chest, and I blink
away the tears that prick my eyes. An unwelcome image pops
into my mind of one of the words within the graffiti on the
side of the Islamic school: *DIE*. I guess this is what Ma meant
when she said that online isn't Lullwood. I knew that prior to
joining *You Truly Assumed*, but I didn't think we were going
to receive that many comments, especially negative ones. But
it seems that as *You Truly Assumed* grows, the amount of nasty
comments do too.

What's said in the comments isn't new. I've heard all of
this stuff before. But none of it's ever been hurled at me so
personally, even though the insults are coming through a
screen. Maybe I need to get a thicker skin like Bri. I've already
learned the trash-and-blast method. Trash nasty comments
and then blast the commentator with a click of the block button. I know Bri probably doesn't like the new method that I've
discovered, especially after we chatted this morning, but she's
much better at handling confrontation than I am. I feel like
it makes the most sense to create as much distance between
myself and the vile comments as possible. I don't really see

the point in letting all of that negativity and hate hang around on the blog when there's a way to get rid of it. The world, even Lullwood now, has too much negativity and hate as is.

I slide my phone into my pocket and stand up, the latest comment repeating itself over and over in my head.

There's a knock on the door, and Aafreen and Lucy come into the storage room. Both of them seem normal, but I eye Lucy. I wonder if she knows that Asher is probably behind the school getting graffitied, or if she even knows that it happened.

"Hello, hello, we came to join you since we're both taking a quick break," Aafreen says, sitting down in the empty chair next to me.

Lucy sits next to her, and an awkward silence fills the room as Lucy and I both look at Aafreen.

"So," Aafreen starts, getting the hint. "Zakat, did you know that Lucy is also into art? She's working on her graphic novel, which is pretty cool."

"That is pretty cool," I say.

"And, Lucy, did you know that Zakat does the art for this really cool blog called *You Truly Assumed*?" She nudges me. "Thanks for sending me the link. I made sure to subscribe so that I can support you."

"That's neat." Lucy turns to me. "What's the blog about?"

"It's a space for young Muslim women," I say, seeing my in. "There's been a lot of Islamophobic things happening, like the boys' school getting graffitied, so the blog is a nice safe space to have."

Lucy frowns. "I heard about what happened to the school, and I'm so sorry."

I scan her face, trying to tell if she's being genuine. "I wonder who did it. Whoever it was is really good at graffitiing based on how it was done."

Lucy's eyes snap to mine, and Aafreen stiffens as she catches on to what I'm trying to get at.

"I'm not sure who did." Lucy shrugs. "But hopefully it won't happen again."

There's a pause, and Aafreen changes the subject to the YA books releasing this month that she's most excited for, and I zone out a bit. Just because Lucy doesn't think Asher was behind the school being graffitied doesn't mean that he wasn't. But even if he was, perhaps I need to separate the two of them in my head. Lucy seemed sorry about what happened, and her tone wasn't defensive. Maybe Aafreen was right and she has changed.

I still want to find out who attacked my home, but Lucy is not the key to figuring that out. And apparently neither is the security footage, since the person was wearing a mask. So no matter how much I want an answer, it seems pretty slim that the community is going to get one.

A knock on the door jolts me out of my thoughts, and Aafreen jumps a bit in surprise.

"Lucy? Are you in there?" the person asks.

"Yeah, Asher. You can come in," Lucy says.

Aafreen steps forward. "Actually, no, sorry, he can't. This room is employees only."

"Really? It can't be that big of a deal if he comes in."

"It is to me," Aafreen says firmly.

Lucy looks between the two of us, a mix of confusion and irritation flashing in her eyes. "Fine, then, I'll leave."

She steps out of the storage room, and I let out a deep breath.

"Thanks for not letting Asher come in here," I say.

Aafreen squeezes my shoulder. "No problem. He's the most well-known graffiti artist in Lullwood. Lucy may trust him, but I don't."

"Yeah, neither do I," I say. "Do you think it was him?"

"I don't know. I don't not think it was him though."

"Fair enough."

"Are you alright though?" Aafreen says. "You seemed a bit antsy when Lucy and I came in."

I smile a little at how well she knows me.

"Just some gross comment on the blog. That on top of everything that's been going on here was just a lot in that moment."

"Yeah, that makes sense. But I've got your back if there's ever anything I can do. I'll start commenting on the blog and fighting anyone who messes with you."

I laugh. "I appreciate that, but there's no need. Thank you though. Are we still on for hanging out at your place after work?"

"Yep, of course."

She gives me a quick hug before leaving to go work the register. With or without Lucy being here, I'm always lucky to have Aafreen as my best friend. And honestly, Lucy may not be that bad either. I may not be able to completely forgive and forget, but I think I can move forward.

I grab a box of books from the storage room and walk over to a half-empty shelf and start filling it back up with books, trying to distract myself. But the comment left on *You Truly*

Assumed plays on a loop in my head, like a paint stain that I can't fully remove. Once I'm done, I fold up the empty cardboard box, toss it into the recycling bin, and head to the register.

"I'm ready to go," I say.

Aafreen nods, stepping from behind the cashier counter. I wave at her mom and then step outside, Aafreen behind me. The sun hangs low in the sky, tinting everything a pinkish orange. I inhale deeply, the rising of my chest reminding me that I'm here. I'm here, and the words and commenters are outside of Lullwood. But maybe the difference between Lullwood and everywhere else isn't as big as I thought it was. That's more terrifying than the message behind the comments.

We walk in silence the rest of the way to her house. Like Aafreen, her house stands out. It's a light eggshell yellow that pops among the grays and dark blues. And while most of the patches of greenery in front of the houses are empty, the one in front of Aafreen's house is full of yellow roses. When we were little, we used to pick the dandelions from around the roots of the roses and make flower crowns.

Aafreen grabs a bag of baby carrots and a tub of hummus from the fridge, and then we head upstairs to her room. During middle school, Aafreen went through a big Pinterest phase and her room still reflects that. Polaroid pictures attached to fairy lights line her walls, and calligraphy quotes are framed all over. There's still a bright orange stain from when we thought that doing papier-mâché on the carpet was a good idea back in third grade. Stepping into her room is like stepping into an open memory box.

Aafreen flops onto her bed, and I sit down in my favorite beanbag chair.

"Is it just me, or has this summer felt really different?" Aafreen asks. "Lullwood feels different."

"It's not just you. Everything feels like it's changing this summer," I say. "Things feel different with the fence, and the graffiti, and even me joining *You Truly Assumed*. I guess I thought that next summer would be the one where everything changed."

"I think Lullwood is being forced to go through some growing pains. Things have been chill since the incident though, so hopefully they'll stay that way. But your change is good. You put yourself out there and took a risk and stood up for yourself," Aafreen says, dramatically dropping her voice to a whisper. "Part of that was spurred by everything going on, which doesn't make everything that's happening good, but I guess it's a silver lining."

"I know, I'm a rebel now. But I guess change is kinda strange because we've never really had to do it. We've both lived here all our lives, went to the same school as everyone else, prayed with everyone else. It's as if up to this point our grade has been a unit and, next year, we're all going to be splitting up for the first time."

"I think that's beautiful though," Aafreen says. "You'll be on your way to Howard, and if I get a scholarship, I'll be at MIT or Duke or Vanderbilt. If not, I'll be at Tech. But either way, we'll be on our way and so will everyone else."

"I know you'll end up where you're supposed to and you'll be a great engineering whiz wherever you go."

She sighs. "You're right. I just feel like there's so much

pressure to not let our parents down and redo the mistakes they made."

"Yeah, that's why I try to understand where they're coming from when they say that I should stay in state."

Both of our parents are first-gen college students who financed their education with really predatory loans that they're still paying back. My parents insist that I major in something other than art precisely because they want to ensure that I can pay back my loans, and they want me to stay in state because they think I'll be more competitive for scholarships that way. I've seen students get into their dream schools and not be able to go because they can't afford it and the hurt that brings, and I hope that Aafreen and I don't have to experience that.

"North Carolina is the closest to DC, just in case you were looking for a reason to bump it up on your list," I say.

Aafreen laughs. "I'm not worried about our friendship at all. We're going to be those people who come back during breaks and always hang out. And honestly, most of our grade probably will too. That distance might change how much we talk and we'll both make new friends, but that won't change the fact that you're my best friend."

"I know, you're right."

Even though most of us will be leaving Lullwood next year, I don't think graduation is really going to be goodbye. I don't think it's possible to permanently say goodbye when Lullwood is such a big part of each of us. I know that at least for me, it'll be with me wherever I go, and it'll always be a place that I can come back to and call home.

"I'm excited," Aafreen says. "I think this last school year with all of us is going to be a special one."

I nod, stretching out in the beanbag chair, and my eyes land on one of the framed photos on top of Aafreen's drawer. It's a picture of Aafreen and me, faces squished against each other's as we smile for the camera. That was the first day of sixth grade, and it's weird to think that was six years ago.

"Doesn't seem like that long ago," Aafreen says, noticing my gaze.

"Yeah, but at the same time it does."

"Time is one of the strangest things, I swear. It moves so slow and so fast at the same time."

I look at the world map that hangs on one of her walls, tiny red pins marking the faded paper.

"I'm going to miss this place so much. I'm excited about what's to come, but part of me is also sad that I know that means I'll be leaving. Is that weird?"

I think back to the doodle I drew recently of a girl with woods growing out of her heart. I'm Lullwood, my roots are here. But I don't know how far I can go without risking the possibility of ripping them out from the soil. And if I lose my roots, then I lose everything.

I'm Lullwood. But that can't be all that I am.

"No, not at all. I feel the exact same way." Aafreen looks over at me. "But no matter where we both end up or how much things change, I'll always have your back."

She sticks out her pinkie finger and I link mine with hers. Just like old times.

★ ★ ★ ★ ★

Beams from the sun hit my back, their intensity reduced by the treetops. I turn onto the main street, which is lined with many shops, including Tiny Treasure Trove, and my feet stop before my eyes understand what's in front of me. Toilet paper is strewn in heaps in front of the store, like a layer of snow. Aafreen's mom reaches for the pieces hanging from the sign on top of the bookstore as they blow in the wind. Yolk runs down the windows, and broken eggshells are scattered in front of the store.

I take a step back, my breakfast churning in my stomach. A scream rises in my throat, but I swallow it, not wanting anyone to hear it. Even though TP-ing and egging a house could be written off as a juvenile prank, the timing doesn't make that so simple. As far as I know, this hasn't happened to any business in this part of Lullwood. The fact that something like this would happen for the first time after the graffiti incident can't be coincidence. That, along with the fact that Asher has been stopping by the bookstore, which he's never done before, is enough to make this disturbing.

I push down the pain and walk over to Aafreen's mom. I can't let her clean all of this up on her own. Seeing the bookstore, her business, like this is probably even more emotionally draining for her than it is for me. It's hard not to feel like the attack in DC has been a match that's lit a bunch of little fires in Lullwood. First the school was graffitied, and now Tiny Treasure has been vandalized.

"Can I help?" I ask.

Aafreen's mom looks up and her gaze softens. "I'll clean this up, dear. You and Lucy can get to work. Aafreen needs some time to process what's happened, so she will be in a bit late, but I can assure both of you that she's going to be okay."

I walk up the narrow pathway to the door, the toilet paper

wrinkling under my feet like a fake red carpet. I want to punch something and cry, but shock and disbelief silence the anger.

"Do we know who did it?" I ask.

"No. I looked at the camera footage from last night, and it appeared to be someone wearing a mask," Aafreen's mom says. "The graffiti incident was reported to authorities, but they have no further leads, so I don't believe they'll be able to do much with this new situation."

I nod, absorbing her answer, and walk inside. Now would be a good time to have my sketchbook so that I could get all of my emotions out on the page to make sure they don't spill out. I wipe a tear away, the emotions fighting to flow, as I head to the storage room to sit down.

I've always been told I'm sensitive, soft, quiet. That my feelings control me more than I control them. My parents were always told, "Zakat, she has a heart of gold. But people rob gold." They realized it a lot earlier than I did that wearing my heart on my sleeve made it easier to get hurt by others. And yet, I still can't keep my heart, and my feelings, in my chest.

The bell above the door rings, and Lucy walks into the store. It's hard to see her expression, but when she takes off her shades her eyes are wide with surprise. She looks around, probably searching for Aafreen, before heading over.

"When did that happen?" she asks as she walks into the storage room. "And does Aafreen's mom need any help cleaning up?"

"It happened last night, and she said she'd handle it."

Lucy shakes her head in disbelief. "I guess people were just out having too much fun."

"I seriously doubt that."

"I mean, why else would someone TP and egg the bookstore?"

"I don't know, Lucy," I say, trying to keep the annoyance out of my voice. "Why do you think?"

"Sorry. If it's helpful, I can ask Asher if he knows anything about what happened. He's much more familiar with the city than I am."

I look at her, unsure whether or not she's capping right now, but she gives me a small smile and I decide that she's not. I still find it hard to believe she doesn't know who Asher is at his core and that she hasn't seen any of his social media posts. Maybe she has and his views don't bother her because they don't threaten her. She may not share his views, but she may accept them. It's hard to know where she stands.

"No worries," I say. "How's your family doing?"

"My sister is doing much better, so the rest of us are doing well. Being in Lullwood has been a nice escape though. I mean, who doesn't like to spend time around books?" Lucy gets up to go work the register since Aafreen still isn't here. "It was nice talking to you."

"Same here," I say.

If Aafreen could've seen that conversation, she'd be really proud. Lucy's comments all those years ago definitely impacted me, but her being here has shown me that her words don't control me. Lucy seems fine, but part of me is still waiting for the other shoe to drop. She's staying with Asher's family, and they spend a lot of time together. But maybe I'm projecting my dislike and distrust of Asher on her, and that's not fair. So for the time being, I'll keep being cordial.

I look out and see Aafreen's mom holding a bottle of glass cleaner and trash bags as she works outside the store, and my heart hurts. Things like this can't keep happening, but Lullwood's idyllic nature is starting to chip away. Nowhere is completely safe. That realization is startling, but I can't give up on my home. *You Truly Assumed* has been making an impact on readers, and maybe I can protect my community here by also creating a safe space for people to share their experiences. There's got to be something, anything, I can do so I can know that I'm not powerless to protect Lullwood and myself.

FARAH

KIRBY, MASSACHUSETTS

I clutch the handle of my suitcase, people and noise streaming past me and surrounding me on all sides. Everyone's moving, moving, moving, and I'm standing in the middle of the airport, still, trying not to get bumped into the chaos of the baggage claim. I sweep my eyes across the sea of people, and everything spins so much that it looks like they're crowding closer and closer. I step forward, the movement making me feel less trapped. I don't know how I'm supposed to find Tommy when I haven't seen him in ages and barely remember what he even looks like. I clutch the handle of the suitcase tighter, as if it's my lifeline, and look down the line of people holding signs, trying to find my name.

"There she is!" a voice says. "Farah! Over here!"

I turn my head, and my eyes land on a middle-aged Black man who's holding his daughter in one arm and has his other arm around his wife, who must be Jess. Jess's high ponytail, boutique leggings, and headband mirror the older daughter who's standing next to her. The wide smile and curly Afro of the son squished between them thaws some of my apprehension.

"Tommy?"

He steps closer, Jess and his stepson on one side and his stepdaughter on his other side. Seeing the five of them all standing in front of me makes me take a small step back. I wish they weren't standing in a line because it feels too much like a wall. And I'm the outsider. I keep my chin held high, but apprehension keeps me on edge as my heart thumps loudly. The small circular birthmark near Tommy's right eye mirrors my own, and that small similarity is both unsettling and endearing. His button-up T-shirt and khaki pants make me feel a tad bit underdressed in my joggers and oversized Lakers hoodie that smells faintly of Riley's cologne. Tommy holds the youngest daughter, who must be Emma, close to his chest like she's the most precious thing, and I wonder if he held me like that when I was little.

Jess steps forward, her dark brown eyes looking me over, and I keep my gaze level with hers. She clears her throat, sticking out her hand. "We're glad to finally meet you."

I nod and shake her hand quickly. She keeps her eyes on me and lips pursed, like she's waiting for me to run away or curse in front of the kids. But she doesn't have to like me and I'm not here to impress her. In the end, Tommy chose her and her kids, and even if that wasn't necessarily her fault, I don't trust her.

The boy, who looks about six, steps forward and sticks out his hand. "I'm Samson! I forgot I had another sibling."

I hold in a snort. You and me both, fam.

"Why are you here?" he asks.

"Nice to meet you," I say, returning the handshake. "They didn't tell you?"

"They said you're here to visit." He lowers his voice. "Don't tell Mom and Dad I said this, but that was a really bad answer."

I laugh. "I like you, Samson. And to answer your question, I'm here because people suck."

From the corner of my eye, I see Jess open her mouth, ready to respond, but Samson nods before she has a chance to interject, accepting my answer.

The girl who's maybe twelve or thirteen skips over to me, the beads at the end of her cornrows clicking together. "It's so awesome to meet you! I'm Ally."

"And this is Emma," Tommy says, bouncing her on his hip. "She's excited to meet her big sister."

I freeze. Emma is actually my younger half sister. Samson is my stepbrother, and Ally is my stepsister. I don't know how all of that managed to go over my head, but it did. And now I'm standing in front of a bunch of people who might want something from me that I have no idea how to give them. The noise of the airport crashes into me again, and all of a sudden it's like the rest of my mind has finally landed and connected with my body in Boston. I'm fully present as a result of that sister comment, and I can feel my hands getting sweaty. I can't handle living in a house with five other people, especially with one of them being a screaming two-year-old. Yesterday, I was sibling-less, and today I now have three.

All five of them stare at me expectedly, and I stare right back.

"So," Jess says, breaking the silence trapping the six of us. "You and Tommy look more alike than I imagined. Almost like twins."

I grit my teeth and mentally face-palm. Part of me doesn't want to have to listen to or engage in small talk, but the other part of me wants to ask Jess to explain what she means more. Besides the same birthmark, I don't see it. I've always been told that I'm a spitting image of my mom, and that's easier to accept than wondering about how much of who I am came from someone who decided I wasn't good enough to stay.

"Well, let's get this show on the road," Tommy says, breaking our silence.

I slip to the back of the group as the family exits the airport. The sky is a foggy gray, and there's a chill in the air since the sun can't break through the clouds. It's a bit like June Gloom. Light raindrops land on my forehead, making everything feel misty. People bustle around, and I can picture Mom and her hustle fitting in perfectly.

"You can sit in the back with me," Ally says as Jess unlocks the minivan.

"Great," I say.

"So how's your summer break been so far?" I ask Ally, only because I can see Jess looking at us through the rearview mirror.

"Good! I've been spending a lot of time on the court. I play tennis, and I'm actually pretty good. And I'm prepping for seventh grade."

I can't help but smile a little at her excitement. I need that same energy going into senior year because, right now, I don't have any.

"What about you?"

"Just working and hanging out with my boyfriend."

She leans in closer, stretching her seat belt. "Ooh, what's he like?"

"He's super sweet, super smart, and he gave me this necklace," I say, tapping the rose charm on the choker.

"Ooh, it's cute. I think I'd like him."

My smile grows. "Yeah, you probably would."

I pull out my phone and send Riley a quick text wishing him good morning and letting him know that I made it to Boston safely. With the time zone difference things are a bit wonky, but I know Riley keeps his phone on silent all the time, so it doesn't really matter when I text him. Even though it's the beginning of the second week of June, I have to improve my text game. I go back and send a sunshine and a red heart emoji and hope they help convey just how much I miss him.

I lean my head against the seat, watching the scenery blow past. Kirby and the Boston area feel a bit quainter than Inglethorne, and the only thing I really know about Boston comes from the Lakers rivalry with the Boston Celtics. Which is probably more than enough information. Jess hops on the highway, and I pop in my earbuds to block them all out. I close my eyes and rest my head against the window, not caring if the jojoba oil on my hair leaves smudges. Before I know it, there's a tap on my shoulder. I pause my playlist and take out one of my earbuds before looking over at Ally.

"Hey, we're here," Ally says.

I rub my eyes and take a look out the window. There isn't a gate, but I can feel the invisible shield of wealth surrounding the neighborhood. The houses are large and made out of gray stones and white bricks, with fenced yards and three-car—or even four-car—garages. They look like the houses on those home improvement type shows that Mom likes to watch. It doesn't bother me that much, but still, the difference in living styles is hard not to notice. This house looks like it might even be larger than Mom's and my apartment and Nana and Grandpa's house combined.

"Home sweet home," Samson says.

"Homeee," Emma babbles.

Grabbing my suitcase from the trunk before anyone else can get it for me, I follow Ally into the house and slip off my shoes after she does. There isn't one speck of dirt on the white tiled floor that shines different colors in some spots from the light coming in through the large stained-glass window right above the wooden double doors. I'm making the space dirty just by standing here.

"Farah, you'll be staying in the guest room. Please make yourself at home."

"Thanks," I say, standing in the middle of the foyer.

Tommy waves a hand. "There's no need to thank us. Thank you for being here."

Well, I didn't really have much of a choice.

There's an awkward pause, and I shift my feet. "So, I'm going to head upstairs now."

"I'll walk you up and show you around," Tommy says.

I follow Tommy closely up the stairs. The last thing that I want to do is walk into the wrong room and make myself even more of an intruder. My eyes land on a sign taped to one of the doors that says Welcome, Farah in large shaky crayon lettering that probably belongs to Samson.

The first thing that catches my attention when I walk into the room is the roses on top of the nightstand. I wonder whether that's a coincidence or a result of careful attention to detail. The walls are painted in this off-white color that's nice enough, and a large bed sits under a painting of a sunset. A desk is tucked in the space between the bed and the wall. There's a walk-in closet, but I'll probably only use the dresser, even though it looks like it's only for decoration. Another door leads to an attached bathroom, and more roses rest on top of the sink.

I want to flop onto the bed, but the covers are so smooth that they look like they've been ironed, and I don't want to wrinkle them. Perching on the edge of the bed, I pick up the small black journal and ballpoint pen on the desk, and the blog *You Truly Assumed* pops into my head. I'm sure I'll have some free time while I'm here to brainstorm how to improve the blog's user interface and make it more eye-catching. Plus, getting lost in a new project will help this trip pass faster.

"I hope this works for you," Tommy says.

"It does."

I stare at him as all of the mental compartmentalization that I've done of boxing Tommy into the past comes undone. Looking closer now, I can see that we have the same thick eyebrows and nose that tips up slightly at the end, and I don't know whether to be glad about the similarities. It's clear that Jess and the kids adore him, and part of me wonders if I'd given him a chance years ago if he'd have done the same for me. Watching him with them makes me wonder if that's what I could've had—or can have now—and if that's even what I want.

Tommy rubs the back of his neck. "Well, I was hoping your trip here could be a great chance to get to know each other better, so I've put together a list of things we could do."

A wave of exhaustion washes over me as the five-hour plane ride and the fact that I'm in Tommy's house catch up with me. The part of me that is trying to get used to taking chances and being more optimistic wants to move forward and get to know Tommy, but the more realistic part of me is saying that a few weeks in Kirby isn't going to fix our relationship. The realistic part of me has gotten me through everything without Tommy so far.

"Why do I have to fit into a plan? Isn't that why our relationship, or lack thereof, is like this now? Because I didn't fit into your plans then? Why are you trying to make me fit into them now?"

Tommy blinks. "I'm sorry, I didn't mean to get off on the wrong foot—"

There's a knock on the door, and Jess pushes it open and steps into the room.

"I have to leave to drop Ally off at tennis practice soon, but I wanted to quickly let Farah know that she has to remember that Ally, Samson, and Emma are kids." She turns to face me. "You can't talk to them like you would your best friends. You can't tell a six-year-old that people suck. I know you just met them, but they clearly already look up to you."

Tommy places a hand on Jess's arm. "Honey, I've got it from here."

Her shoulders drop. "Okay, sure. You deal with her."

She gives me one last hard look and leaves the room, slamming the door behind her.

"Did Jess not want me to be here?" I ask.

"The plans for you to come out and visit were a bit last minute, but that's no one's fault. We had to reschedule a family vacation, which was supposed to happen this month, but it wasn't that big of a deal. Your mother was adamant that June was the best month for you to visit, so that's what had to be done. But I can assure you that Jess doesn't hold any of that against you. It's just that she's protective of her family, and she wants to make sure that you'll be good to the kids. No need to worry."

"Right. I'll be sure to stay out of her way."

"That won't be necessary. The expectations of you in this house are fairly straightforward. As long as you're respectful and you're kind to the kids, I think your visit will go off without a hitch. Everyone is excited that you're here, so I don't think you'll have any difficulty with getting into the swing of things."

That's simple enough, almost too simple. Ally, Samson, and Emma all actually seem fine, but I'm still a bit wary of Tommy and Jess. My original plan of keeping my head down and getting through these next three weeks seems a bit better than trying to insert myself into a dynamic that doesn't have space for me.

"How about we go—"

"Maybe later, Tommy. I'm tired."

He moves to close the door behind him. "Right, of course. Okay, well, I'll leave and let you get settled in. I'm looking forward to getting to know you."

I rest my head on a pillow and go to the news app on my phone. My fingers hover over the screen, the headline "Four Injured, One Dead in Attack Outside Black Boston Mosque" catching my eye. I read the first few sentences and scroll past, not clicking on the full article. I only follow LA news because trying to keep track of everything is too exhausting. Nana was right when she said that some things don't change, they morph. Though it's ironic that Mom sent me out here in part to avoid any retaliation because of the terrorist attack and now something similar has happened in the very place I was sent to escape to.

But there really isn't any way to escape hate, and I can't keep running.

My phone buzzes, and I look down to see Bri's name flashing across my screen.

"Shit," I mutter, grabbing my laptop from my backpack.

Scheduling my first meeting with Bri an hour after I landed probably isn't the most ideal timing, but I knew I could always say I was tired from my flight if I needed an excuse to get away from Tommy or the rest of his family. I open up the document that has all the questions I want to ask Bri about how she wants the site to look.

I throw my braids into a messy bun, slide into the desk chair, and hit Accept.

"Hey!" Bri says as she pops up on my phone screen. "How are you doing?"

"I'm doing alright," I say.

Silence comes from the other end, as if Bri is waiting for me to say more.

"Well, I'm glad to hear that. And thanks for taking the time to talk with me. I'm really excited to have you on the team."

"Of course, I'm glad to be a part of *YTA*. So, I have a list of questions prepared, but if you want to start off by telling me what you had in mind for the blog's design that'd be helpful."

"Yeah, definitely. So, I was thinking that the color palette could be based off the colors that Kat used for the potential logos, which I'll send to you in a sec. I also want the blog to be more on the minimalistic side so that Kat's drawings can stand out, and I want the overall layout to be straightforward and easy to navigate."

My fingers fly across the keyboard as I take notes, and ideas for the design start to come together in my head. Excitement washes away some of the numbness from reading the news headline. Maybe being a part of the blog will be a way for me to pause and stop running for a bit.

POLITICS OF PROSE

Okay. I'm not going to lie, the title of this post is an ode to one of my favorite indie bookstores here in DC. But it's also a reminder that language can be political. Recently, we've received a few hateful comments. For some reason, looking back after blogging for a few weeks, I feel like I should've expected to get comments like those. But I didn't, and I don't know if that means I'm naive or that I still believe in the intrinsic good in people and the world. I also wanted to apologize to you all for having to see those horrible comments when you're trying to interact with others in the *You Truly Assumed* community. The admin team is trying to figure out how to best navigate them, so if any of you have suggestions we're all ears (as always!). But the comments, as horrible as they are, have made me reflect on something that I haven't consciously thought about in a long time.

I'm constantly aware of my existence, my being, being politicized. As a young Black Muslim woman, I've gotten used to having all three identities politicized. Or having others try to separate the three and try to act like just one is central to my existence. I used to try to do the same, until I realized it was impossible. I'm Black and Muslim and a young woman. Have you all ever felt this before? Feeling like you have to separate your different identities in order to fit a particular space? Is there an identifier that you think carries more weight in your life? Feel free to answer any or none of these questions in the comments. We love engaging in the discussion within the comments with you all!

Though I can see how *You Truly Assumed* can be considered political, I've never thought of my writing on this blog as really being political in the same way that I sometimes view my own identity. I primarily see *You Truly Assumed* as a space for a bunch of us young Muslim women to connect and chat about different things, whether that be talking about politics or talking about our love for the *Great British Bake Off*. I'm curious to know what you all think. Do you consider *You Truly Assumed* to be political?

I do view my thoughts and my writing as an extension of myself, so I guess in that way I can see how they'd be viewed as political. Not that being political isn't important because it is, but with *You Truly Assumed* we're just trying to create a space for us to be able to be our full selves. But if our being is politicized, does that mean everything that's an extension of ourselves is politicized too? I'm interested in hearing what you all think about this.

Words themselves have the power to be anything. I want *You Truly Assumed* to be the same way. I hope this is a space where we can just be.

On a bit of a different note, you may have noticed that the blog looks a little different! YTA 2.0 is live all thanks to Rose, and we hope that you all like it. There's also a new "resources" page that has a growing list of organizations that either are doing relief work or are Islamic charities, nonprofits, or organizations. Hopefully the page will be helpful in pointing you all in different directions if you want to get involved.

Until next post,
~Bri

SABRIYA

ABINGTON, VIRGINIA

The small rusted yellow metal bell rings as I walk into the café. Coffee Café, more affectionately known as CC, is the place where all the students at my school go to get the iced coffee that they use as their excuse for being late to class. Which is a valid reason because the coffee at CC is elite. It's only a block away from campus, so it's the perfect place to make a snack run in between classes or during lunch when school is in. A few people sit in the cluster of worn armchairs near the window, but most of the wooden square tables are free. The dimness makes the small space feel cozier, and the neutral colors of the walls and decor add to the calming aesthetic.

I sit at one of the empty tables, tap on Zakat's and Farah's numbers, and type, Hey, it's Bri! This is the YTA group chat. It's been a week since Farah joined the team, so the shared group chat is much more active now that the whole admin team is complete.

My phone buzzes, and I look down.

> It's Zakat! I'm excited to be working with the both of you. 😊
>
> this is Farah

I smile. The *You Truly Assumed* admin team is truly starting to come together. Even though *You Truly Assumed* has only been officially running for a little over a week now, it feels so much longer than that.

> **Me:** We can get to know one another or we can jump straight to business.
>
> **Zakat:** I feel like getting to know each other better IS business, especially since we're going to be working so much together!!
>
> **Farah:** ^^ agree
>
> **Zakat:** Maybe we can play a game of 20 questions?

I bop my head to the folksy song playing from the speaker that sits on top of a small bookshelf in the front corner of the café and type out my response.

> **Me:** That's a great idea! Are we all in the same time zone? I'm in EST.
>
> **Zakat:** I am in EST as well!

Farah: i'll be in EST for this month, but I'm usually in PST

Me: Okay, noted! Does 1pm for a game of 20Qs work?

Zakat: Can we do 2pm? I need a couple more hours.

Me: Yep, ofc!

Farah: works for me

Me: Awesome! Text y'all later. Have a great rest of your day!

My phone buzzes with goodbyes and TTYLs, and I go to my text messages with Morgan. Zakat and Farah both seem like cool people. People that I could not only work with but maybe also become friends with. Hopefully getting to know them over text won't be awkward. I switch gears and text Morgan that I'm at CC and go to the counter to order.

"Hey, Bri."

I look up from my phone to see Hayat behind the counter, with an apron and a name tag. My eyes widen in surprise, but once it wears off, I give him a small smile.

"Well, I guess I'm just bumping into you everywhere now," I say. "First the hip-hop studio and now here. Are you sure you aren't following me or something?"

He laughs. "You're the one that showed up at my job."

"Fair point, fair point. Working at CC seems like a solid summer job though."

"It's pretty lowkey, and it's definitely not the worst way

to make a little coin. Especially since applying to college is pricey. But I only work here on the weekends, so it doesn't interfere with volunteering or anything like that."

I lean forward, resting my arms on the counter. "I thought you had some recruitment interest."

"I do from two schools, but I want to be prepared in case neither of those pan out."

I raise my eyebrows, and he rolls his eyes.

"You're not the only who likes plans, you know."

"Oooh, burn," someone says from behind me, and I turn to see Morgan.

"Hey hey," I say as she steps up to the counter next to me.

Morgan looks at me, trying to hide her smirk. "Was I interrupting something?"

"No, no, definitely not," I say. "I was just talking to Hayat. He goes to school with me."

She grins. "Nice to meet you, Hayat. I'm Morgan, Bri's ballet bestie. She's told me so much about you."

If both of our feet weren't so sore from hours spent in pointe shoes, I'd definitely consider stepping on her toes because what in the world is she doing? I settle for nudging her with my elbow in hopes that she'll get that I'm internally yelling, *Shut. Up.*

Hayat grins wider. "Oh, is that true now?"

Morgan turns to me, waiting for me to get something that I'm clearly not.

I turn back to Hayat. "Uh, ignore her. Can I please get a medium iced coffee with two shots of vanilla syrup and a medium iced matcha latte?"

Hayat nods and punches in the order, and then I hand him

the cash. Usually I always keep my change, but when Hayat hands mine to me I drop it in the tip jar.

"It was good seeing you, Bri," Hayat says.

His words warm me unexpectedly, and my stomach flips. There's more to Hayat than I originally thought, and not going to lie, it's hard not to like what I see.

"Thanks, Hayat. You too."

I can feel Morgan's questioning excitement radiating off her as we move toward the end of the counter to wait for our drinks.

"Is that the same Hayat from your English class that you used to complain about? Isn't he Aliyah's brother?" Morgan asks once we're out of earshot.

"Yes, he is."

"Well, I didn't know you two were so buddy-buddy. I can't believe you didn't spill the tea."

"That's because there's no tea to spill. We were being cordial, that's all."

"If you say so. But did you see the way he reacted when I told him that you talked to me about him?"

Before I can answer, my name is called.

"Thank you," I say to the barista.

I pick up my iced coffee and hand Morgan her latte as we head outside. The seats in front of CC are metal with floral designs on the back, and I put the table umbrella up because I've learned from experience that the metal gets hot in the summer.

"Thank you for getting my drink," Morgan says.

"Of course, it was my treat." I take a sip of my coffee. "How have you been doing? How's your mom been?"

She sighs. "I'm alright, I think. I'm going to be back in the studio soon because I miss classes. My mom's got a cast on her wrist since she broke it when she fell on the train platform, and she's been having bad nightmares. She's going to therapy, which helps, and of course she's off work. My dad has been taking on fewer contracting jobs to be home with her, which is good. But medical bills are expensive. She's not working, and he's working less, so I applied to a couple of jobs to help out. It seems weird to be worried about college apps right now, but those are starting to stress me out too. So, it's just been a lot."

"I'm sorry, Morgan. Is there anything I can do? I can share my scholarship spreadsheet with you if you want."

"That'd be helpful. Thank you. You reaching out and getting me out of the house is more than appreciated, and all of the meals have been super helpful. I think we just have to move forward as best we can, you know?"

"Yeah. Well, I love you, so if there's anything else that I can do for you or your family I'm always a text away."

"I know, thank you." She gives me a small smile. "It definitely sucks, and I ask myself all the time why the attack had to happen. But I'm also grateful that my mom is still here because I know things could've been so much worse. It's weird to be stuck between anger and gratitude."

I reach over and squeeze her hand, and she squeezes mine back.

"You know what would cheer me up?" she asks.

I shake my head. "What?"

"You spilling the tea about Hayat. Oh, and catching me up on whatever I've missed in ballet."

I can't help but burst out laughing, and when Morgan joins in it only makes me laugh harder. No matter what happens, present or future, I know that we'll always have each other and that our friendship will never change.

Time passes as we talk about anything and everything, and after two hours pass, Morgan stands up from the table to leave.

"Thank you for this," Morgan says. "I needed it."

"Anytime, no need to thank me."

She hugs me before she goes, and then it's just me. I glance at the time on my phone to see that there are a couple of minutes until Zakat, Farah, and I are supposed to text. Maybe eventually we'll FaceTime, but small steps first. I look up at the sound of footsteps to see the person who was working behind the counter with Hayat walking toward me.

"Hey, this is on the house."

They set a plate with a caprese sandwich and kettle-cooked chips down in front of me, and I blink.

"Wow, thank you so much. Was this Hayat's idea?"

His coworker winks at me. "I'm not able to disclose that info, but I hope you enjoy the sandwich."

I grin. "I will. Thank you so much."

Before I can overthink and analyze the meaning of the gesture, Zakat's name pops up on my phone.

> **Zakat:** Hi! Are we still texting now?

> **Me:** Yes!

> **Farah:** hey

I take a sip of water. So far so good. It's cool getting to know Zakat and Farah—not just Kat and Rose.

> **Zakat:** There were two tomatoes and one fell and went splat. The other tomato told the one that fell, "Ketchup, pal."

I laugh, spitting out some of my water.

> **Me:** I might have to tell that one to my friend. He loves jokes.

> **Farah:** that...was bad...

> **Zakat:** Don't worry, I have many more where that one came from!

I eat my sandwich with one hand and text with the other. A wave of contentment washes over me, and I soak it in. Today's been a pretty solid day, and it's not one that I could've ever planned for. But in this moment right now, things feel pretty close to perfect.

★ ★ ★ ★ ★

Mom turns off the Mariah Carey CD as she pulls into a parking spot in front of the school. The good vibes from yesterday still linger in the air, and I hope the same energy will carry into today.

"Have a good day, Bri-Bri," Mom says.

"Thanks, Mom. You too."

I hop out of the car and head to the faculty kitchen. I blink, my eyes adjusting to the bright fluorescent lighting. Faint classical music plays in the background, and a box of bagels and a box of donuts sit on one of the front tables. Major shout-out to whoever brought those in. The kitchen feels light, and there's a bounce in my step as I head toward the station in the back.

Mr. Smith clicks his tongue. "Sabriya, good morning!"

His gravelly voice makes my skin crawl, but I keep walking to my station.

"Your post about the politics of prose was a great read. It paired well with my morning cup of joe. That being said, I'm going to need you to keep up more today."

I pause, not turning around. "Excuse me?"

"Our group was short five dinner meals during the last delivery run. The families we're helping deserve the exact number of meals that we promise them."

My stomach sinks a little, and I grip the edge of the table that marks my station. "I apologize. I'll make those meals up today."

"That's okay. It won't be necessary."

The room falls silent, and everyone who was pretending not to be listening to the conversation now turns toward Jonathan and me. I rub my arms, the tension in the air itching my skin.

"I'll do better on our next assignment."

Mr. Smith nods. "Good. Your new assignment is to join Hayat in delivering the meals from this point forward."

"It was just one small mistake, and Bri wasn't the only one who was preparing the meals," Hayat says.

Mr. Smith turns to face Hayat, and I can tell that the knife that Hayat tried to use to cut the tension is about to ricochet and stab him in the chest. All the energy in the room shifts to him, but it feels less tense now that it's off me. I start packing up the prepared meals, blocking out Mr. Smith and his need for drama. I'll do this new assignment so well he won't have a reason to call me out again.

"You two will be responsible for delivering the meals to our assigned families." He points to the packed tote bags resting by the door. "You can start now."

I step around him, not meeting his eyes but not lowering my head. I feel people's eyes on my back as I pick up two of those reusable square bags that people use at the grocery store. Each of our assigned families gets a bag full of prepared meals for breakfast, lunch, and dinner. The bags are stuffed, but at least there aren't that many of them to carry. Hayat holds the door to the staff kitchen open for me as we step into the hallway, bags full of cooked meals in our hands. His footsteps fall in time with mine, and the sound echoes off the walls. The hallway is so dimly lit that it looks as gray as it is outside. Out of the corner of my eye, I spot the principal walking down the hall toward her office.

I hesitate, part of me wanting to run after her and let her know how rude and borderline disrespectful Mr. Smith has been treating me. I'm still not exactly sure what his problem is or why he continues to single me out, but it's clear that it's becoming more than a onetime thing. I'm not the only Black person in our group, which makes me think that maybe Mr. Smith has a problem with me because he knows that I'm Muslim. Or maybe I'm reading too deeply into his comments, and he has a problem with me for reasons that I can't figure out. But if I talk to the principal and she talks to Mr. Smith, that could get back to my dad. I don't want to say or do anything that will make things harder on him, but I also don't want Mr. Smith to think that he can continue to walk all over me. Not to mention the fact that he also sits on the school board, and even though Mom's worked at this middle school ever since I can remember, this is still her job. If I'm going to do something, I've got to play my cards right.

"Hey, if I were to talk to the principal about Mr. Smith could you back me up?"

If I use Hayat as a witness of sorts, then it won't seem like I'm the only one who has problems with Mr. Smith. My word should be enough, but I know that sometimes it's not. If I'm going to talk to the principal, I've got to make sure that she'll take me seriously. Even if that means asking Hayat to back me up.

He nods. "Yeah, of course. No problem."

"Thank you."

I start walking down the hall, and he falls into step next to me.

"Hello," Principal Barry says when she sees us approaching. "What can I do for the both of you?"

"I wanted to let you know that one of the group leaders, Mr. Smith, has made some remarks toward me that have made me uncomfortable."

Principal Barry pushes her glasses up her nose, as if she's trying to get a different look at me.

"Very well. I'll look into your claims."

"What exactly does that mean?"

"It means that I'll look into your claims. Can you provide examples of some of these remarks that you say that he's made?"

I can tell that she doesn't fully believe me, or she isn't fully taking me seriously, but I'm in too deep to backpedal now.

"He continuously singles me out in front of our group and solely blames me when our group has a shortcoming."

"She's right," Hayat says. "Mr. Smith gives Sabriya a harder time than the rest of us in the group, and he has done so on more than one occasion."

The principal nods. "I will make sure to bring your concerns up with Mr. Smith."

"Okay, and exactly how long is it going to take you to look into what I'm saying?"

"I cannot give you a specific time frame, but I can assure you that your claims will be looked into."

She gives a firm nod before she continues walking toward her office, leaving Hayat and me standing in the hallway.

I sigh. "Well, I guess that went as well as it was going to go."

"Hopefully something will come out of it, but I'm glad that you decided to talk to the principal. I know that probably wasn't the easiest decision."

His understanding makes my stomach flip, and I give him a small smile as we head toward the front doors of the school.

"Bri," Hayat says. "Knock knock."

I look over at him. "Who's there?"

"Cash."

"Cash who?"

He shrugs. "No thanks, I prefer peanuts."

A smile tugs at my lips. "All of your jokes are dry. How do you actually get people to laugh with these?"

"People laugh at them because they're bad. Sometimes that's

all it takes. I do have a few good ones stored deeper in my pocket, so don't worry." He pauses, his eyes locked on me. "Is it me, or is it weird that we're the only Black people in the group and he chose us to leave?"

I look over at him, surprised by the seriousness of his tone. "Yeah, I was thinking the exact same thing, but I didn't want to say it in case people thought I was being too dramatic. And I guess he does need someone to deliver the meals."

We step outside, and I tilt my chin up toward the sky and smile. It's been raining on and off for weeks, and today thick gray clouds block out all of the sunlight. It feels like being grounded, trapped in a bubble of impermeable sky. Cloudy gray days always make me feel rooted and more aware of the fact that my feet touch the ground.

"That's true," Hayat says as we weave between the parked cars. "And before I forget, Mr. Smith gave out his email address before everyone came in, but he also put it up on the whiteboard if you missed it. I don't think he's big on texting, so he said if he needs to reach us, then he'll email us." He hands me his phone. "And it's zero not *O*, for some reason. I typed it in wrong the first time."

I type the email address, *Jonathand0e23@xmail.com*, into my notes, and Hayat clicks the button on his car keys, and we start to move in the direction of the beep.

"Okay, thanks." I pause. "And is it me or is it weird that he always brings up my blog when he talks to me?"

"It's weird, and I'm not sure what he's trying to get at."

"Yeah. If he keeps it up, I'll talk to my dad. Anyways, let's bounce."

Hayat twirls his keys around his finger. "On it."

I walk next to him, side by side, toward a cherry-red SUV. It's hard not to notice his arm brushing against mine, but he doesn't move and I don't either.

"Shanice, Bri. Bri, Shanice."

"You named your car?"

"All the cool people do." He opens the back door and puts the bags in, and I get into the passenger seat.

The upholstery has that clean car smell, probably from the car freshener that hangs from the rearview mirror. A bunch of Post-it notes with reminders and cheesy motivational sayings are stuck on the dashboard, and I can't help but grin at how that definitely seems like something he'd do. A small square photo of him and his family is tucked in the speedometer, and I lean in to get a better look.

"We're cute, huh?" Hayat asks as he slides into the driver's seat.

He puts his phone in the glove compartment before starting the car, and I know if Mom was in the car with us she'd say, "Now that's what safety and a good head on your shoulders looks like."

"I mean, you bring down the quality of the photo. But otherwise, it's a good family pic. Hey, are you okay if we use your phone for directions, so I can use mine while you drive? I have a charger in case you're worried about the battery."

"It's totally fine." He smirks at me. "Unlike some people, I don't always need my phone to be at one hundred percent."

I roll my eyes. "It's called being prepared, Hayat." I get his phone. "Password?"

"Four, five, six, nine."

"Why the nine?"

"To shake it up."

I shake my head and type the address into his phone. Hayat turns on the radio, and I relax into the seat and go to my texts. I sigh, seeing another one about a new nasty comment.

"You good?" Hayat asks, turning down a residential road.

"Yeah. I'm fine."

He nods, not pushing. "You know, your blog is pretty cool."

I turn toward him so fast that my neck cracks a little, and I let out a sharp burst of laughter. Even though *You Truly Assumed* has grown and made its way across the country, and even the world, I never thought that it'd make its way to Hayat.

"How'd you even find it? And you're not saying that to make me feel better, are you?"

"No, not at all! I looked it up after Jonathan talked about it, and it looks super cool."

My heart warms a little.

"Yeah, well, not everyone thinks that."

"What do you mean?"

"Just some anti-Muslim and racist trolls who have nothing better to do than leave hateful comments about us and how all Muslims should die. You know, the usual."

"Yeah, those are the worst," he says as he pulls around a cul-de-sac. "In my experience, the best way to deal with them is to go on and live your life. That's what they say they're mad about anyway. But really, they're upset because despite trying to tear us down, we're still here."

"So, you're saying don't react?"

"Nah, not necessarily. I think living your best life is the best reaction."

"But what if their comments are keeping me from living my best life?"

"I don't know. I guess the way I see it, our ancestors went through too much for me to not at least try."

I uncross my arms, leaning forward a bit. "So, tell me, Hayat, are you living your best life?"

He flashes a lopsided grin. "I'm trying."

"Aren't we all."

I look at him, really look at him. The crescent moon and star charm that rests on his chest, the way the sunlight makes his amber eyes seem gold, and the light dusting of freckles across his cheeks make my heart flip.

"You aren't as bad as I thought you were," I say, interrupting the moment.

"I'm hurt that you would ever say such a thing," Hayat says, putting a hand on his chest dramatically. "But now that we're spending so much time together, we're going to be friends."

I roll my eyes. "That's a stretch. Nuri and Morgan, the person whose house we're going to second, both think doing the dance would be a good way to step out of my comfort zone, especially since hip-hop isn't my key strength as a dancer," I say. "Stepping out of my comfort zone isn't something that I really find fun. At all. But I'm doing this because I don't want to disappoint Aliyah, because I know she works super hard at the studio and she and Nuri are friends."

"Yeah, I understand. It took Aliyah two weeks to convince me to try out a hip-hop class. Partly because I was too busy sulking but also because I was scared of failing at it and embarrassing myself. Plus, I have bad stage fright."

I give him a look. "But you play a sport and are one of the top players on the team. Aren't eyes always on you?"

"Yeah, but it's different. I'm confident on the field. In the studio, I'm still getting there."

"How do you expect to get onstage at the end of the summer for Aliyah's dance?"

He shakes his head. "Honestly, I have no idea, but I'm going to do it for Aliyah. She more than deserves it."

"Aw, that's so sweet."

My phone buzzes, and I reread the notification.

"How did Jonathan get my email address?"

"Why? Did he send you something?"

I nod, clicking on the email.

"Probably from our registration info sheet. We had to put down our email address."

"Oh, true."

To: ballerinabri@xmail.com
From: Jonathand0e23@xmail.com
Re: Can you cook beef?

Bri,
One of our team members had to leave early and couldn't finish cooking the last pans of lasagna. Can you take over that when you get back, or do you also not know how to cook beef?

I snort and read the message to Hayat.

"I can't tell if he's being serious or not," Hayat says.

"Same. Is this lowkey offensive or just funny?"

Hayat laughs. "I honestly have no idea."

"Me either. He's definitely still annoyed that I didn't cook the bacon, but that's whatever."

"He'll get over it." Hayat turns to me. "By the way, can I tell a joke when we drop off the food if I need to?"

"I mean, sure, you don't need my permission. But why would you need to?"

"I'll let you in on a secret."

I laugh, leaning back in the seat. "Hayat, you're an open book."

"Eh. I actually hate being around new people."

I raise my eyebrows. "Really?"

"Yeah, I always feel awkward and never know what to say. When I was little I had a really hard time talking to new people—I still do sometimes—and my dad suggested that whenever I met someone new and didn't know what to say to tell a knock-knock joke. I never really let that go, I guess."

I reach out and squeeze his arm. "Whenever you're with me, moe, you can tell your crappy knock-knock jokes."

"Great. Wanna hear one?"

"No."

He laughs, tapping the steering wheel as he drives off. "I don't actually need them with you. You're pretty easy to talk to."

And for some weird reason, it feels like my heart flutters a little at his words.

The GPS alerts us that we're five minutes from our first destination, and I look down at my phone to see a text from Zakat: Bri, you need to see this asap. Alarm bells start ringing in my head. Zakat almost always ends all of her sentences with an exclamation mark, so there shouldn't be a period. I click on the link she sent.

"Oh, shit," I say as the website pops up. "Crap."

"What's wrong?" Hayat asks, pulling in front of our first destination.

"Nothing. Just something came up with the blog, that's all."

"Okay, I'll run the food in. You want to come with?"

"Um, are you comfortable going alone? I want to check *YTA* real quick."

He nods. "Yeah, no worries."

He grabs one of the bags of food before closing the car door behind him. I focus on the website that Zakat sent. The title of the page is "Sites to take down." The tagline on the homepage reads, "Protecting American values online and abroad," which is a warning sign in and of itself. I scroll to the bottom of the website, titled *Free the Right*, and sure enough, *You Truly Assumed* is on the list. *Free the Right* spouts a lot of terrible garbage that usually isn't based in facts, and the whole point of their site is to radicalize their base. Every so often one of their posts will go viral on Twitter because it warrants strong criticism, and most of the things that they write about minority communities are extremely toxic. I've done my best to never interact with the website, and that's never been a problem until now. My eyes start to sting, and I take a sharp breath, trying to center myself as my surroundings start to spin. This must be why the nasty comments have been increasing. People who support or belong to this *Free the Right* site are literally trying to force us to shut down *YTA* by flooding us with comments. And they didn't link the blog, they listed it, so there's no way for us to remove ourselves from that list.

"Oh my gosh," I say, tears pooling over. I sniffle and wipe them away before they can fall.

I fight down the feeling of entrapment rising in my chest and bile rising in my throat and go back to Zakat's message, my hands shaking. I text Zakat with wobbly fingers and tell her not to engage and that I'll try to figure out what to do. I wipe my face so that I don't look a hot mess when Hayat gets back in the car and slide my phone in my pocket so that it's out of sight.

"It's fine, Bri," I say to myself. "You'll come up with a plan. You always do. Everything will be okay. Everything will be okay."

But I'm not sure I believe it.

ZAKAT

LULLWOOD, GEORGIA

I eat my bagel and scroll through Instagram looking at the latest posts on my feed from all the various art accounts that I follow. I've always gone back and forth about creating my own, but I'm not sure I'd be that good at marketing or branding myself and my art. I do have an eye for aesthetics, and my feed would definitely be on point, so maybe I'll give it a go eventually. It'll be another step toward expanding and putting myself and my art out there. My phone buzzes, and I click on the email notification that pops up, humming with the feeling that comes right before telling a secret.

I uploaded my first comic strip this morning, and I've been looking forward to reading the comments ever since it went up. I decided to chronicle how Bri, Farah, and I came together with *You Truly Assumed*. The style is much more animated than I usually do, and I used a lot more color this time around. But the comic strip is super bright and cute, and I

YOU TRULY ASSUMED   183

really like how it turned out, so I'm telling myself that that's what matters most. Sharing my artwork is like sharing secrets, each one lifting a tiny weight off my shoulders. Comics take more time, and I poured myself into the first one that was going to go up on *You Truly Assumed* because I wanted it to be well received. If I'm going to put myself out there, I might as well put out my best self.

> **LynneR07:** Though the writing and drawings are both well done, I think that the subject matter is unnecessarily polarized.

Well, no one asked what you thought, Lynne, did they?

> **Mimi_Reads:** As a Muslim teen, I wanted to say how much I love reading YTA.

My insides warm, the comment wrapping me in a tight hug.

> **WillieK:** Muslim hoes.

> **DJ_101:** This blog isn't going to change anything. Complete waste of time. Don't know what dreams y'all have, but y'all might want to let those go.

I twist my lips and shrug, clicking on the next email notification. I may not have the thickest of skins, but it's not like a super drunk Lullwood High student hasn't said that to my friends and me before. I sink farther into the beanbag chair, waiting for another email notification to load. I read the next comment: This blog is disgusting. The Muslim ban should've stayed in place so you all could stay with all of the terrorist gangs since you're all terrorists. This blog is run by Muslim n******.

I recoil at the last sentence, the words slapping me. Even though *Bloggingly* blocked the racial slur, the message still rings clear. I press Delete, but the sting still lingers on my skin. Though there were more positive comments today, the hateful ones still seem to be rising. It went from one hateful comment per post to three, to five, to twenty, to now forty-five. Maybe trolls have shared the blog's URL among themselves since the alt-right site is trying to get *You Truly Assumed* shut down, or maybe the increase is a consequence of the blog's growth.

Bri said the sting would fade over time, but it seems to be the exact opposite. She said eventually the worst of the comments would slip through my fingers like water, but it seems as if they're drowning me. Or maybe I need to get more used to these types of comments.

But if Bri knew that these comments were rattling me she'd start worrying, and I don't want to make her worry. I joined *You Truly Assumed* to be helpful, not a hindrance. And if she and Farah are dealing with the hateful comments fine, then I don't want to be the only one who isn't and disappoint them. Being part of a team is nice, and it does make all of this easier. I don't think I could be a part of *You Truly Assumed* without Bri and Farah. The online world can be ugly, but there's a lot of beauty too. I guess it sometimes takes a while to find.

I send off a quick text in our group chat asking if they want to chat later and then get to work organizing a box of books to donate to the homeless shelter in the neighboring town, humming to myself as I work. I turn on some light jazz, and the music fills the small space. I wish I could talk to

Baba and Mama about the comments. They didn't grow up in Lullwood, so they probably have good advice about navigating around hate and not absorbing it. But I know that if I tell them about the comments, they'll think that I'm putting myself in danger. And then I'll have to explain to them how much *You Truly Assumed* means to me and watch them not get it. Telling them will only lead to disappointing them, and that's the last thing that I want to do. For now, it's better if I keep this all to myself.

Because before this summer, I thought I was the only studious Black Muslim girl whose voice echoed among the trees. But I've realized since joining *You Truly Assumed* that my art is my voice and it can be heard beyond Lullwood. If I put my pencils and pens down, I'll be giving in to hate. And I can't let hate win.

I go to the group chat named "Islamic School Seniors" and type, If you're free at four this afternoon, let's meet at the masjid. We need to figure out who's targeting Lullwood and how we want to respond and move forward. Together.

I hit Send and brace myself for the responses like "you've got the wrong number" or flat out "who is this?" which is a fair question. People know of me, but they don't know me and that's how I've always liked it. But I want Lullwood to feel safe again, and in order for that to happen I have to speak up and out. If I want to protect Lullwood, I can't keep being silent.

My phone buzzes, and I look down.

Aafreen: I'll be there.

And even though it's only one response out of one hundred possible ones, a small flicker of hope sparks in my chest.

★ ★ ★ ★ ★

I slide into the seat next to Aafreen, and she reaches over and squeezes my hand. Our classmates crowd into the Sunset Room. It's one of the most underrated rooms in the masjid. The dark yellows and rusted oranges make the space feel warm and homey, and sunlight always spills in through the tall windows. Bits of conversation bounce around, and the air buzzes with energy.

"Should I say something?" I ask Aafreen.

"Yes!" Aafreen squeezes my shoulder encouragingly. "This is your meeting to lead."

I set my shoulders back. I can do this.

"Hi, everyone!"

My words get sucked into the cacophony of voices, no one batting an eye.

"Hi, everyone!" I say a little louder, trying to project.

My voice slices through the array of conversations, and the weight of people's eyes falls on me.

"Um, hi, I'm Zakat. Most of you probably know that. This is a quick emergency meeting to air any thoughts about how we want to address recent incidents, as incoming seniors and as the Lullwood Islamic community as a whole."

One of the girls who does debate with Aafreen and me raises her hand, and I nod at her to begin.

"I'm honestly so glad you called this meeting because I've been feeling at a loss about what to do about everything. And I think everyone is to some degree because nothing like this has ever happened in Lullwood before. I'm angry. Really angry. And I want to acknowledge those who are too.

There's nothing wrong with anger. Wallow in it if you need to, and let it push us forward. I think anger can be converted to hope through action, and I think this meeting is one of those actions."

A few people snap after her words, and one of the top soccer players from the boys' school raises his hand. I nod at him to start.

"I know we're not talking a lot about this, but I wish more people were taking steps to find out who's doing these crimes and hold them accountable. I personally think that Asher Anderson is either the person who did it, or he's at least somehow involved."

Loud cheers ring through the room, and I snap in agreement. People sit in all the chairs, lean against the wall, and spread out on the soft maroon carpet. The fullness of the Sunset Room warms my heart, and it reminds me that we're here. We take up space too.

Someone else raises their hand. "While I agree that finding out whoever's doing this would put a lot of us at ease, I also think we need to be realistic. We need to keep in mind that Lullwood means different things to different people, which is part of what makes this place so special. But our reactions and plans to move forward are going to be different too, and it's okay if we don't all agree."

"That's a good point." I take out my pen and notebook. "Speaking of plans and moving forward, how do we as individuals and as a group want to accomplish that?" I pause, taking in everyone and the connectedness that holds us all together. "How do we want to create change?"

Silence washes over the room, and doubt starts to creep

in. This is where the meeting falls apart. Maybe I should've phrased the question differently. Maybe it's too big, too daunting.

But then Aafreen raises her hand. "I have an idea. What if I were to throw a small get-together at my place at like seven? Asher's cousin, Lucy, is in town, and she'll come, which means Asher and his friends probably will too. Then we can ask around and see if any of them know anything. Who knows? Maybe Asher will slip up and spill the tea."

"That's actually not a bad idea," someone says. "But the people who are instigators are going to show, and we'll all have to be prepared for that."

"I can't believe this is only the second week of break and we're already trying to pull off an operation, but I'm in," someone else in the room adds.

I turn to Aafreen. "You're sure you're okay with doing this? Your parents will be fine with it?"

"I should be able to pull it off." She turns to the rest of us. "I'll send out details to confirm everything, but I think this could work if we play it right."

Everyone cheers, and the noise sounds a little like hope.

I finish laying out my outfit for tonight's get-together, which is really just a ploy to find out who's behind the boys' school and the bookstore being damaged, and anticipation makes my stomach churn. Hopefully we can all pull this off without anything going wrong. If Asher and his friends show up, they'll be outnumbered, but they could still make a scene somehow. My alarm rings, and I shift my focus away from tonight as I grab my laptop and sit down on the nook bench. After I texted in the *YTA* group chat to see if we could talk, Bri suggested that we Zoom. Baba and Mama have always warned against talking to or meeting up with strangers online, but I don't think that's why I'm jittery. This is the first time we're actually seeing each other, so I just want to make a good first impression. Or maybe second impression, since we've technically all already met?

"Well, this is interesting," I mutter, signing into Baba's Zoom account. A notification pops up that Farah's waiting to be let into the room, and I hit Accept.

Farah waves. "Hey, Zakat!"

"Hey, it's awesome to see you! Give me one sec, I've got to admit Bri into the room."

Farah nods. "Okay, great."

My cheeks start to hurt because I'm smiling so hard. I can't believe we're actually doing this. There's a little ding, and Bri's face pops up on the other side of my screen.

"Bri! Hi!"

"Have you ever Zoomed before, Zakat?" Bri asks.

"Yes, I have, but I'm still so excited." I clap. "I mean, I'm actually seeing you both! At the same time! Though I guess I know what you both look like because we follow each other on social media."

"Wow, that didn't sound creepy at all," Farah says, resting her chin in her hand.

"You know what I mean! Zooming or FaceTiming is the next best thing to talking face-to-face."

Bri nods, her movements a little jerky from the lag. "I get

what you're saying. This is kind of a big step in our collective friendship. So, how's everyone been doing?"

"I've been working at a bookstore," I say.

"I'm in Boston," Farah says. "Spending some time with some people."

"Let me guess, you haven't finished unpacking yet."

Farah raises an eyebrow. "What makes you say that, Bri?"

I laugh. "It's not like we can't see the open suitcase and piles of clothes on the bed or anything."

Farah rolls her eyes.

"So are we going to talk about the comments and being on that site?" Bri asks.

"Yes." I sit up a bit straighter. "We've been getting a lot more of them. This one said, 'Hijabs are ugly. I'm so sorry that you're all oppressed by your religion.' Another one says, 'I thought Muslim women weren't allowed to read.' Like, what the heck? Oh, this comment made me laugh. It said, 'This blog is trash. Keep your opinions to yourself.' And there are a bunch more telling us that Muslims need to die, but I'd prefer not to read those."

"Wow, that's a huge yikes," Farah says. "I guess it's a good thing that I don't check the comments often, because I don't know if my mental health can handle reading those types of comments all the time."

Hearing that makes my shoulders drop a little as relief erases some of my own worry. I know the comments get to Bri too, but I still thought that I was overreacting to them. It's nice to know that I'm not alone in finding them overwhelming.

"What do you all think could be causing the rise besides being on the *Free the Right* site?" Bri asks.

Sighing, I rub my temple and rack my brain for an answer. Perhaps it's because the number of national incidents of hate crimes committed against Muslims have seen an uptick since the attack in DC. That could definitely be a parallel. *You Truly Assumed* is growing and getting some more exposure from other blogs, but it's all been pretty lowkey and positive until the blog appeared on that list.

"What if I made a post showing some of the bad comments?" Bri asks, tapping her fingers against the desk. "That way everyone will know that *YTA* isn't backing down."

I shake my head. "I don't think that's wise. That might make the people who run that *Free the Right* site come for us more."

"I agree with Zakat, fam," Farah says.

"I still believe using the block button is the best option," I add.

A post with all the comments would only be a target. We need a shield.

"We'll come up with something," Farah says, breaking the silence. "No need to overstress about it."

Bri nods. "Yeah, you're right. And I've already reported the list that's up on *FTR*, so hopefully that's taken care of."

"Have either of you started working on your college essay yet?" I ask, changing the subject.

Farah groans. "I hate having to write about myself. I'm boring, and I'm okay with that."

"Well," I say. "Hopefully this summer has given us all something cool to write about."

"Seriously, it has. I feel like I've already learned so much," Bri says.

"If you write about us and *YTA* to get into college, I'll honestly feel so honored," I say.

We all laugh, and even though the connection starts to waver, the sound rings through solidly.

"So, I'm actually going out to a party tonight," I say.

Bri puts her hand on her chest. "Aw, look at you. They grow up so fast."

"Have fun and be safe," Farah says. "Are you going with friends?"

"Yes! It's at my friend's house, and I'm going to walk over in a couple of minutes."

"Before we finish, what are you wearing?" Bri asks.

"One sec, I'll show you both." I get up from the nook and grab the pair of jeans and blue floral blouse. "It's not much, but I think it'll work."

"It definitely works! That top is so cute," Bri says. "Okay, well, I've also got to run, so I'll talk to you both later. Have fun, Zakat."

Farah waves. "Bye!"

"Goodbye. I hope you both have a good rest of your night!" I say.

The laptop screen goes fuzzy as the call disconnects, and I get up to change before heading downstairs.

"Mama, I'm heading out!"

Light footsteps get closer to where I stand at the front door, and Mama appears from the living room.

"The party is at Aafreen's, yes?"

"Yes, Mama."

Mama gives a firm nod. "Okay. Text me when you get there."

I press a kiss to her cheek. "I will."

Mama closes the door behind me, worry in her eyes, and I start walking down the block. It hurts that Mama has to worry about me more now, but hopefully once whoever's attacking Lullwood is caught that worry will fade. My fingers reach for my earphones, but I decide against it to stay present.

I feel the bass thudding from the house as I walk up the front steps of Aafreen's house. The sun still shines brightly, and I can feel the buzz in the air. Aafreen's mom waves at me as I enter, and I give her a quick hug. I send a quick text to Mama and make my way down to the basement, the thudding getting heavier. I squint through the darkness, trying to find Aafreen. Squeezing through everyone feels like swimming upstream, and I can already tell that my ears are going to be ringing tomorrow morning.

Despite the number of people that are packed into the basement, the space feels light. My classmates and peers spin and pop and sway, a kaleidoscope of movement. People wave at me as I pass, and I can hear the laughs and the cheers above the pop remix that's playing. Even though I can already feel a headache starting to form, I feel like I belong in this moment. And I know it's because I know the people here, because they're who make Lullwood what it is.

I spot Aafreen in the back of the room, standing with Lucy near the kitchenette where bottles of water sit on the counter. I make my way through the crowd toward her, letting my body move with the music. I probably have no rhythm and look super awkward, but if no one else is judging me, then I should try not to judge myself either.

"Hey," I say.

Aafreen hugs me. "Hey. Thank you for coming."

Lucy smiles at me. "Good to see you."

"Thanks," I say. "Did Asher come with you, Lucy?"

She nods. "Yeah, he's around here somewhere. And there are a few other people from Lullwood High too, I think."

"Alright," I say. "I'm going to go mingle for a bit, but you two have fun."

Aafreen nods, and I make my way through the crowd, looking for anyone who isn't familiar. Between the two Islamic schools, there are about one hundred people in my grade, and we all know each other by name. I spot someone that I don't know near the snacks, and I make a beeline over to them. No matter what, I have to play it cool. I can't push too hard. I've got to be smooth and subtle or what I'm doing will be too clear and won't lead to anything.

"Hello," I say. "I haven't seen you around before. What's your name?"

The person turns to me. "I'm Jay. Aren't you one of Lucy's friends?"

I nod. "Hi, Jay, nice to meet you. And I am—we actually work at the bookstore together."

"Doesn't your mom own the bookstore?"

"No, you're thinking of my friend who works there with us too. Did you hear what happened to it?"

He nods, but nothing changes on his face. "I did, but I'm sure whoever did it was just playing around."

I try to push down the tiny spark of hope that flares in my chest. Jay may not say anything helpful, even if he didn't initially brush me off.

"What do you mean?" I ask.

"People play around and things like that happen." Jay shrugs. "It really isn't a big deal."

I try not to frown. "Why do you say that?"

Something crosses Jay's face, as if he realizes that I'm not agreeing with him. "I've got to go catch up with my friends."

He leaves, and I watch as he joins Asher and a group of others toward the back of the basement. Jay says something to the group and Asher looks over at me, but it's hard to figure out his expression with the dim lights and the distance. I start to head back over to where Aafreen and Lucy last were instead of moving on to the next unsuspecting person. Hopefully my classmates are making more progress than I did. I didn't get anything out of that conversation with Jay. Maybe finding out who's behind both incidents isn't going to be solved with a get-together.

"Hey, Zakat," Asher says from behind me.

I jump a little and turn around to face him. "What do you want?"

"I heard that you were talking to Jay about me."

I make a face. "A, I wasn't, and B, not everything is about you."

"Well, I could say the same thing to you. You're always whining about how you and this part of Lullwood have it so bad, but you really don't. Look what's happening to Black people. They have it way worse."

I blink, taking a minute to fully process the dual punch of anti-Blackness and Islamophobia.

"I am Black though—"

"Hey, is everything good here?" Aafreen says, appearing next to me. "Because if it's not, I will make you leave, Asher."

Lucy steps next to Asher, crossing her arms and giving him a questioning look.

Asher raises his hands. "Hey hey, I'm just here to enjoy a good party." He shrugs. "And rumor has it, this is where the 'Book of Secrets' is kept."

Asher winks at Lucy and disappears back into the crowd. I glare at Lucy, but she ignores my stare. I don't know what that exchange was, but I don't like it. Still, I didn't expect her to stand up to Asher like that.

"Hey, Aafreen," Lucy says. "Why would Asher be looking for the Journal of Secrets here?"

Aafreen laughs. "First off, that's not what we call it. And I really can't say."

I take a sip of water, fighting to keep my expression neutral so that Aafreen will also succeed at doing the same. Aafreen cares about Lucy, but she wouldn't spill the beans. At least I don't think she would. Not when Lucy would take any information straight to Asher.

"I'm going to run to the bathroom. Be right back," I say.

Aafreen nods. "Sounds good."

I look at myself in the mirror as I wash my hands and try to collect my thoughts. I can't let Asher rattle me. If anything, his comment only makes me want to try harder to find out the truth and get answers. He's got to be connected to the bookstore being egged, and I'm going to prove it.

"Come on, let's go," Aafreen says when I step out of the bathroom.

Lucy links her arm through Aafreen's, and Aafreen nudges her. Lucy makes a face but extends her other arm out toward me. Aafreen nods at me encouragingly, and I link my arm with Lucy's. Together, we make our way onto the dance floor. I make out fragments of people I know, seeing flashes of them illuminated by the disco lights.

Amina, one of my classmates, runs over to us. "Aafreen, Zakat, could I talk to you two for a minute alone?"

Her sky blue hijab goes super well with her patterned long-sleeve tunic, but I don't have time to admire how cute her outfit is because of the panic in her voice.

"Yeah, of course."

Lucy gives us a small nod and heads over to Asher and his crew, and Amina leads us to a corner where there are a bunch of people from our grade standing and murmuring. The vibe doesn't seem good, but I have no idea what's wrong.

"You all need to see this," Amina says, holding out her phone to Aafreen and me.

The air suddenly feels thicker, and my heart drops as I zoom in on the photo of a faded page from the "Book of Secrets."

"Oh, no," I say at the same time that Aafreen says, "Shit."

"Whose Instagram story is this on?" Aafreen asks.

"Jay Jacobs," Amina says. "But this is just a screenshot. His account is private."

My stomach sinks. If that's the same Jay as the person that I was talking to earlier, then my approaching him might have spurred him to do this.

"How would they have found the closet and gotten into the box?" Amina asks, her voice rising in panic. "And did they take the book?"

"We'll go check," I say.

The "Book of Secrets" is kept in a locked wooden box in a closet that's tucked all the way at the end of the hall. We walk in silence, both of us lost in our own thoughts. Aafreen opens the closet at the end of the hall and pushes aside the jackets that hang from the rack above.

Aafreen gasps, and I reach out to steady her. The left side of the wooden box is splintered and dented in the middle as if someone hit it in one spot until it gave way. The rest of the box is intact, but the clasp that kept it locked shut is broken. I start to search through the closet as desperation claws at my throat, but the "Book of Secrets" is gone.

Aafreen starts to cry. "I had one job, and I couldn't even do it. The 'Book of Secrets' got taken because of me and this bad idea."

I reach out and hug her. "It'll make its way back to us somehow."

"I'm sure some Lullwood High people knew about it," Aafreen says. "But they've always respected what it means to us."

The thought of Lullwood as a whole being stripped bare by people who aren't in the community makes me feel sick.

"Lucy asked about the 'Book of Secrets' a couple of days ago, and Asher mentioned it tonight. They've got to be the ones behind this," I say. "We have to tell everyone else that it's missing."

"I know," Aafreen says, her voice a whisper. "And you're right."

The possibility of Lucy gathering info about the book from hanging around Aafreen and me and then passing it along to Asher is very likely. There's no way she'd accidentally let things slip without having some idea of what he'd do with that info.

We close the closet behind us and go back to the party.

"Asher and his friends are gone," Amina says as soon as she

sees us. "We were going to go talk to them right after you two left, but by the time we turned around they were already gone."

"Because they took the book," Aafreen says. "That's the only reason why they came."

Concern, shock, and disbelief ripple out through the group.

"What do we do now?" Amina asks.

"What can we do?" Aafreen asks.

The feeling of powerlessness that has been present ever since the fence appeared around the masjid washes over me so strongly that I feel dizzy. This is the third time in two weeks that my community has been violated in some way, and it's been hit after hit. Tonight, we tried to fight back, but even that didn't work.

"How about we all go to bed and recharge? We'll figure out how to best handle this in the morning," I say.

People nod and start to filter out. The tone is somber, everyone's disappointment and anger heavy in the air, and all of the joy and laughter has been squashed. It's as if we've been a flame, fighting to keep burning amid strong winds, and the "Book of Secrets" getting taken blew us out. Without a spark, there's no way to reignite that flame, and right now all that's left is the smoke from the flame that once burned.

FARAH

KIRBY, MASSACHUSETTS

The alarm on my phone rings, and I roll over, snuggling deeper under the covers. I'm not going to lie, this bed is mad comfortable. But I won't be able to go back to sleep if I don't hit the snooze button. I fumble around, trying to reach my phone that rests on the nightstand before I jolt up as a realization hits me. That alarm was a reminder to wake up and Face-Time Riley. He wanted to talk when we were both free, even if that meant it was six in the morning his time. Bless his heart.

I crawl out of the bed and head to the attached bathroom. My stomach flips with nerves, even though I know I have nothing to worry about. It's just that Riley and I have never really FaceTimed before. Whenever we wanted to hang out, it was in person, and we texted in between. FaceTiming feels like new and uncharted territory, but if our relationship is going to become long-distance, then this is going to become our main way of communicating. So I'm willing to try now.

I glance at myself in the full-length mirror attached to the back of the door. It's weird to see my full self in this space that isn't mine. The only mirror that's at my house in Inglethorne hangs above the sink in the bathroom, and it only shows from the shoulders up. Everything about this room—and even Tommy and his family—seems so polished and put-together, and though I do my best to come across as put-together, I know that I'm not that polished. I've always thought that being a bit rough around the edges was part of my charm, but here it feels like something that needs to be dry-cleaned or wiped down. The apartment that Mom and I share may be small but it's homey, and the guest room here feels like a museum. Pretty but for display, and I'm not supposed to touch.

After washing my face and brushing my teeth, I throw some of my box braids into a topknot and put in my hoop earrings. For some reason, both the hairstyle and the type of earrings both give off a very confident vibe. My phone rings, and I rush over to accept the FaceTime call.

"Hey, babe!" Riley says. "You look good."

His desk lamp sends beams of golden light across his face, but his smile shines brighter.

"You don't look half-bad for it being six over there," I say, resting my chin on my hand. "What have you been up to?"

"Missing you," Riley says.

I laugh, and my cheeks warm. His smoothness and genuineness are an irresistible mix, and his words replace my nerves with something that might be close to butterflies.

"But I've also been keeping up with the internship and

hanging out with the boys. Other than that, I'm just trying to relax and enjoy—"

He falters, unsure if he should finish his sentence, and I give him a small smile.

"You should be enjoying the rest of your time in Inglethorne. I want you to," I say adamantly.

He nods. "Thanks, I appreciate that. But enough about me. How are you? How is the family?"

I shrug. "The kids are fine, and I guess Tommy and Jess are too. It just feels like I have to walk on eggshells because I don't want to mess anything up."

"I'm sure Tommy and Jess are a bit nervous. They probably want to make a good impression, so perhaps that's why it feels like that."

"Maybe. I just don't know how much is really going to change in the next few weeks."

"Keep an open mind. They might surprise you."

"Yeah, I'll try." Actually talking to him, even if it's through a screen, is making me realize just how much I miss him. "I'm excited to see you when I'm back."

Before Riley can respond, the door opens and Samson peers in.

"Good morning," Samson says.

I turn toward the door to talk to him. "Hey, I'll be right—"

He starts running, and before I can yell at him a huge weight crashes on top of me, causing me to almost drop the phone. Samson starts laughing, and the adorableness of his smile with the three front teeth missing wipes away my annoyance. He's so cute, and I want to reach out and squeeze him or ruffle his hair.

"Samson, I was talking to someone," I say, trying to sound annoyed as a laugh slips out.

He climbs off me and rests his elbows on the bed. "Who?"

Riley laughs, and Samson sticks his head near my shoulder so that he can see the screen.

"Hi, I'm Samson, Farah's brother. Nice to meet you."

His introduction takes me by surprise, and I can't help but grin.

"Hey, Samson, it's nice to meet you too. I'm Riley, Farah's boyfriend."

Samson waves and turns to me. "Mom told me to tell you that breakfast is ready," he says, dropping his voice to a whisper.

"Thank you, I'll be down very soon."

"Okay," he says, flashing me an adorable smile and leaving the room.

"Well, it looks like I should let you spend time with the fam," Riley says. "But I'll text you later."

"Sounds good."

He blows me a kiss, and I laugh and pretend to catch it and throw it back.

"Talk to you soon," I say. "Wait, should I hang up or should you?"

"You can do the honors, if you want."

"Alright," I say. "Miss you."

"Miss you more."

I give a little wave before hanging up. That actually wasn't that bad. I was worried that I wouldn't know what to say or that this would be awkward, but our conversation flowed just like it does when we're talking at Tate's. Plus, watching Riley and Samson meet was really cute. I didn't think those two spheres of my life would intersect, but they do so really well. Maybe long-distance is worth giving a shot because walking away from Riley at this point seems like it'll hurt more than the future hurt that I'm trying to protect myself from.

I quickly make the bed, instead of leaving the blankets in a rumpled heap like I usually would back home, and then head downstairs.

Jess looks up as I walk into the dining room. "Good morning, Farah."

I nod. "Good morning."

"These pancakes are delicious, Dad," Ally says.

I unfold the white plastic chair that's off to the side and slide it into the empty space between Emma's high chair and Jess's chair. They look like a picture from out of a family or home magazine, but my added plastic chair completely ruins that whole aesthetic. The smell of maple syrup and chocolate chip pancakes is the only thing carrying me right now. That and the pure excitement over my computer science seminar buzzing through my veins. I probably don't need this much sugar, but oh well.

Two stacks of pancakes, three different syrup options, and a fruit spread that could make the cooking network jealous cover the table.

Tommy jumps up. "Let me get you a plate, Farah. I thought I set out an extra one, but I must not have."

"It's not a big deal," I say, sitting down.

He hands me one when he gets back from the kitchen, and I load it with pancakes, eggs, and pineapple chunks. I can't remember the last time that I ate pineapple.

"Do you want any bacon?" Ally asks.

"No, thank you. I don't eat pork."

"Really?" Samson asks, munching on a piece. "Why not?"

I shrug. "I'm Muslim, so I'm technically not supposed to eat it. But I'm pescatarian too, meaning I only eat fish, so that's also why."

"Cool! We're Christian." He pauses. "Wait, if you only eat fish, does that mean you can't eat chicken nuggets?"

"Nope, no chicken nuggets."

"Then what do you eat at McDonald's?"

"The fish sandwich is my go-to."

Jess sits down at the table, the screechy sound of her chair against the floor making me wince. "Who's ready to share what they're excited for?"

Ally raises her hand. "Oh, oh, oh! I want to go first!"

"Since Farah's our guest, why don't we let her go first and you can go after her, Ally." Tommy turns to me. "Every morning, we go around the table and we each share something about the day that we're excited for to help center ourselves in gratefulness. It can be as small or as big as you want."

Jess turns to look at me, and the suspicion and wariness in her stare makes the pancakes in my mouth turn to glue. It's like she's waiting for me to say or do the wrong thing, or maybe she's still upset that me coming here threw a wrench in her family's vacation plans. I want so badly to say something to ruffle her feathers, but I'm not going to break my promise to Mom over her. Mom's trust is worth way more than a few minutes of personal satisfaction and the couple of seconds it takes to come up with a good diss.

I turn back to Tommy. "I'm excited about the computer science seminar."

That's probably the thing that I'm most excited for about this entire trip. Even though it's only from ten to two during the weekdays, it'll give me a reason to be out of the house. Maybe I'll even gain some skills that'll help me with the blog or my app. The seminar is for rising high school seniors and college freshmen, so hopefully I won't be the only high schooler in the summer seminar. But even if I am, I'm sure I'll be able to hold my own.

I listen to everyone else share and finish the rest of my food. I look around the table, unsure if I can get up and leave like I can back home or if I have to be excused. As much as I want to just go, I don't want Jess to hold that over my head if it ends up against a house rule or something like that. But also, I'm not really here to make Jess like me. I slowly start to stand up, and everyone looks at me.

"Um, I'm finished, so I just thought that I'd go get ready," I say. "But the breakfast was good."

Tommy nods. "Of course."

I give an awkward smile and then hurry back up to the guest room. For the first breakfast with the family, that wasn't actually that bad. I mean, the food was good, so there's that.

I grab a pair of joggers and an old sweatshirt and throw them on. A brief flash of longing for the hot summer LA sun runs through me as I slip my laptop in my backpack and slide on my knockoff Vans.

There's a knock on my door.

"Farah, I'm ready to leave," Tommy says.

"'Kay!"

I grab my backpack and head out of the guest room. The winding spiral makes it hard to go down the stairs very fast, and I grip the railing so that I don't trip and embarrass myself. Tommy kisses Jess and the kids, and I give a quick wave before we leave. My eyes widen when I notice a Google ID badge on Tommy's lanyard. He works at Google? I get in the passenger seat, and my eyes go to the logo in the center of the steering wheel and they widen.

"You can pick the music," Tommy says as we drive out of the neighborhood.

"I don't really care what we listen to."

He nods and turns up the volume, and a summery pop song blasts through the speakers.

"Samson loves this song. But how can you blame him, it's a bop."

I bite my lip to keep from laughing as he bops his head along to the beat. I can't tell whether or not I think he's annoying, endearing, or a combo of both. He seems to be trying but also not trying at all, and I still don't know which I prefer.

We ride the rest of the way in our own little worlds, and before I know it, we're in the city. I take in the tall buildings and the beat of honking cars. Cars are tightly packed in traffic, but it's nowhere near as bad as LA traffic. Pedestrians weave in between the cars, and bikes zoom past. It's all one big kaleidoscope of motion. Besides the noticeably cooler and wet weather today, the similarities between the Boston area and Inglethorne are a bit comforting.

"Here we are," Tommy says, pulling into a parking space.

I look over at the dull gray building, excitement surging through me.

"Do you need directions?" Tommy asks.

I shake my head and hold out my phone. "No, I'll be okay. I have the seminar info and a map of the building I found online, so I should be able to piece everything together."

"Alright, then, have a good day! I'll be here to pick you up at two."

"You get off work that early?"

"I have some flexibility in my schedule, so I'll be able to get you on time."

I nod, closing the car door behind me. Anticipation swells in my chest as I walk toward the entrance of the building. I take the elevator up to room 203 and walk into the computer lab. I sweep my eyes across the room and frown when I notice that I'm the only person of color out of the twenty students here so far. I was expecting it to be bad but at least a little bit better than this. Tommy did drop me off a couple of minutes early, so hopefully more Black students will get here. The seminar description said that it was a preparatory skills course for 200-level classes at the college and provided more practice with Java, Python, and C++, which I could use. But maybe people decided to skip the course and jump straight to the 200-level classes, which I would probably do if I was in that situation. But for now, I'm hoping that gaining more experience with the various programming software will give me a head start when it comes to the compsci classes that I'm going to take next year.

I take a seat in the third row, perfectly in the middle.

"Good morning, everyone! Welcome to Computer Science 102. I'll be your teacher for the next couple of weeks. I know this is a beginner-level class, but has anyone here had any experience with coding, web design, or anything of that nature?"

I raise my hand, and someone snickers.

"Stop showing off," someone behind me hisses. "You already stick out enough."

I stop my mouth from falling open. Honestly, whoever said that was really outta pocket. Maybe they're upset that I'm in the same class as them, but they need to get over it. I couldn't care less if me raising my hand makes anyone feel embarrassed. As much as I want to turn around and cuss this person out, I take a deep breath and keep my hand up.

★ ★ ★ ★ ★

"Class dismissed," the teacher says.

The loud rustle of movement as students begin to pack up erupts, and I close my laptop and slide my notebook into my backpack. Besides that rude guy who was sitting behind me, today was actually enjoyable. For this being a 100-level college course, it wasn't all that bad, and I think I'll do fine. It was cool to get a small taste of what college might be like in the future, and the computer lab here is ten times better than the one back at my high school. It's a bit strange to be in an entirely new space with access to different resources, like really good discounts on all of the required software, but I think if Mom could see me here on a college campus, she'd be really proud of me. Being in the college-level seminar is a small glimpse of everything that she's dreamed for me and everything that I've been working toward. It's exhilarating to think that this could be my life a year from now.

I start to head out, and I spot the guy who sat behind me

and called me a show-off watching me as he talks with a few of his friends near the doors.

"Ignore him," the Black girl next to me says. "You're new, and he knows the rest of us here well enough to know that we don't take his shit."

"Oh, I don't either. I just didn't want to make a scene."

"Making scenes is what I do. That's why I got here fifteen minutes late." She grins. "I'm Jamilah."

"Nice to meet you. I'm Farah."

"Hey, I know we're just now meeting, but I'm trying to get the word out about something really important to me." She hands me a flyer, and her voice softens. "I'm not sure if you've heard, but my mosque was attacked earlier this week. One of my close friends, Khadijah Ibrahim, was killed." Her shoulders drop as her eyes well with tears. "She was only seventeen, looking forward to her senior year and enjoying her summer, like the rest of us. But her future was cut short by hate."

"I'm so sorry."

Jamilah holds out her phone, and I see a picture of a Black girl, eyes crinkled with laughter and smile glowing. There's a crescent moon and star ring around her index finger, similar to the one Mom always wears, and it hits me how much this girl, Khadijah, full of love and light, could've been me.

"I'm organizing a vigil to honor her."

I take the flyer. "Is there anything I can do?"

If I walk away from this, I'll be running away again. And even though I'll never meet Khadijah, I know her smile and her joy and the largeness of the life she had to live. I can't walk away from the reflection of myself I see in her and her death.

"There's going to be one or two more planning meetings to make sure all the details of the vigil are ironed out," Jamilah says. "I can text you the details."

I give her my phone. "Sure. I'll try to swing by to the meetings, and I should be able to come to the vigil."

I'm not sure what Tommy will think about me getting involved with the vigil, but it's not like I necessarily need his permission. I can always pay for my own Uber if he doesn't want to take me to the meetings, and even though I don't know this area well yet, getting involved might be one way to do so. If I'm going to be in Kirby for the rest of the month, I might as well make the most of it, and the vigil is really important. Black girls, especially Black Muslim girls like me, rarely get the justice that they deserve, and while the vigil won't bring Khadijah back it will bring her some of the justice that she deserves.

I fold the flyer and slip it into my pocket. Until I leave Kirby, I'm going to do what I can to take a stand for Khadijah. And for me.

I head out of the classroom alongside her, the flyer heavy in my pocket but filling me with lightness. There hasn't been much that I've been able to do to stop the growing number of hateful comments on *YTA*, but I feel like I can do something about Khadijah's death.

"Great, I hope to see you there," she says, as we step outside. "I'm really sorry about your friend."

"I am too." She slides her backpack up on her shoulders and gives me a small smile. "You seem new here. Would you like to grab lunch with me and a few of my friends?"

Agreeing to go to lunch with someone I just met is completely out of my wheelhouse, but this trip is all about build-ing new connections, I guess.

"Um, I'd love to. Just let me ask the person that I'm stay-ing with real quick."

Calling Tommy by his first name throws people off if they don't know me, and it doesn't feel right to call him my father. So, for now, he's the person that I'm staying with. I pull up his number and cross my fingers that he picks up.

"Hey, I'm about five minutes away," Tommy says, picking up on the first ring.

"I was actually wondering if I could grab something to eat with a friend that I met in the seminar," I say. "But I under-stand that it's a bit last minute."

"Sure, of course! Text me the name of the restaurant where you end up going, and I can swing by there in an hour."

"Sounds good. Thank you."

I put my phone in my pocket and turn toward Jamilah. "I'm in!"

"Great, let's go."

We head outside the building and start walking.

"I feel like you can't visit the Boston area and not go to the Prudential Center," Jamilah says. "There's this Asian fu-sion restaurant that's so good I swear that I eat there at least once a week."

"Dang, well, now I'm excited."

I look up, and a silver tower looms over the rest of the buildings. I follow Jamilah inside, and the bright white lights and streams of people appear in full force, flowing up and down the escalators. Various department stores line both sides of the walkways, and I try to keep up with Jamilah, who weaves in between people like she's done this a million times before.

"Here we are," she says, slowing a bit.

Two people who are sitting at a table in front of the restaurant stand up and wave, and we walk over to them.

"Everyone, meet Farah! She's in my compsci class, and she's interested in helping out with the vigil." Jamilah turns to me. "Farah, this is my girlfriend, Nadira, and this is Lulu."

I give a little wave. "Nice to meet you both."

We go inside the restaurant, and a spicy aroma greets me. I can already tell that lunch is going to hit. The lighting is a bit low, and a mix of booths and tables with wooden benches fills the space. Bits of conversation filter past, and the vibe of the restaurant is warm.

The waiter leads us to one of those wooden benches and hands us menus. Water is in a cute glass bottle that rests in the middle of the table, and I pour some into my cup.

"So, Farah, before we get into the details about the vigil, what brings you to Kirby?" Jamilah asks.

"I'm visiting some family for a bit, but that's pretty much it! In terms of the vigil, I think I'll be able to help spread the word outside this area, if you wanted to. I'm a part of this blog called *You Truly Assumed*. It's run by myself and two other Black Muslim teens, and it's basically a small online community for young Muslim women. I think the blog could be a good way to get word out."

"Wait," Nadira says. "You're part of *YTA*? I love that blog. I even voted in that poll that Kat put up about potential logo ideas. Can you pass along that she should go with option A?"

I laugh, my shoulders dropping a little. "I'll try."

"Option B was better," Lulu says.

"Clearly, I'm late," Jamilah says. "But I'll be sure to sub-scribe too. And I think your idea is a good one. Right now, the plan for the vigil is to walk from the community center to the mosque. It's a simple route that's about twenty min-utes, so I think that'll work."

The waiter comes back over with a smile. "Are you all ready to order?"

I look at the menu, a little overwhelmed.

"I say go with the curry and swap the chicken for tofu. It's my go-to," Jamilah says.

I nod and order that along with one of the fresh juices, and the waiter writes down numbers on each of our paper placemats.

Jamilah pulls out a thick notebook from her backpack. "Okay, Imam Muhammad has said that he'll speak at the vigil on behalf of the mosque, and Khadijah's mom is going to speak as well. So that's set."

"Did they find out who was behind the attack?" I ask.

"Yeah, some random white guy who turned out to have connections to a hate group," Nadira says. "I wish I could say 'surprise, surprise,' but really there's no surprise there."

The rally that happened back in California pops into my head, and I nod in understanding.

"Are we still using #JusticeForKhadijah to spread the word?" Lulu asks.

"Yes," Jamilah says. "I don't like that her life has to be boiled down into a hashtag, but it's simple and will get the message across."

As I listen to the conversation, inspiration surges through

me. Is this what Bri felt when she decided to grow the blog? Or how Zakat felt when she called that emergency meeting? This tingling in the fingers and the weighted feeling of believing that change can be created.

★ ★ ★ ★ ★

"Kiddos, dinner's ready," Tommy yells.

Surprisingly, his voice carries up the stairs and down the hall, despite the largeness of the house. Back in our small apartment, Mom and I could hear each other's whispers no matter what.

I close my laptop, set aside the problem set that is due tomorrow, and head downstairs. The smell of freshly baked garlic bread wafts from the kitchen, and I follow it to the dining room. The white plastic foldable chair sticks out among the dark brown wooden chairs that match the table, but seeing it still makes me feel a sliver of belonging.

Tommy places the steaming bowls of Alfredo pasta, chicken, and broccoli on the table, and everyone sits down. I watch as the rest of the family close their eyes, bowing their heads in silence, and I do the same. I hear a rustle of movement, and I look up to see that they've finished their prayers.

"So, Farah, is there anything you learned in class today that you would like to share with the rest of us?" Tommy asks.

Ally and Samson look at me, like they forgot I was here. Which is probably a good thing because that means that they're starting to get used to me. I chew and swallow slowly, awkwardness swirling in the air with the steam from the food.

"It was good. But I actually learned more from one of my

classmates today than the teacher. Did you hear about Khad-ijah Ibrahim's murder and the attack on the Black mosque? One of her close friends is in my compsci class. She's orga-nizing a vigil, and I'm helping her with that. And I'm defi-nitely going to go."

"Can I come with you?" Ally asks. "One of my friends goes to the mosque that got attacked. She's really sad about what happened, and I want to support her."

I smile. "Yeah, of course you can come with me."

It's just walking, so I don't mind Ally coming with me to support her friend. As long as she sticks with me and doesn't get lost, us going together shouldn't be a problem. Plus, I like Ally and Samson so far, and stepping into a big sister role doesn't seem to be as overwhelming as I thought it would be.

Jess's fork slips from her fingers, the metal clattering against her plate. "No, Ally, absolutely not. It'll be too dangerous. There's been talk about threats at the vigil, and I don't want you to be in an environment like that." She turns to me, her expression sharp. "Please don't talk about the vigil anymore."

I pause, not exactly sure how I should respond. For starters, I'm pretty sure that Ally's thirteen and would be fine going to the vigil with me. I haven't heard any speculations about threats, and even though I won't write them off completely, I think if Ally wants to stand up for her friend and for what's right, then Jess should support her instead of trying to shield her. Not everyone gets the privilege of being shielded. But hey, what do I know?

Tommy clears his throat. "Ally and Samson, can you two please go eat in the living room? Take your placemats with you and try not to make a mess. One of you please take Emma."

Ally looks at me, guilt in her eyes, but I smile at her. She has nothing to be sorry for, and honestly, it felt like it was only a matter of time before I slipped up and did something else that upset Jess.

"As much as I feel bad about what happened to Khadijah, my main concern is keeping Ally safe," Jess says, once the kids leave the room. "She's still young. There are some things that she isn't ready to see yet."

I blink in shock. The fact that Jess thinks that she can hide Ally from seeing hate and injustice reminds me of the white mom who was walking with her son the day I was called the N-word in elementary school. She had looked at the car the slur had been hurled from, at me, and then she tugged on her son's hand and kept walking. Maybe Jess has the privilege to look away, but she shouldn't make Ally do the same.

"You know what? Fine," I say.

It's not worth fighting with Jess, especially when I'm only going to be here for two more weeks anyway.

She sighs, turning to face me. "Look, I've lived in Kirby since I was your age, and nothing like this has ever happened here. I want you and Ally to have a relationship, but I don't think that the vigil needs to be a part of that. In fact, you might want to reconsider going to the event yourself, Farah."

I look at Tommy, waiting to see if he'll disagree with her. But his silence is the only answer I get.

"You two really don't get it," I say.

Now that I'm a part of *YTA* and helping Jamilah organize the vigil, Jess's reasoning and Tommy's silence bother me more than they would've two weeks ago when I was back in Inglethorne. I used to hope things would change—and that was fine—but now I'm trying to *make* things change. And neither of them is supporting that.

"If Khadijah wasn't Muslim and the vigil wasn't going toward the mosque, would you still be saying this? You know, just so we can be on the same page and everything." I pause, looking at their shocked faces. "Do you even understand what a death like this means?"

Jess gives me a hurt look. "A death like this?"

"Actually, forget I asked," I say, standing up from the table. "But I think Ally would be fine at the vigil, and it's clearly important to her."

"Farah—" Tommy says, but I shake my head.

"I'm not here to argue. I don't even want to be here in the first place." I shrug, hoping it hides my hurt. "I'm going whether or not Ally comes with me, so I'm good either way."

I head upstairs to the guest room and take a deep breath as my head spins. I've done absolutely nothing wrong, and I deserve better than what just went down at dinner. For some reason, I feel let down. I guess I expected a bit more from Tommy and Jess, even if I was trying not to. If they really cared, perhaps one of them should've volunteered to come with Ally and me instead of simply saying she shouldn't go. Them choosing to look away from what happened to Khadijah makes it seem like they don't see me, or if they do, then they don't care. Things were actually going really well today and then this happened.

I dig my nails into my palm, trying to fight the urge to kick the bed. I need to talk to Riley. Or Mom. Or both.

A death like this. A death like this death. A death like mine. A death like Mom's. A death like Khadijah's. A death like Bri's. A death like Zakat's. A death. A death. A death.

WHY DREAMS DIE

I'm starting to realize that I may be overdoing it with these blog post titles, but they're honestly so rewarding to come up with. In fact, I was choosing between "why dreams die" and "the death of dreams." But the former just had that extra artistic touch, you feel?

I was going to make this post more political like the past couple of posts have been. But in all honesty, the rising amount of hateful comments has been really stressful and draining for me, and it probably has been for the *You Truly Assumed* community as a whole. So I wanted to switch it up and do a more fun story-time kind of post that was inspired by a discussion you all were having in the comments. A comment convo of sorts. So gather around, it's story time.

One of the hateful comments that we got a few days ago was about how we should let go of whatever dreams we had related to *You Truly Assumed* changing anything. It wasn't totally horrible, as far as comments go. But it hit a nerve, and until our comment convo I couldn't pinpoint exactly why.

I did some internal reflection, as one does, and I realized it was because that comment echoed a sentiment I've heard way too many times before. A sentiment that many minorities in this country are told at all times, whether explicitly or not. That our dreams don't matter. In elementary school, a few of my classmates and I would play Disney Princess. We'd always vote to decide who got to be the princess, the crowning role. And recess after recess, I'd lose. Finally, I got the nerve to ask our group's ringleader why I never won. She patted my arm and said in the sugary-sweet way that only first graders can that I couldn't be a Disney princess because I didn't look like one. When I went home that day, I threw away all my Disney princess coloring books and told my parents I didn't like the movies anymore. That was when my first dream died.

Eventually, I got into dance. All styles, but ballet was the one that captured my heart. But as the level of intensity grew, from beginner to intermediate to advanced to pre-pointe to pointe to preprofessional, I became one of a handful of Black ballerinas in the studio. The transition from intermediate to advanced was the one that almost killed my dream of dancing professionally. It's when I started being told that I stuck out in dances, that my bun wasn't slick enough, that my lines weren't sharp enough.

I took a season away, unsure if my dream was worth the amount of insecurity I was wading through. But I missed the eight counts, the adrenaline that comes with nailing a difficult turn sequence, the feeling of weightlessness when leaping. I missed it all, and I went back with one mantra: no one can destroy my dream. And that mantra has carried me through everything thus far.

And as these hateful anti-Muslim comments add up, I keep reminding myself of that mantra. No one can take away my dream. Have you all had a similar experience? Has there been a dream that you were told didn't matter? Did you hold on to it, or did you let it go? How do you protect your dreams? I'm interested in hearing what you think about this topic, and if any of you have a story to share feel free to drop it in the comments. I love getting to know more about you all!

And to those of you in a similar situation, don't be afraid to bring your dream inside, like how plants are moved inside when it gets cold. Share it with those who you trust to prune it and water it when you don't think you can make it grow anymore. Don't be afraid to keep it away from those things that are weeds, even if it means taking it away from the sunlight for a bit.

Sorry for the weird dream/plant metaphor (sometimes I go overboard with metaphors, if you couldn't tell that already from the titles), but in short, don't let anyone or anything diminish your dreams. They matter, and they deserve to live and breathe and grow.

Until next post,
~Bri

SABRIYA

ABINGTON, VIRGINIA

My phone dings as I head downstairs to the kitchen.

Zakat: Just checking in!

Farah: thx. have either of u heard about Khadijah Ibrahim?

I steal a handful of grapes from Nuri's plate and pop them into my mouth as I set my breakfast down on the table on my placemat.

Me: I think I saw a post about her on social media.

Zakat: Me too! Wasn't she killed while at the masjid?

Farah: yeah, in the city where i am staying. i'm going to a meeting soon to help plan her vigil. i'm a bit nervous.

Me: We're here for you!

Zakat: What Bri said! You're living the mission of YTA off the screen. That's brave.

I text a quick You've got this! and slide into my seat at the dining room table across from Nuri. Breakfast is one of my favorite times of the day because I almost always see my sister. With my dance schedule and her lacrosse practices we're usually so busy that we're like objects constantly in motion, always passing each other but never colliding.

"I have news," I say.

Nuri raises her eyebrows, the cereal bowl covering half of her face as she slurps down the sugary milk.

"I think Hayat can come off the Siddiq Sister No List."

"Really?" Nuri sets the bowl down, a milk mustache above her mouth, and laces her fingers together. "I never really knew why he was on the list to begin with, so tell me more about this development."

"He was on there because I disliked him more than I didn't like most people. And because of sister solidarity." I shrug. "But he's actually not that bad. He's still annoying, but in an endearing sort of way."

Nuri sighs. "His brother can come off the list now too, I guess. Aliyah is one of my best friends, so she outweighs her brothers." She pops a blackberry into her mouth. "How did you and—"

"Mr. Smith. He basically forced Hayat to work with me."

"That's not bad at all. He could've paired you up with someone worse."

Hayat's freckles pop up in the furthest corner of my mind, and I shake my head, trying to push the image out of my mind. But then the image of him smiling pops up, and I groan internally. Who gave this guy permission to take up space in my brain? Because I sure didn't.

I chug the last of my milk. "Yeah, I guess that's a fair point."

Nuri laughs, getting up from the table. "I'll see you later, sis. I've got to head to practice."

"Have fun!"

I grab a granola bar to go and slip on my Vans. A faint breeze greets me as I step outside and close the door behind me. The weather signals the slow approach of July. Humidity sticks to my skin, and the mugginess causes beads of sweat on my forehead. There aren't any clouds to help block the sun, so there's no relief from the heat. I should've sprayed more anti-humidity mist on my twist-out because as soon as mid-June hits, summer frizz starts to come out in full force. It's hard to believe that this is already the third week of June. Maybe it's because there's so much going on right now, but this month is zooming by.

I walk down a couple of blocks and head farther into my neighborhood. The townhomes eventually give way to larger detached homes. Having moved to Abington at the beginning of junior year in order to be closer to school and to allow Mom and Dad to have easier commutes, I haven't spent much time getting to know the neighborhood beyond my street. As I get closer to the Taylor family's house, it hits me that this time next year, I'll have graduated and so much will be different. Even though the DMV feels like home, Abington doesn't yet, and I wonder if it will by the time I'm leaving for college.

I spot Hayat's car, Shanice, parked in front of the Taylors' house, and I speed up a little. Hayat gets out the car and waves as I get closer.

"Hey, how are you?" I ask once I'm next to him.

"I'm doing alright! How are you?"

"I'm good. I've never walked a dog before, so I guess we'll see how this goes." I reach into the pocket of my jeans and pull out a small crumpled ball of plastic bags. "Just in case."

Hayat laughs. "Always prepared."

"You know it."

We head up the walkway that leads to the Taylors' house, and I hesitate before pressing the doorbell. Footsteps sound from the other side of the door, and a couple of seconds later it flies open. A tiny golden dog runs toward the front door, dragging its leash behind it.

Mrs. Taylor says, scooping the dog up, "Hello, are you two the volunteers who are assigned to walk Coco today?"

I nod. "Yes, we are."

Mrs. Taylor sets Coco down outside and hands me the leash. My hand starts to sweat, and I'm not sure if it's because of the heat or because of my fear that Coco will make a mad dash before I can stop her.

"Coco is very well-behaved, and a good twenty- to thirty-minute walk will suffice. And thank you both for volunteering to walk her." She gives us a grateful smile, but it doesn't hide the worry in her eyes. "I'm a labor and delivery nurse, so my shifts are extremely long, and my partner is still healing from the burns that she got during the attack. Coco keeps her company, but she can't walk her as much as she used to just yet."

"Of course, it's our pleasure, and I hope that your partner is having a speedy recovery," Hayat says.

Mrs. Taylor leans down and gives Coco a kiss. "I'll see you soon, Coco. Be a good girl. You all have fun!"

She gives us a wave before closing the front door.

"Bri, you good?"

I look away from Coco. "Yeah, I'm fine. Why?"

"You were doing that thing you do when you're thinking hard about something. You get this crease in your forehead."

I set my shoulders back and smooth out my features. I get tense when I'm overthinking, but no one's ever noticed before. The fact that Hayat pays that much attention to me makes me want to ask him what else he has noticed about me.

"Does Coco lead? Or do we lead?" I ask.

"I think we just walk and Coco will go along with us."

We start walking and sure enough Coco falls into step a couple of paces in front of us. Now, as long as a squirrel doesn't jump in front of Coco, we'll be good. I set a timer on my phone to make sure that we can get back when we're supposed to. If Coco can feel my apprehension, she doesn't show it as she continues padding along.

"So," Hayat says, breaking the comfortable silence between us. "How's life been?"

"What kinda question is that? I mean, it's a little better than your jokes, but I see you all the time during the week."

He shrugs. "I thought it was a pretty solid convo starter."

What he told me about using jokes to start conversation pops into my head, and I instantly feel bad.

"Sorry, I was just teasing. I think it's starting to hit me that a year from now my life is going to look completely different in ways that I can't even imagine yet. It's disorienting."

"Ah, college. I'm trying not to think about how much writing I'm going to have to do for college apps until at least August."

I roll my eyes. "Writing isn't that bad. Now that I think about it, applying to college is a lot like dance auditions. You put yourself out there, and someone who doesn't know you decides if you're a good fit, or worthy, or whatever."

The college process seems so nebulous, and I just hope that I end up going somewhere where I feel like I belong. Somewhere that makes me feel like *YTA* makes me feel. But I know that someone can be a perfect candidate and still not get accepted, which isn't that far off from nailing every move and still not getting the part. If I think of the college process in terms of dance, it isn't as overwhelming.

"That's true. But I think we're going to be fine in the end."

"Yeah, I guess I shouldn't worry too much about the outcome of stuff that hasn't even happened yet."

"I'm sure that this time next year, we're both going to be happy."

"That's very good vibes only."

He shrugs. "There's nothing wrong with a little optimism. After my injury, I didn't think I was going to be able to bounce back, and now I have recruitment interest from colleges."

Before I can respond, Coco pulls on her leash, and I stumble forward. Hayat wraps his hand around my arm, and I jolt a little as sparks erupt. Coco tugs at her leash again, making me even more off-balance.

"Coco," I yell.

She turns at the sound of her name, and just when I think she's calm, she leaps at me and presses her front paws to my legs. My foot catches on her leash, and I shriek as I start to fall. Hayat grabs my wrist, and I hold on to his arm tightly in case he decides to let go. My stomach flips, but I'm sure it's because I was a second away from bruising my butt and not because I can feel Hayat's muscles flexing under my fingers.

"You good?" Hayat asks as he pulls me up.

He's so close that I can smell the fresh scent of his laundry detergent and whatever cologne he wears. That, on top of his nearness, makes my head spin.

I nod and bite my lip so that I don't say anything embarrassing. Hayat's eyes follow the movement, and when he leans in closer, my heart goes into overdrive and my thoughts fade away. Coco barks again, breaking the spell between us, and I try to take a step back before realizing that Coco's leash is still wrapped around my ankles.

"What has you so frazzled, Coco?" I ask.

I lean down to untangle myself, and once I'm good, I hand the leash to Hayat. We walk back to the Taylors' house, and the silence crackles with unspoken words and unacted upon feelings. If Coco hadn't interrupted, would Hayat have kissed me? Was I going to let him?

The alarm on my phone goes off, and we both jump. Coco starts to speed up as we head up the walkway, and she barks happily when Mrs. Taylor opens the front door.

"There's my girl," Mrs. Taylor says, taking her leash from Hayat. "Thank you both again. It looks like Coco had a great time."

We say our goodbyes, and Hayat and I get into Shanice to drive back to the middle school. I feel like I should say something to Hayat, but there's no plan for me to go off of. Or maybe what happened wasn't that big of a deal, and I'm overthinking everything.

To distract myself from thinking about him as we drive, I scroll through the hateful comments on *You Truly Assumed*, trying to match the usernames to those in the *Free the Right* comments. But the numbers and letters blur together, and doing this is making me feel even less in control. I click on an email, and a comment pops up.

> **JohnD0e23:** You girls are in over your heads. If you knew what was best for you, you'd end the blog. Or it will be ended for you.

My mouth falls open as I reread the comment. I only know one person who puts a zero in Doe, and that's Mr. Smith. I guess anyone could make that change though. Plus, the whole point of using John Doe as a username is anonymity, so there's no way to tell who it really is. Mr. Smith also doesn't spell his first name with an *h*, so I'm probably jumping to conclusions. Still, my stomach turns, despite the logic.

But what if it is actually him? Mr. Smith has done and said enough questionable things that I wouldn't put this past him. But even if I did want to speak up, he's still Dad's new boss. There's no way I could say anything against Jonathan without inscrutable evidence, especially since doing so would destroy everything Dad's worked for. Maybe it's just better if

I let it go, for Dad's sake. Besides, Jonathan's the least of my worries right now.

We're stuck between shutting down *YTA* and continuing to face an onslaught of terrible comments. And this is all my fault. I should've turned off the comments when we started getting more hateful ones. I should've never dragged Zakat and Farah into this. I should've never said yes to making the blog public. Damn it. How do I fix this?

"Bri, we're back."

I look up from my phone to see that we're parked in front of the school.

I take a deep breath. "Okay, sorry about that."

"No worries." He pauses. "Are we good?"

I nod. "Yes, of course."

Hayat gives me a small smile, and we both head inside. Everyone is chatting with each other as we walk into the faculty kitchen. My hip hits the sharp edge of one of the tables, and it rattles as I try to pass it. I bite my lip to keep from cursing as Mr. Smith's laptop falls off the edge. My shoulders drop in relief as I scan the screen, not seeing any cracks. I'm in the clear. I set the laptop down, and I notice how many tabs he has open. My eyes go to the tab next to the music player out of curiosity, and I do a double take. But the *Free the Right* site still sits in the tab to the left.

A mix of anger and shock moves my hand forward, and I click on the tab. There on the *Free the Right* site is Mr. Smith's comment, the cursor blinking. I squint, and I can make out the title of the post: "Sites to take down." I take a step back, shock jerking my footsteps. I read through those comments minutes ago, and it was a ton of people agreeing to go after

YTA and the other blogs on the list. He knows me beyond the blog, and he could easily dox me by releasing private information about me. Not only that, but I have no idea how much he knows about technology, which means I have no idea what he could do to the blog. He could hack *You Truly Assumed* or somehow do something even worse. I sneak out my phone and take a photo, capturing his unfinished comment about how there needs to be increased surveillance of Muslim communities inside and outside the DC area. Mr. Smith turns from where he's standing across the room, his eyes locking on me. "Why are you using my laptop?"

My heartbeat quickens as everyone in the group turns in their chairs toward me. I tighten my grip on my phone and my stomach clenches.

"I bumped into the table and accidentally knocked over your laptop. When I went to pick it up, I noticed you had a ton of tabs open. One of them caught my eye."

"Oh, that's fine," Mr. Smith says. He gives me a weird look as though I'm telling him something that's irrelevant. "Please be more careful next time."

I blink. He's got to be kidding me. For him to just look at me and act like he's done nothing wrong is beyond me. And the worst part is, he probably thinks he's done nothing wrong. Mr. Smith probably thought he'd never get caught commenting on the *Free the Right* site. He's likely felt not even an ounce of anxiety or paranoia, unlike what many Muslims have felt since the terrorist attack. And then for him to have the nerve to tell me to be more careful. The privilege.

As much as I don't want to take away from the work that Dad's done to get his new job, I also can't keep holding my tongue. I know my worth, and I've been raised to speak my mind. That applies even when a situation is complicated. I don't want to drag Dad down, but I think he'll understand why I need to rise up. I don't want to be seen as the stereotypical angry Black woman, but in this moment I realize there is nothing wrong with my anger.

"No, it's not fine!" I yell. "I saw your comment on the *Free the Right* site. The same site that has been attacking my blog. Yes, I shouldn't have been nosy and clicked on another tab, but I did." I pull up the photo of his comment on my phone. "And now I know that you believe that 'Muslims need to be held responsible for the terrorist attack.' And that 'we're not safe with them in our country.' Now I know."

Mr. Smith's smug look slips. "I simply think you and your little friends, Kat and Rose, are in over your heads."

"No one cares what you think," I snap.

"Is this true, Mr. Smith?" Hayat asks.

Others in the group nod, echoing his question.

"Did you really write that?"

"How could you?"

"Is she making this up?"

"Your little blog isn't going to change anything." He lets out a short, sharp laugh. "Besides, you three broadcasted to the world that you were Black Muslim girls. You seriously thought you weren't going to get any negative comments after putting that on display? I know you're not that naive."

There's a collective gasp around the room.

"What the hell, dude," Hayat says, and everyone's voices erupt.

Loud enough to almost drown out my anger.

Something inside me snaps, the urge to chuck his laptop off the table and see the screen crack into pieces washing over me. "You know what, Jonathan? Fuck you."

I turn on my heel, tears streaming down my face too fast for me to wipe them away.

"Bri!" Hayat yells, but I don't look back.

Not until I'm outside. A sob forces its way up my throat, and I keep stumbling farther from the school. Working on *You Truly Assumed* was my new plan, but now I have nothing. No plan and no destination. All I know is that I'm not going back. If Mom wasn't teaching summer school, I'd ask her for a ride home, but for now Uber will have to do.

I click on the app, my fingers shaking. Sure, Jonathan is beyond annoying, but I never thought that he was so hateful. And does Dad have to put up with this kind of treatment at work every day? Or is Jonathan just showing his true colors because he isn't on the job? Since he's taking mornings off work to volunteer, I expected him to take this seriously, but I never expected this.

I hear footsteps behind me, and I turn to see Hayat running over.

"Hey. I'm not going to ask if you're okay because I know that's probably not the best conversation starter when you're not, but I did want to ask if you'd like a ride home."

My lips quirk up a little as memories of our dog-walking outing that felt like a date but definitely wasn't a date pop into my head. He may not think so, but somehow Hayat always knows exactly what to say to put me at ease.

I sigh. "Yes. Thank you, I'd appreciate that."

I swipe out of the Uber app and follow him over to Shanice. I plug my address into the GPS and put my phone on the dashboard, making sure not to crinkle any of the Post-it notes. I buckle in and go to my messages with Mom. I don't have the energy to explain what just happened and answer all of the questions that she'll probably ask, so I stick to the basics.

I'm not feeling well, so I left early.

Once I settle into the passenger seat, exhaustion and numbness start to replace the adrenaline and shock, and I fight to keep my eyes open. I jolt when I feel a hand touch my shoulder and hear a soft whisper telling me to wake up. My eyes snap open, and I turn to see Hayat looking at me with concern written all over his face.

"Hey, sorry to wake you up, but we're here."

"Oh, right. Thank you again for the ride."

I start to reach for the door handle when Hayat clears his throat.

"Um, I'm here if you ever want to talk about what happened. Not that you have to or anything, but I'm here."

I give him a small smile. "I'll keep that in mind, thanks."

I close the car door behind me and give him a small wave as he pulls off.

"Breathe, Bri, breathe," I say to myself as I walk inside the house.

Forcing myself to keep moving, I head upstairs to my room. I know I need to text Zakat and Farah about what happened, even though it doesn't change the fact that we're still stuck on that list. But I really don't want to dump this on them. Not when they're already going through so much because of *You Truly Assumed* and me.

I punch my pillow. I should've spotted Mr. Smith's prejudice from the beginning. All the signs were there, but I was hoping that I was wrong.

Stop, Hayat's voice says, popping into my head. *You can't blame yourself for this.*

Sighing, I burrow farther under the covers. I don't want to think about next steps or coming up with a plan right now. I just want to watch the *Great British Bake Off* and go to bed.

My phone buzzes, and I see two new text messages.

> **Aliyah:** Hayat told me about what happened. I understand if you don't feel like coming to rehearsal today.

> **Hayat:** Are you okay?

No part of me feels like dancing. I don't want to tell Aliyah that though, so I force myself to kick off the covers and click on her text message.

> **Me:** I'm on my way.

Send.

I can figure out how to deal with disappointing myself again later. But I've let down Zakat, Farah, and basically my entire relief work group in one day, and I don't want to add Aliyah to that list. I have to do something—anything—right.

★ ★ ★ ★ ★

"Okay, that's all for today!" Aliyah says. "Good work, team. Please practice. And yes, I'm looking at you, Hayat."

I drop my hands from Hayat's shoulders, and he moves his hands away from my waist, both of us gulping in air. I take a small step back, putting some space between us. I can't tell if my racing heart is from the intense hour of dancing or if it's because I was so close to him that I could see how thick his eyelashes are.

My breaths start to steady as I guzzle down water. I was so close to canceling on this rehearsal, but I'm glad I didn't. I forgot how much dancing can take my mind off things, and I really needed this. The basement at the Prices' house has been converted into a dance studio for Aliyah, and the purple walls, the panels of wall-length mirrors, and the shiny polished hardwood floors all lifted my mood.

We all walk upstairs to the main level. Amir looks up from where he sits at the dining room table eating, and he gives us a small nod of acknowledgment. Mrs. Price places three glasses of water on the kitchen counter, and I take one and gulp it down.

"How have you been doing, Sabriya?" Mrs. Price asks. "Aliyah told me about your blog! She's an avid reader."

Aliyah gives me a sheepish smile. "It's good."

The compliment is a nice reminder of the reason why I decided to make *You Truly Assumed* into a blog in the first place, especially since that reason has gotten lost recently. *You Truly Assumed* is a positive space for so many people.

"I've been doing alright. Thank you for asking, Mrs. Price."

"I'm glad to hear that. Please tell your parents that I say hello."

I nod. "I definitely will."

"I'm going to go catch the four o'clock news, but let me

know if you need anything. It's always good to see you, Sa-briya."

"Thank you, Mrs. Price."

She goes into the living room, and Aliyah claps her hands.

"Our next rehearsal is on Saturday." She hugs Hayat, gri-macing at his sweatiness, before turning to smile at me. "Thank you so much again, Bri. You make this dance one hundred times better. No offense, Hayat."

I laugh. "My pleasure."

She nudges Hayat's shoulder. "I'll let you two be, but don't forget to practice!"

Aliyah waves and heads upstairs to her room.

Hayat turns to me. "That wasn't that bad."

"Yeah, not at all."

"How long do you have until you're getting picked up?"

I sit down on a kitchen stool in front of the counter to un-lace my dance street shoes and slide on my regular sneakers.

"It should be five minutes, but knowing my mom that could also easily be twenty minutes."

Hayat laughs. "Okay, we can hang out in the kitchen or go up to my room if you want to?"

My cheeks warm, even though he's not implying anything. "Sure, why not."

He gives me a crooked grin that makes my heart skip a beat, and we leave the kitchen. I notice the Islamic art on the wall that leads into the living room. The script is painted dark brown and is in Arabic, so it's probably a verse from a Surah in the Quran. It's pretty and matches the dining room table and china cabinet.

"Here we are," Hayat says, opening the door to his room.

My eyebrows rise as I take a look around. "It's neat."

Hayat rolls his eyes but doesn't hide his grin.

There isn't a stack of clean clothes that needs to be folded in sight, and his bed is neatly made. His lacrosse stick, gloves, and sports bag are strewn in a corner, and my heart melts when I spot a framed picture of his family on his desk. A few posters of lacrosse players hang on the walls, but his room is much more minimalistic than I expected. Maybe I need to start letting go of my expectations about Hayat because somehow he always seems to flip them around.

"It's cute," I say.

"Thank you," Hayat says, his voice teasing. "I'm glad you think so."

Silence falls between us, and I drum my fingers against his desk.

"I know I asked this earlier, and it still probably isn't the best question, but are you okay?" Hayat asks.

I look up, my eyes locking on his amber ones and gorgeous lashes.

"I'm fine. I mean, did I think Mr. Smith was part of an alt-right site? Well, no, I didn't see that one coming. But I've decided that it's time to tell my parents about what's been going on. I don't think they'll be disappointed or upset, but I wish I would've been able to handle this on my own."

"I'm sorry, Bri. But for what it's worth, I think telling your parents is a good idea. You don't have to do everything on your own. You've got a lot of people in your corner."

"Yeah, you're right." I give him a small smile. "This rehearsal helped me get my mind off things though."

"I'm glad."

My phone buzzes, and I look down to see a text from my mom letting me know that she's outside.

"Before you head out, I just wanted to say if there's anything at all that I can do, just text. But don't let Jonathan's words, or the words of any of the other commenters, keep you from writing yours."

I roll my eyes. "That was corny."

"But true?" he asks, raising an eyebrow.

"But true." I bite my lip to keep from smiling. "Um… I've got to go but I'll, um, catch you all on the flip side."

I cringe as soon as the words leave my mouth. The flip side? What is this, middle school?

Hayat laughs. "Yeah, I'll catch you on the flip side."

"Bye, Bri," Aliyah says, popping out of her bedroom at the end of the hallway, and Hayat gives me a wave.

I head downstairs, and Mrs. Price walks me to the front door. She waves to my mom, and I'm surprised that she doesn't come outside and start up a fifteen-minute conversation.

"Is everything alright, Bri? Did something happen earlier?" Mom asks as I slide into the passenger seat next to her.

"I'm feeling a little better."

Mom looks at me, her eyes searching my face, and I fight not to fidget.

"You know I'm here if you want to talk," Mom says.

"I know, Mom."

Even with all the explanations I could give, Mom will never fully understand what happened or what it means to be Muslim despite her proximity. But I also know that she's always been proud and supportive of who I am and what I do, including *You Truly Assumed*. She's always been accepting of Islam and my faith, and even though I'm nervous that I might've screwed things up, I'm not nervous that she won't believe me.

"Um, actually, Mom, something happened today," I say.

"Yes, I'm listening, dear."

"Mr. Smith is Islamophobic and involved with an alt-right site. He's singled me out in our group from the very beginning, and I tried my best to deal with it because I know he's Dad's new boss."

The words tumble out in a rushed whisper, all of them coming in one breath, and I look over at Mom to see her reaction.

Mom pulls onto a side street and parks before she turns to me. "Oh, Bri. You should've come to your father and me with this as soon as it started, and I'm sorry if we made you feel like you couldn't. Did you report him to the principal? Because I'll most definitely be having a conversation with her and making sure that he loses his spot on the school board and that he can't volunteer at the school anymore. He can take himself somewhere else. Is there anything that you want me to do? I'm here to assist you in whatever way you want me to."

"Thanks, Mom."

"Of course, Sabriya. I'm always going to be on your side. You did nothing wrong here, and even if you did, that doesn't warrant an adult who's supposed to be in charge treating you like that. Trust and believe that I will be getting to the bottom of this."

Tears rush to my eyes as her words settle. I was putting so much pressure on myself to do the right thing, and it's a relief to hear that I didn't have to be perfect.

"Are you absolutely sure I didn't mess up all the work that Dad put in to get his promotion? Because I kinda blew up…" I say, sniffling.

"No, no, baby, you didn't mess anything up. You don't have to worry about that." Mom reaches over and wipes away my tears. "Sabriya, my beautiful girl, your power is immense, and I'm glad you drew from it today. And thank you for telling me about all of this."

"Thank you for having my back."

"Always, baby girl. Always."

ZAKAT

LULLWOOD, GEORGIA

Aafreen sits down across from me at the table in front of Tiny Treasure Trove, her movements blending with the constant breeze whipping past. Exhaustion clings to me, and the events from the get-together last night play on a loop in my mind. The bell above the door rings as customers enter and leave the bookstore.

"How are you?" I ask.

"Well, I'm wearing my shades because I only got five hours of sleep last night and my eye cream is not getting rid of these bags this morning," Aafreen says. "So, in short, I've been better."

"This month has felt like a year," I say.

"We only have to get through one more week, and then it's over. Hopefully July will be a reset."

I sigh. "Hopefully. Do you want to talk to Lucy, or should I?"

"We'll tag-team," Aafreen says. "I feel like I should've listened to you more. You were right not to trust her."

"She took advantage of your trust, but that's not your fault," I say, getting up.

Aafreen stands, and we walk into the bookstore together. Lucy looks up from where she's working the register, but she drops her gaze when she sees us. She has to know where the "Book of Secrets" is.

Anger, hurt, and shame swirl in my stomach. Aafreen may have trusted Lucy, but I also gave her the benefit of the doubt. I don't know how yet, but Aafreen and I are going to get the book back. Lucy could've been an ally if she had stood up against Asher, but she went along with him just like the rest of his friends. She may not be guilty, but she's complicit, and I'm not going to let her acting as a bystander last night go unchecked. I wait until Lucy finishes ringing up a customer before stepping behind the register next to her.

"Hey," she says.

I cross my arms. "Did you do it?"

Her smile slips. "Do what?"

"You know what! Did you take the book and then share photos from it?"

Lucy's eyes widen. "What? No! I would never do something like that."

"But you asked about the journal at the party last night."

"Yeah, as a joke!"

"I'm not sure I believe you."

Lucy laughs. "You're being serious right now? I promise I didn't do it."

Aafreen steps forward and takes off her shades. "Then who did? Where is the book?"

"I don't know who has it, okay?"

Aafreen frowns. "That can't be true. You were there with Asher and his friends, and you left with them. The book may not be with you or Asher, but he was definitely the ringleader. Why are you protecting him?"

"Because he's my family and I know him better than either of you."

I snort. "Please. You only see what he wants you to."

Lucy shakes her head, standing up. "I can't believe you both. Your little journal was in a wooden box that anyone could've gotten into. Or so rumor has it. This town's too small for secrets. That's why I don't like being here." She takes a step toward me. "And you were there at the get-together just like the rest of us, Zakat. Who's to say you didn't do it?"

"I would never hurt Lullwood."

"Don't turn this on Zakat," Aafreen says. "You know something about the book whether or not you're telling us, and we'll figure it out eventually. Lullwood takes care of its own, and if you think our community is going to let this go, you're wrong."

"To you, I'm only an outsider. And that's all I'll ever be. When you want to have an actual conversation instead of yelling at me, you know where to find me."

She walks past me, brushing against me so that I stumble to the side.

"Can you believe that? She wants to be mad at me?" I ask Aafreen, who takes Lucy's place behind the register.

"It's ridiculous," Aafreen says, scowling.

My phone buzzes, and I pull it out of my pocket to see a new notification. I frown, signing into my school email. No one's sent anything to my school email since summer break began, except for colleges trying to convince me to apply in the fall. I click on the email.

To: zumar@lis.org
From: landerson@elakehs.org

I know where you live, Kat. Or should I say Zakat Umar. End the blog.

Numbness washes over me, and I freeze until a sob rolls through me, ripping me apart. I run to the bathroom at the back of the store as Aafreen's question of if I'm alright bubbles in my ears like I'm underwater. I rest my forehead against the door and cry. I've had enough of the ups and downs, and this is a low that I never thought would happen. Baba and Mama warned me that this was a possibility, and I didn't listen. I was trying to push myself to try something new for a change, just for this to happen. Maybe I should've stayed inside the safety of my comfort zone. But I've always equated that with Lullwood, and if Lullwood isn't safe anymore, then do I even have a comfort zone anymore? This is all too much. If this isn't some disgusting prank and the person who sent this email actually is a threat and knows where I live, I can't put Baba and Mama in danger. They've done everything their whole lives to make sure I don't have to live in fear, and they don't deserve to live in fear because I ruined all of their hard work. I love being part of *You Truly Assumed*, but I love Baba and Mama more. This is a line I can't cross. I can't do this anymore. I can't.

I lean over the sink and gag, but nothing comes up. If this is what fear feels like, I'm not leaving Lullwood. I can't leave. Everything starts to shake. The room, my hands, my heart, my thoughts. Everything feels like it's shaking to the brink of collapse. Another sob rips through me as I start typing out a message to Bri and Farah. I wish I didn't have to abandon them, especially now with *You Truly Assumed* being on that awful site, but I'm not built for this. I thought I was. I thought I could handle being a part of *You Truly Assumed* and use a pseudonym and everything would be alright. I thought I could handle this world outside of Lullwood.

But I was wrong.

Don't engage, that's what Bri told me earlier after we found out about the list. Don't engage. Don't engage. I never should've engaged in the first place. I should've known that something like this would happen. I should've known that the more I made myself visible, the more I was making myself a target. And I do know that. I can't exist without always knowing that, but I guess some part of me didn't want to believe it. Some part of me thought that as long as I stayed physically in Lullwood, I'd be okay. But stepping virtually outside of Lullwood is as bad as stepping out physically, and now I truly understand where Baba and Mama are coming from.

I wipe my cheeks with the rough paper towels and pray for the world to stop spinning. I take a deep breath and leave the bathroom.

Aafreen leans away from the wall where she was waiting for me. "What's wrong? What happened?"

"I got a really horrible message," I say, fighting the tears threatening to fall. "I think I'm just going to go home."

"Of course. I'll tell my mama that you weren't feeling well, so no worries. And I'll call you later to check in."

"Thank you," I say.

The bell rings, almost deflatingly, as I leave the bookstore. I look up at the large expanse of green, watching the way the treetops ruffle in the wind. A few pine leaves fall around me like rain, as if the woods are hugging me. I inhale, letting the air seep into me and focusing on the rise and fall of my chest.

"Zakat, how was work?" Mama asks as soon as I close the front door behind me.

And as much as I want to tell them everything, I don't want them to hurt because of me. They don't deserve to drown in my feelings. I can't disappoint them. I promised I wouldn't. They tried to warn me, and I should've listened.

So I smile and hope my eyes aren't a dead giveaway.

"I'm fine."

"Zakat, you are not fine," Baba says. "You can tell us what's wrong."

I look at both of them, guilt churning in my stomach. They're never going to trust me again because of this. What if joining *You Truly Assumed* was a big, impulsive mistake?

"I received a threat to my school email about *You Truly Assumed*. I know I shouldn't have gone against your wishes and joined, and I'm sorry. I'm so sorry."

My voice cracks, sobs shaking my shoulders.

Mama runs over and hugs me. "Oh, dear child of mine. I am disappointed, but I am not mad, and I'm sure your baba isn't either. Do we need to call the authorities about the threat?"

I sniffle and shake my head. "No, it's fine."

The last thing I want is to turn this into a bigger deal.

"Well, let us know immediately if that changes," Baba says.

"But this is what we told you would happen, and you chose not to listen to us. Unfortunately, there are some lessons that you have to learn on your own," Mama says.

Though her embrace is warm, her words shoot daggers into my already bruised heart.

"I learned a lot from being a part of *You Truly Assumed*," I say, leaning away and brushing away my tears. "The blog gave young Muslim women a communal space, and I met a lot of great people through it. And a lot of people liked my art."

Mama frowns at my pushback. "You will not rejoin that blog under any circumstances, Zakat. Do you understand? Someone is threatening you, and I'm your parent so what your friends or readers choose to do is none of my concern. Who knows who is behind that threat? I simply cannot stand for it. No more, Zakat. I will take away your computer and phone if I have to."

Tears spill down my cheeks. Even though I know that Mama is trying to come from a good place, I wish she was responding differently.

"But blogging makes me happy," I say.

"But it's also putting you in harm's way," Baba says. "There are safer opportunities for you to share your work and challenge Islamophobia. You have weakened our trust, Zakat, and your mama and I are hoping that this time you'll listen to us. No more blogging."

I nod, unable to utter any sort of confirmation or push back harder. It feels like everything—*You Truly Assumed*, my new friendships, my joy—is being sucked out of me. And nothing remains that can bury the onslaught of hate and the threat of danger lurking behind the words in that email. Right now, I'm just a mess of bones and a heart still trying to beat even though the world keeps breaking it.

I head to my room and shut the door behind me. I pull up the threatening email, bile rising in my throat as I reread it, and I copy and paste the sender's email into Google. A school named Erwell Lakes High pops up along with its address in DC. I go back to the email address, and it hits me. L Anderson has to be Lucy. She mentioned the name of her school when she called Lullwood High "L-High."

Some of the tension and fear leaves me as my shoulders drop. Now that I know who sent the email, things don't seem as scary. But why would Lucy send a message like this? Especially after the conversation that Aafreen and I had with her today. She has to be trying to make a point, and anger and shock create a ball of energy in my chest. Lucy might think that sending this email has knocked out my flame and my fight, but little does she know that this is a spark.

I'm reignited, and if I'm going to go down trying to protect Lullwood, then I'm going down blazing.

FARAH

KIRBY, MASSACHUSETTS

I tap lightly on the side of the Porsche, the bright sun reflecting off its pearly-white color. Tommy unlocks the car, and I slide into the back instead of the passenger seat next to him.

He turns down the radio. "How was class?"

"Fine."

He looks at me through the rearview mirror. "Do you want to talk about what happened with Jess?"

"What's there to talk about?" I ask, not meeting his eyes.

He was the one who wanted me to visit so badly. I didn't come to listen to Jess's privilege and arrogance. The first flight back to Inglethorne leaves this afternoon, and my bags are still packed. One of them can say the word, and I'll bounce.

"Well, I wanted to apologize for Jess's tone," he says as he begins to drive. "Her brother was injured during a protest against police brutality when they were growing up, so the idea of Ally going to the vigil is hard for her."

"That does suck, and I guess it explains a bit why she reacted like that. But I'm sure it's hard for Khadijah Ibrahim's family too."

He nods. "Definitely much harder. Jess and I both want you to feel comfortable in our home. I hope you'll attend the vigil, and I think Ally should go with you, if she chooses."

"Sure." I glance out the window. "Hey, why aren't we heading back to your place?"

"It's a surprise."

I glance at him, trying to see what caused Mom to think that he was worthy of being in her life all those years ago. Trying to see how I'm connected to him. Trying to see what she wanted me to find during this trip. But right now, I still feel like I'm coming up empty.

Tommy turns onto a bustling street lined with shops. The buildings seem a bit old-fashioned with the rustic faded brick and period decor. Though Boston is one of the oldest cities in the country—and that's definitely seen in the architecture—the various stores and boutiques we pass all seem shiny and trendy. There's a mix of buildings that look like skyscrapers, like where I had lunch with Jamilah, Nadira, and Lulu, and then there are buildings that look like they were inspired by the medieval era. It's an eclectic mix of old and new, but I like the vibe it creates.

"Welcome to Boylston Street. It's one of the streets that make up the heart of Back Bay."

"This is pretty cool," I say. "It's such a big city."

Tommy swings into a parking garage, and excitement surges through me. I pull my zipper up a little as we begin to explore the area. I turn in a circle, trying to capture everything. People speed past, and bits of scattered conversation carry with the breeze. Trees that are equally spaced apart line the street, but other than that there's nothing but foot traffic and some cobblestone side streets that seem less crowded. I've never seen snow, but I imagine the street would look pretty during the winter with the fancy buildings and a few flurries.

I notice Tommy next to me, his steps falling in time with mine. Honks and bits and pieces of conversations fill the gap between us. And even if I wanted to get rid of that gap, I have no idea what to say.

"Here we are," Tommy says.

My eyes widen, reading the sign on the door. "Gelato?"

"Yep. Gia's Gelato is some of the best in Boston. I figured it's hard to go wrong with gelato, and it's one of my favorite places in the city. Hopefully you'll like it too."

"I do have to agree that it's hard to go wrong with gelato," I say, stepping inside.

I go up to the counter, my eyes sweeping across all of the creamy deliciousness. The shop is pretty dark, but lights shine over the giant tubs of gelato like spotlights. There are so many different colors that I almost want to be annoying and try a sample of everything.

"What's their best flavor?"

"Honestly, everything here is good. Their Crema Fiorentina is a personal favorite of mine." I must make a face because he quickly adds, "It's vanilla custard with citrus."

I point to the magenta-colored gelato. "I think I'm going to go with Rosa."

Tommy nods. "Very fitting. I haven't had that flavor before, but Ally likes it."

"What are you going to get?"

"My usual. A medium Crema Fiorentina."

"Sounds good to me."

Tommy gets in line, and I take a moment to study him. He stands the same way I do, left foot slightly in front of the right, as if caught midstep.

One of the workers scoops out the Rosa gelato, and my mouth waters. My taste buds are already shook. This surprise is nice. I wonder how he knew about my belief that sweets make everything better.

"Thank you so much," I say, taking the small cup of creamy, delicious goodness into my hands. I turn to Tommy. "Tommy, can you take a picture of me and the gelato and then send it to me?"

"Of course." He pulls out his phone with one hand, and I pose holding up the gelato next to my face. "Is this good?"

I look at the picture. I'm not centered, and Tommy's finger blurs one corner of the photo. But my smile is wide, and I'm a little shocked by how happy I look.

"Eh, it'll do."

We sit down at one of the circular black metal tables, and I dig into my gelato and try to ignore the silence between us. Even if he thinks Ally should come with me to the vigil, I'm not going to get involved and risk getting into another argument with Jess. There's no need to hold on to what happened last night or set up any expectations for the future. I came on the trip like he and Mom both wanted me to, and I guess that's really all there is to it.

Tommy clears his throat, breaking the silence. "Farah, I also wanted to apologize for making you feel uncomfortable last night in regards to the vigil. I hope that I didn't minimize the impact that Khadijah and her death may have had on you or the importance of her vigil."

"Um, thanks, I guess."

He sets his gelato down and laces his fingers together, and I can tell from that gesture that this conversation is about to go down a completely different route.

"I know that being out here is new for you," Tommy says. "It's also been an adjustment for Jess and myself, and I hope that our nervousness didn't come across as apprehension."

"Sure, okay."

The sooner this convo is over, the better because if Tommy keeps going, my expectations are slowly going to tick upward. I can't have that happen again.

"I do have to say that Jess was a little overwhelmed by the idea of you visiting on such short notice, and I think she was a bit worried about how you and the family would gel. You're her main interaction with my life in Inglethorne, besides my parents, and I believe that threw her for a bit of a loop. Ally and Samson were so young when Jess and I got married, and their father has been absent for most of their lives, which is why they both call me Dad. Jess is very protective of them, but I know she does genuinely want to get to know you, as do I. Plus, the kids seem to adore you."

Even though I don't agree with Jess when it comes to whether or not Ally should come to the vigil for Khadijah with me, I can relate to her a bit. Trying to bring two completely different aspects of your life together when you're not sure if they'll fit is nerve-racking.

"Thanks for the explanation, but you really didn't have to say all that. I'm going to be out of everyone's hair at the end of next week."

"I know it's going to take more than this trip alone, but I'd love to be a bigger part of your life if you'll let me. Maybe you can visit during a school break, if you'd like to."

My heart pounds in my chest, as if my body is waiting for the gotcha moment that might be around the corner. Even though it doesn't seem like Tommy would do that now, I'm not sure how much weight his words carry or how much trust I can put in them.

"Why now?" I ask.

"I've always tried to respect your wishes as you got older when it came to wanting to visit, and I didn't want to step on your mother's toes when it came to raising you. I thought keeping my distance was helping and protecting both of us, but I was wrong. I've realized that keeping that distance has hurt our relationship because it didn't convey how much I love and care about you.

"You're going to be graduating and going off to college next year, and I knew that if I didn't start to bridge that distance now I'd risk there coming a day when it'd be too late to do so. I regret not making a stronger effort to reach out sooner, but in truth I was scared. You're an amazing young woman, and I had no role in that. I wasn't sure if I was worthy enough to be in your life, but I want to be if you'll have me. I've been feeling this way for quite some time, but your mother was the one who convinced me that it wasn't too late and that now was the right time."

I sniffle, and my eyes sting with unshed tears. Some hardened part of my heart loosens and thaws with his words. I didn't realize how much I needed to hear Tommy say everything that he just said until now. This conversation doesn't erase the years of hurt that I've been carrying around, but it does make it lighter and put it in a different perspective. He left, and that part of the past can't be changed. But he's here now, and he wants to be here in the future. And maybe that's enough to start with.

"It's not too late," I say shakily.

Tommy stands up and holds out his arms, and I walk into the hug. He rocks me back and forth, and a few tears spill over. I guess a gelato shop is as good a place as any to start fresh. This moment feels like a release, and I let my walls lower a bit and give Tommy a chance. What he does with it is on him, but I did something that I've been scared to do for years. And it didn't hurt me like I thought it would. Tommy pulls away and pats my shoulder, a huge smile on his face.

We leave the gelato shop and head back down Boylston Street toward the parking garage. I want to talk to Mom and Riley and tell them about what happened, and it hits me that Riley is one of the few people that I want to run to when I have good news. Today gave me clarity on where I stand with Tommy, but I also think it helped me figure out how I want to move forward with Riley. If I can give Tommy a chance, then I can definitely give Riley one, especially when he's always been there for me. I settle into the passenger seat and pull out my phone to see that there are a ton of new messages in the *YTA* group chat.

> Bri: On top of whoever sent the threat to Zakat, we got two more comments that had the N-word. I'm going to turn off the ability to comment for now, and I'm also thinking of temporarily shutting down YTA. I don't think this is a good idea anymore.

I start texting back, but the rumble of the garage door interrupts my thoughts.

"Oh, no," I murmur, scrolling through the rest of the texts that I've missed.

Things with the blog must've spiraled, and my stomach sinks as I read Zakat's message. I text Zakat back apologizing for my late response and letting her know that I'm here for her and I'm glad the blog brought us together. My stomach gurgles, either because I've eaten too much gelato or because ever since Zakat put the link to the *Free the Right* site in the group chat I've wanted to puke.

The whole site is disgusting, full of racist, sexist, homophobic, and xenophobic trash posts. I wish I had the technical skills to shut it down myself instead of waiting for some blogging platform to get around to doing it. But at least now we know where all of the gross comments are coming from. A couple of weeks in Kirby, and now I'm getting harassed by alt-right trolls. Welp, that escalated quickly.

There's no way we're getting off that list, so it makes the most sense to wait it out. People will get bored eventually, and since the blog isn't directly linked to the site, only named, there's nothing I can do to speed up the process. Which is almost the part that sucks the most. I can't do anything to help the community that I've come to consider home.

"Thanks for the gelato," I say over my shoulder to Tommy as I head upstairs.

Emma's bedroom door is open, and I hear her babbles, which means she's not napping so I head down the hall. She grins when she sees me, and her excitement and toothy smile lift some of my stress. I've never really been fond of toddlers, but seeing Emma is like getting some sunshine. It does wonders for my mood.

"Fah–Fah–Fah," Emma says, dropping her toys and running over to me.

She throws her arms around me and lifts up her head, her tiny chin digging into my leg.

"Ugh, you're too cute for your own good, Em."

I set the gelato down on top of her dresser and lean down to pick her up, and she giggles.

"I-cream?" Emma asks, reaching for my gelato.

"It's gelato." I scoop a tiny spoonful and hold it up to her lips. "Here, taste."

Her face scrunches up at the coldness, and I laugh at her expression.

"Down. Down," Emma babbles, and I let her go.

"Bye," she says, running out the door and taking off down the hall.

I start to chase her. "Emma, I'm going to get you!"

Jess appears at the top of the stairs, and she gives me a small smile. I nod in acknowledgment. We may never be close, but we don't have to be. As long as we're not enemies, I think we'll be fine. I don't need her to be thrilled that I'm here, but I guess I need her to tolerate me.

Jess gives me a forced smile. "I don't mean to interrupt your fun, but it's time for her nap."

"Yeah, of course," I say before heading back to the guest room.

I sit down at the desk and cringe when the *Free the Right* site pops up when I open my phone. Guilt swirls and bubbles in my stomach, not mixing well with all the gelato that I just ate. Part of me feels like there was more that I could've done to keep the blog from getting added to that list since I'm supposed to be the tech guru. The whole reason that Bri brought me on to the admin team was to make the blog look pretty and keep it running smoothly. Between that list and the flood of hateful comments that we've been getting, the latter has been really hard to do. Perhaps I could've been more proactive and done research on security software or something like that, but I've been so caught up with trying to find my place in this family and thinking about what to do with Riley that the blog has been on the back burner a bit.

Striking a balance between Farah and Rose is harder than I thought it was going to be, but I can't give up on Bri and Zakat or the blog. I've got to figure out a way to get us all through the storm that's going to come from being on this list. But if there's one thing that I've learned so far from this trip, it's that there's really no other way around some things but through.

YIKES ON BIKES

Hey, everyone!! Due to some life stuff, we wanted to share that Kat will be stepping away from the blog for a while. Not going to lie, the past couple of days have been pretty shitty. Full of bad vibes and negative energy. This post is shorter than usual, but the one for next week should be back to normal length. Thanks for sticking with us throughout all of this. We're lucky to be a part of the community that you all have put so much love and strength into. I tried to come up with something fun to write about, but nothing came to mind.

Spread the happiness and positivity and good vibes. We could all use some more.

Until next post,
~Bri

SABRIYA

ABINGTON, VIRGINIA

I *chaîné* across the floor, taking comfort in the spinning. I watch my reflection ripple in the panels of mirrors that line the wall as the music fills me with movement. I always thought that life was like spotting while turning across the floor. Because even though you're moving, you're still focused on one point. There's still an anchor. Morgan and I *jeté* across the floor, and I put all of my anger into propelling me off the ground.

Dancing has always been my anchor. But like blogging, it's also broken me. And if I go back to *YTA*, I won't be the same.

"Good job, girlie," Morgan says as we leave the room.

We pass one studio room full of five-year-olds going through the different positions. I spot two Black girls toward the back, and I send all my love to them. I'm sure they look up to Misty Copeland and Michaela DePrince like I do. And who knows, maybe someday they'll look up to me too.

I grab my water bottle and guzzle down my power drink, sweat dripping down my face, and sit on one of the benches.

"So, I've noticed that Hayat's been doing deliveries on his own this week," Morgan says as we throw our clothes on over our leotards and tights.

"Yeah," I say, taking off my pointe shoes. "I'm taking a break from relief work. This is the last week of volunteering anyway since the shifts stop at the end of this month."

"Oh, did something happen?"

"It turns out that Mr. Smith, my group leader, is actually a bigot, so I don't really want to be around him right now. And everything going on with the blog is a hot mess. We're getting so many terrible comments right now, and I have no power to get us off the list I was texting you about. That's the only way they're going to really stop—or at least subside. I've already reported the site, but there's nothing else I can do. And—"

She steps over and puts her hands on my shoulders, and I realize how tense I am.

"Deep breaths. Everything is going to be okay. I'm sorry to hear about the comments, but don't beat yourself up about this, and don't let them take away from any of the great work you've done with *YTA*." She squeezes my shoulders. "And you should text Hayat. He's been asking about you."

"Hayat? He has?"

She throws her hands up. "Wow, I love how Hayat's name stuck out to you more than my pep talk. Which was pretty good, if I do say so myself."

I laugh. "It was. I needed it. I wouldn't still be dancing if it weren't for you." I put my dance bag over my shoulder. "But why has he been texting you?"

"He's trying to give you your space, so he hasn't texted you. But he's been texting me to see if you're doing better. So maybe put him out of his misery."

I grin. "Maybe."

She smirks but doesn't say anything. "I'll see you tomorrow."

"Yep, same time same place."

I wave at her as I walk out of the studio. It's hard to think that almost a month ago, I was walking out of these doors the day of the terrorist attack. It feels like so much has changed since then but also like everything's still the same.

My eyes land on Dad's car, and my stomach sinks. I scroll through my texts with Mom, trying to see if I missed something over the past couple of hours. Because last time I checked, she was picking me up.

Dad unlocks the door as he sees me coming, and I slide in.

"How was your time in the studio?" Dad asks.

"It was good." I pause, realizing this is the perfect time to tell him what's happened. "But there's actually something that I've been wanting to talk to you about."

The words rush out, lifting a weight off my shoulders.

"I heard about the Jonathan thing."

"Yeah, I figured that Mom told you since I told her yesterday. I'm sorry that I might've messed things up for you at your job. I know you worked really hard for your new position, and I didn't mean to blow it."

"Sabriya, I'm not upset with you in the slightest." Dad looks over at me. "I know that your mom is already planning on talking to the principal at her school, but I'm also planning on having a conversation with Jonathan myself. He was completely out of line in how he treated you."

"Thanks, Dad."

"No need to thank me, dear. Jonathan is extremely professional at work, but people often go after those they believe have less power than them. Perhaps he had issues with me, but decided to take them out on you. Either way, his behavior toward you was uncalled-for, and that's not even taking into account his actions on that website your mom told me about. He will be dealt with."

Tears well up in my eyes, and I wipe them away.

Dad looks over at me. "You know, I don't tell you how proud I am of you often enough."

"Oh, Dad, not you too. First Nuri went mushy, and now you are too."

He laughs, tapping the steering wheel. My mind goes to Hayat doing the same thing during our drives, and I scowl at the image. I'm not sure why he's been popping into my head more recently, but my mind needs to quit it. I keep the furthest corners of mind locked for a reason.

"Sabriya, you may not be able to move through the world like others, but if you keep holding on to the rope of Allah, then you'll get all the good that He intends for you to have."

I smile at the reference to my favorite verse from the Quran. I anchor my soul on verse 3:103, that if I keep holding on, Allah will keep holding me up.

"As Mom says, if God says yes, nobody can say no," I say.

Dad nods. "Absolutely." He looks at me briefly and grins. "It's hard to believe that this is your last summer before you're off to college. It makes me feel old."

"That's because you are, Dad."

"Girl, I'm not even fifty yet. I'm as young as a spring chicken."

I cover my face. "Oh, Dad, please don't say that."

"On a more serious note, all of this has reminded me that when you leave to go to college I won't be able to protect you as easily." He turns down the radio. "Have I ever told you what happened when I got accepted to Swarthmore?"

"Yeah, Granny and Granpops went a little bit ballistic. But in a good way."

He nods. "They were really happy, the whole family was. But there were people outside of my family who felt that I didn't deserve the acceptance."

"Why am I not surprised?"

"Yep, they said I only got in because I ticked off the majority of their diversity boxes. I was Black, Muslim, and first-generation, a triple whammy. And I let that get into my head. I hid for the first month of freshman year."

"So what changed?"

"I realized that I wouldn't be at Swarthmore if that wasn't where Allah wanted me to be at that moment in time. And if He wanted me there, was I really going to waste my time hiding? Nope, I was going to be the best me I could possibly be. Not to prove anyone right, and not to prove anyone wrong. For me. Because I owed that to myself and to the people who had helped me to get there. And I owed it to Allah. No breath should be taken for granted, and I wasn't going to spend mine hiding."

I nod.

"Your breaths, your life, are too precious to spend hiding, Bri. Spend it laughing, and healing, and making mistakes.

You don't have to prove anyone right, and you don't have to prove anyone wrong. You only have to be you for you."

I squeeze Dad's arm. "Thank you, Dad, I needed that."

He pulls into the garage. "Anytime, Sabriya, anytime."

I walk into the house and head up to my room. Flopping onto my beanbag chair, I set my dance bag on the floor. I pull out my phone, opening a new text message with Hayat. Hey hey. I start typing but then delete it, chewing on the inside of my cheek. I type out the full text, cringing, and I replace the exclamation point and press Send. Hey, you down to chat? The three bubbles pop up on my screen, and my stomach clenches. Probably cramps from the two hundred crunches Morgan made us do earlier.

Hayat's text pops up on my screen, asking if I want to Face-Time instead of texting because it may be easier than going back and forth. My stomach jumps, and I groan. That's definitely not cramps. If what I think is happening is actually happening, I'm never going to believe in plans ever again.

My fingers hover above the screen, and I bite my lip before I type, Sure. Send.

My phone rings immediately, and I click Accept before I can talk myself out of it.

His face fills my screen, and he grins when he sees me.

"Bri! How are you?"

I sit up in my bed, my back against the wall and my legs hanging off the side. "I'm doing better."

"That's good. Better is good."

"Yeah." I clear my throat. "So, uh, Morgan said you've been asking about me."

He rubs the back of his neck. "Yeah, I wanted to make sure

you were alright, but I also wanted to give you your space. I thought about texting Nuri, since I still have her number from that time I was forced to drive her and my brother to the movies."

I burst out laughing. I remember how pained he looked standing on my front porch because Nuri didn't come when he honked and Amir was too scared to come up to the front door.

"Well, I appreciate it."

He tilts his head to the side, his signature smirk–smile on his face. "Of course. We're friends."

I feel a pinch in my heart, and warmth surges through me so unexpectedly that I almost drop my phone. I'm officially screwed.

"Yeah, I guess we're friends."

He smirks. "I'm sure that wasn't in your summer plans."

"You're absolutely right," I say, grinning. "In fact, it explicitly said to avoid you."

"I'm hurt."

I lean forward, even though I'm sure that means my forehead looks super huge. "Guess what?"

"What?"

"You were also on the Siddiq Sister No List."

"What's that?"

"It's a list of people that Nuri and I don't like."

He gasps, dropping his phone, and I clutch my stomach as a wave of laughter rolls through me.

"I'm deeply wounded," he says, picking his phone back up.

"You're off the list now, if that makes you feel any better. You're welcome."

"Was it my knock-knock jokes that got me off?"

"Nope, definitely not."

"My charming personality?"

"Eh." I laugh. "I have to get going."

"No worries! It was good to hear you laugh."

My traitorous heart flutters.

"Well, I don't want to take up too much of your time. I just wanted to make sure that you were alright."

"You never take up too much of my time," I say before I can stop myself. "Thanks for checking on me. Talk to you soon?"

His grin spreads wider. "Talk to you soon."

"Bye."

"Bye, Bri."

He waves at me and then my screen freezes, disconnecting. I slide off my bed and go through the joint bathroom to Nuri's room.

"Hey, sis, whatcha need?" Nuri asks.

She taps the empty space on the bed, and I flop down next to her.

"I've realized something, something big."

"What are you talking about?"

"Um, I think I like Hayat."

"Oh, that?" She laughs. "I knew that."

I roll my eyes. "But it's okay because I have this all under control."

"How?"

"By acknowledging the feelings and letting them pass. Hopefully this will all be over in a week."

"You're not going to tell him that you like him?"

I make a face. "Uh, no, I'm not. That's definitely not in my plans for the foreseeable future."

She pats my shoulder, standing up. "If you say so, but definitely let me know how things are going for you at the end of the week."

I stick my tongue out at her, making my way toward the door. "You suck."

"Just doing my job as your sister."

"Oh, and one more thing," I add, turning back around. "I think I'm going to go back and finish volunteering. I'm not going to let Mr. Smith run me off."

"Period," Nuri says. "I'm really proud of you, Bri."

"Thank you, sis."

"Yeah, yeah. Don't forget to update me at the end of the week!"

I laugh, closing her door to the joint bathroom behind me. I like Hayat. I didn't see that one coming at all. But I do, and I have a plan. Doing nothing and letting the feelings pass. Sure, there could potentially be some small possibility that Hayat likes me too, but I'm not planning on finding out. There's a reason I've never dated or even told anyone I liked them. The thought of giving my heart to someone, knowing that they could break it at any moment, is terrifying. Because all the plans in the world wouldn't be able to save me.

★ ★ ★ ★ ★

I plug in my earphones and log in to Zoom. I lean back in my desk chair, propping my feet up on my desk. Within seconds, Zakat and Farah appear on the laptop screen in front of me.

"Hey, you two!"

"Hello!"

"What's up?"

I rest my chin in my hand. "How are you both doing?"

"I'm…well, I'm hanging in there."

Farah shrugs. "Same ol', same ol'."

"Yeah, same here, I guess."

"How's the dance going?" Farah asks, wiggling her eyebrows.

Zakat grins. "Yeah, how's Hayat?"

I roll my eyes. "Shut up, you two. Farah, how are you and Jess getting along?"

"Ugh, she's the worst. She out-petties me, and that's hard to do because I'm as petty as they come when I need to be. But it's whatever. I don't want to talk about her."

I take a deep breath. "There's something that I really need to talk to you both about."

Their eyes snap to me through the laptop screen.

"I've decided to permanently shut down *You Truly Assumed*."

"What?!" they both yell, and I cringe as the sound vibrates through my earphones.

"I thought that was only supposed to be temporary?" Zakat asks.

"I think it was only meant to be a summer project, and I don't want to continue to hurt the people I want to help. I've shut down the comments, and I've been going through the comments that came in before I did that to approve the ones that aren't harmful and reject the ones that are, but there are way too many to go through now that we've been added to the site and it's overwhelming. Plus those comments make me anxious and they're super triggering. So, unless there's a way to deal with the comments, I think shutting the blog down is the best route. We could technically continue the blog and keep the comments off, but then that would get rid of the community aspect. The readers wouldn't be able to communicate with one another, and that's part of what makes *You Truly Assumed* so special. I don't want to do the blog halfway, and those comments aren't going to stop. We're always going to be a target as long as we're on that *Free the Right* list."

Not only that, but Mr. Smith isn't gone from volunteering yet. So far, he hasn't faced any consequences for his actions, which means he could still feel emboldened to do something to *YTA*, or anyone of us, and I'd much rather eliminate that possibility. Especially since now he knows that I know about his connection to the alt-right site. Hopefully Dad's and Mom's actions will put Mr. Smith in his place, but until then I don't want to take any chances. From here on out, I'm keeping a low profile.

"I completely understand, and I get why you're worried. Getting that threatening email made me feel the same way," Zakat says. "But I think even if you keep the comments off and the three of us never post again, *You Truly Assumed* should stay up. For all the negative comments, there are so many positive ones."

"I see what you're saying, but I don't know. I'm scared of making the wrong decision."

"Whatever you decide, we support you," Farah says.

My heart swells at their words. I never thought that anyone would end up caring about *You Truly Assumed* as much as I do.

And I never thought I'd meet Zakat and Farah, and so many other young Muslim women who care so much about changing the world. Despite the recent flood of nasty comments, I'm constantly inspired by the readers that chatted in the comments among each other. Their dreams and passions and hearts are so big and beautiful. It's like being constantly surrounded by amazingness, and I'm always in awe. *You Truly Assumed* is more than me, and it's more than the three of us, and I guess shutting it down would erase that essential part.

"Have I ever told you both how awesome you are? And how much I appreciate having you both as friends?"

"Maybe once or twice." Zakat smiles. "But seriously, *YTA* has helped me so much. Before joining, I'd never shown my comics and drawings to anyone. I didn't think they were important enough. *YTA* has helped to show me that they are important. Joining this team has made me push myself in a way that I never have before, and as a result I've been able to befriend both of you and find the voice I use to make change."

Farah sighs dramatically. "Since we're apparently being sentimental, I'll add something too. Being a part of *You Truly Assumed* has helped me seek out more ways to help out here in Kirby since, before joining the blog, I hated working on teams. I'm not the greatest at relying on people. You all both showed me that collaboration is aight. I adore you both."

I fan my face. "You're about to make me start crying."

But as I wipe away a tear, grinning so hard my cheeks ache, it hits me that in order to create change I have to be able to face what needs to change.

"Alright, we'll leave the blog up, even if we don't keep posting new content," I say.

Zakat and Farah cheer loudly before breaking out into a conversation about some stickers that Zakat made for us, and a spark of inspiration hits me. I grab the new journal I stuffed in the bottom drawer of my desk, turn to a blank page, and write.

I never realized how easy it could be to let hate have the last word. To stop fighting and accept things as they are. But I wasn't raised to do that, and I don't think it's in my DNA to do so. Despite the lessening of my trust in the world, I don't want to silence my voice. I can't silence my voice. I have to keep speaking so that when other young Muslim women come after me and they speak, their voices don't only echo in isolation. But their voices and their words move mountains, create waterfalls, mend hearts, and make this world closer to what it could be.

ZAKAT

LULLWOOD, GEORGIA

I sit on one of the benches outside of Tiny Treasure Trove, and I wipe away the sweat on my forehead. As June prepares to blend into July at the end of this week, the temperature will only get hotter. Maybe I should reconsider my plan and wait for Lucy inside. The sound of footsteps approaching gets louder, and I turn down the volume of the latest episode from my favorite art podcast.

Lucy starts to walk past me to the door of the store, and even though I know she must see me she doesn't look in my direction. I stand up from the bench before she passes, and instead of feeling nervous about the confrontation, I feel energized. Up until now, I've done my best to avoid confrontation with my parents and Aafreen by trying my hardest to put them all first. But if I'm going to paint my own future, then I can't have people-pleasing on my paint palette. It only muddles the rest of the colors.

"Hey, Lucy," I say, crossing my arms.

"What do you want? Are you just here to attack me again?"

I laugh dryly at her thinking that Aafreen and I attacked her while we talked to her yesterday when Lullwood has actually been targeted and attacked multiple times this month.

"I got a threatening, and quite frankly disturbing, email sent from your school account, landerson@elakehs.org," I say. "It crossed my boundaries, and if something like this happens again, I'm going to have to report you."

Lucy opens and closes her mouth as she struggles for words. "I didn't send that email."

I make a face. "Why are you lying? That's clearly your email address."

She pulls out her phone and presumably goes to her email. Her face pales, and her eyes are glassy when she looks back at me.

"I'm so sorry, Zakat," Lucy says. "I didn't send this email, but I'm going to find out who did."

I can't tell if her tears are genuine or for show, but they're unsettling.

"I don't know why I should believe you, but whatever you do from here is on you," I say. "I have nothing else to say to you."

The last sentence lifts a weight off my shoulders, and the lightness in my chest feels unfamiliar. I guess I've carried that weight for so long that I eventually got used to it. When Lucy visited during the summer before fourth grade, I never got closure. I froze, shocked and not sure how to confront her. But I've grown since then, and this time around, I stood up for myself and what I needed. I put myself first.

Lucy doesn't say anything as I hop on my bike and pedal away from the bookstore. The sunlight streams through the canopy of the treetops and casts beautiful shadows against the leaves that reflect onto the pavement. I park my bike and walk into the masjid, which glows in the setting sun. I slide my sandals off and put them on the shoe rack, and then I head toward the Sunset Room. I relish the way my feet sink into the soft carpeting, and I let the beauty of the masjid wash over me. The large maroon bookcase takes up an entire wall of the Sunset Room, accompanied by plush armchairs and shiny coffee tables. It's the perfect place to go when I need to call an emergency meeting or just want a change of scenery when studying or reading.

"Assalamu Alaikum, Imam Farad," I say as she walks into the room.

"Walaikum Assalam," Imam Farad says.

Imam Farad and Imam Bashir are basically Lullwood's collective parental figures to Muslims and non-Muslims alike. They're the glue that holds the community together. They host an Eid party open to all of Lullwood at the end of every Ramadan. They also lead a lot of interfaith events with the church on the other side of Lullwood. Imam Farad and Imam Bashir can be found at all of the community events, and they help to run the programming at both Islamic Schools. They come to all the graduations and every person's Eid parties, no matter how many there are. It's hard to imagine Lullwood without the both of them.

"Your mother said you had something you wanted to discuss, and I'm all ears if you would like to chat."

I nod. "Yes, definitely."

I sit down in one of the big fluffy burgundy armchairs, and she sits across from me. Imam Farad is not that much older than me, maybe ten years or so, and she used to go to the Lullwood Islamic School for Girls. She has the best posture, and her winged eyeliner is always on point. She's so regal and respected, and I'm glad I have her to look up to.

She also gives some of the best advice in town. She listens to everyone, no matter who and no matter how trivial a problem may seem. I've come to her for help about what classes to choose, how to find my passion, to do mock interviews for college admissions, and to ponder on the true meaning of life.

"Lately, I've been feeling a bit overwhelmed and lost. Besides getting into college, I have no idea what I'm moving toward. Which is also making me worried about college. Plus, I'm not sure I'll be able to find a college that I can call home like I call Lullwood home, which is also making it hard to know how to move forward. It won't be the same, and I'm scared of how big that difference is going to be."

"I see. That's completely normal." She leans back in her chair and laces her fingers together. "Only Allah truly knows whether or not you're indeed lost. But as long as you continue to have faith, He will lead you to the straight path."

I nod. "Of course, I know. But I feel like the path is a bit murky right now. Or maybe I'm running in circles or zigzagging around the path. I really don't know."

"I don't believe you are lost. I believe what is affecting you is that you think you're running in circles or zigzagging."

I pause, turning the thought over in my head. "So I'm moving forward, but it feels like I'm not even though I am?"

"Yes, that's how I see it."

"That actually makes sense." I smile. "I feel like I have been moving forward this summer. I joined this blog called *You Truly Assumed* and started sharing my art more publicly. It made me feel confident enough to think that going to Howard was a good idea. But then all of the Islamophobic incidents that have happened this month have made me question whether or not leaving Lullwood, and Georgia as a whole, is smart."

"What about the incidents has made you begin to question?"

"I'm scared of being so far away from Lullwood that I won't be able to protect it. If something like this happens again when I'm in college and I'm too far away to get back here and help, I'll be devastated."

Imam Farad nods. "I understand your concerns, Zakat, and I was in a similar position when I was trying to figure out my college plans and, by extension, my future. My best advice would be to follow your heart, and because Lullwood is a piece of your heart, it too will guide you. There's no right or wrong answer, only the answer that's right for you."

I nod. "Thank you for listening, Imam Farad."

She stands up. "That's part of my job, Zakat, no need to thank me. I'm here to serve the community, and that means listening and engaging in conversations. And, Zakat, the world is so big it's a part of life to get lost in it. Have a good evening, and please tell your parents that I give salaam."

"I will!"

I leave the Sunset Room and take a seat on the bench outside, the sharp scent of pine greeting me. Whatever path Allah put me on, though still confusing, feels a bit more well lit. Lightness flows through me, and hope sparks my fingertips. Imam Farad made me realize that I've taken a lot of steps forward this summer that I never, ever thought I would take.

Right now, I'm still unsure whether or not to confront Asher. Even though he's likely involved in some way with the graffitiing of the boys' school and the "Book of Secrets" getting taken, I have no solid proof, just my intuition. There's also the tension with my parents and figuring out how to rebuild the trust I damaged when I went against their wishes while also finding a way to remain involved with *You Truly Assumed*. Both of those conflicts have been making me feel stuck, and I want to move forward on my terms, like I did with Lucy earlier this morning. But after talking with Imam Farad, I feel like I just have to trust myself. Everything else will work itself out.

I look up at the sky and the wispy clouds. Ideas for new sketches pop into my head, and I smile to myself. One sketch could be a girl covering half her face with a hand made of stars, and the second sketch could be of a girl crying stars. Those sketches would be perfect for the blog, though I've never shared any of my sketches with other people before. But it's definitely something that I want to explore, and I'm glad Bri decided to keep *You Truly Assumed* up so that I can do so at some point in the future. I don't know when it'll be—or if it'll even be soon—but I'm going to return to *You Truly Assumed*. I love sharing my drawings and comics and helping others feel seen, and I'm not going to let fear keep me from being my full self and being visible. I'm going to keep creating my own path.

★ ★ ★ ★ ★

The back door of the store closes behind me as I bring the empty recycling and trash cans inside. I glance at my watch and let out a sigh of relief. The air feels heavy with tension from Lucy keeping her distance from Aafreen and me. Aafreen's usual bubbly and outgoing energy is dimmed, and I know she's still getting down on herself about the book getting taken. I wish there was more that I could do to cheer her up.

Looking one last time at my cardboard display for this fall's favorite YA books, I grab my belongings and head out of the storage room. The materials already came in for the fall display, and even though there are still almost two full months left of summer, Aafreen's mom wanted me to get started early. I look both ways for any signs of Aafreen or Lucy before weaving through the bookshelves.

"Zakat," Aafreen says, popping out from behind one of the shelves. "Look at what Amina just sent me."

She hands me her phone, and I look down to see a blurry picture of Asher grinning. He's flipping off whoever took the photo, his own phone held in front of the open "Book of Secrets." The background of the photo is dark, so it's hard to tell if it was taken at Aafreen's get-together or some other place. I frown, waiting for the anger to come. But a wave of numbness washes over me instead. My intuition was right.

"I'm not surprised." I hand Aafreen back her phone. "Do you think he has it?"

"He probably does, and if he doesn't, then he knows who does," Aafreen says.

"Then he's in the same position as Lucy, who by the way sent me a threatening email related to *You Truly Assumed* a few days ago. When I asked her about it today, she said she didn't send it."

Aafreen's eyebrows furrow. "She did what? I know you said you already took care of it, but do you need me to do anything? Because I will throw hands. No cap."

I laugh a little. "I think I'm good, but thank you. I am going to go talk to Asher and get some things off my chest."

"He's probably down at the field for soccer practice. Amina said she saw the team over there." Nudging my shoulder, she sticks out her pinkie finger, and I link mine with hers. "Thank you having my back through all of this. I love you, you know that, right? A to Z always."

"A to Z always," I say, squeezing her pinkie. "And I know. Love you too."

Because like the trees, which sway and bend and whose branches sometimes snap, the roots of our friendship will always remain, Insha'Allah. I head out of the bookstore and hop onto my bike. I pedal through the woods, taking in the light piney scent of the air, the familiarity calming. The sound of the crushed nettles and pine cones beneath my tires provides a soft blanket of comfort. Words jumble around in my head as I run through what I'm going to say when I see Asher.

I cross the street that connects both sides of Lullwood, the backdrop of the trees fading. The air smells different over here. Everything in me is screaming for me to turn back around and go back home, but I pedal forward. I stop at the bottom of the soccer field, whistles and cheers piercing the air. Lullwood High and the Lullwood Islamic schools always have weekend soccer scrimmages, but hopefully today's has finished. The last thing I want to do is make an awkward entrance and have everyone stare at me.

I take a few steps up the incline of the hill and head toward Asher, who's stuffing his cleats in a drawstring bag at the end of the bleachers. I spot Jay and a few other people that came to Aafreen's get-together, but no one from either of the Islamic schools is here since the Lullwood High team has the field reserved for right now. There are about ten people still packing up and joking around, but if I wait for all of them to leave I might miss my chance to talk to Asher. My heart starts to race, my jacket suddenly feeling too hot.

I can do this.

"Excuse me, Asher?"

He looks up, eyes narrowing. "Yes? What do you want?"

I set my shoulders back and slide my hands into my pockets. "I'm not here to make you see my side of things or anything, that's not my job. I'm here for me because I needed to get this off my chest." I take a deep breath, collecting my scattered thoughts. "Taking photos of or with the 'Book of Secrets' was rude and an invasion of privacy, and though you claim not to be behind the graffiti incident, I don't believe it."

"That doesn't matter to me. You have no proof."

I nod. "You're right, and that's not the main reason I came here to talk to you. I'm not scared of you, Asher. Not anymore. And I will keep fighting so that Lullwood doesn't have to be scared of you either. Your actions, or supposed actions, will not make me feel powerless and unsafe in my own home anymore. You don't get to take that away from me or my community."

He rolls his eyes. "Are you done blabbering?"

The jab stings, but I keep my shoulders back and chin up, and I don't break eye contact.

"You and your friends will never crumple Lullwood, and I hope you get everything that you deserve."

His eyes drop at my tone, and I turn and head back down the hill. I brace myself for his response, but it never comes.

I pull out my phone, my fingers shaking from adrenaline.

> **Me:** I did it! I stood up to the Islamophobic butthole in my town.

My phone dings instantly.

> **Bri:** You. Did. That. So proud of you!

> **Farah:** ^^very proud. how do u feel, fam?

I grin, energy flowing through me as I hop on my bike and cross the street leading back home. For the first time in a long time I feel completely free, bound by nothing but Allah, gravity, and air that smells like home.

> **Me:** I feel invincible.

FARAH

KIRBY, MASSACHUSETTS

I tap my fingers against the desk in the guest room and close out of another YouTube video comparing various security software for websites. Most of the info was easy to digest, but the price of those software systems is a bit harder to do so. Most of the internet security softwares that provide more than simple antivirus protection are around eighty to one hundred dollars. But if we split the price up among the three of us, then maybe the investment won't be too bad. The internet security software won't get us off the list on that disgusting site, but it'll give us the capability to block spam emails and a firewall to block hackers, both of which would be helpful for the blog.

I pick up my phone to text Bri and Zakat and see that I have a text from Nana that simply says, Call your mom. My anxiety spikes at those three words, but maybe the tone of the message is coming across more intensely than she meant it to since she doesn't text all that much. She always calls me instead, which only makes her message more alarming. But I'm sure Mom's fine. Nana would tell me if she wasn't.

I sit on the edge of the bed, and my hands shake as I dial Mom's number.

"Farah?"

"Mom, are you okay?" I ask. "Nana told me to call you."

Mom sighs. "I told her not to bother you. I'm alright. There was a bit of an incident at the community college where I take my night classes, but everything's fine now."

"Wait, what happened?"

"There was a series of emails sent to the college LISTSERV that targeted many marginalized communities. The college administrators shut down all of the buildings while I was at class, so it took me a while to get home last night."

"I'm glad you're safe, but why weren't you going to tell me?"

"Because I'm fine. Your nana was just a bit shaken, that's all, but she's fine now too."

I sigh, my shoulders dropping. Even though she's fine now, what happened is a stark reminder that something could've easily gone wrong and I wouldn't have been able to help. Though she has Grandpa and Nana, I'm used to basically always being there for Mom. I guess I can't be in two places at once, no matter how much I want to be, but that doesn't give me much comfort.

"Farah," Mom says, her voice gentle. "I can hear you thinking through the phone. I'm alright, and I don't want this to take away from your trip or make you think that you have to go to college close to home or anything like that. Keep moving forward, okay?"

"Yeah, I know. I'm just used to having your back."

"And you still do. The distance between us doesn't change that," Mom says. "How's the trip going? Only one week left until I get to see you."

"I'm excited to be back on the best coast. But the trip has been fine for the most part. It feels weird not to be home for Juneteenth though."

Even though I haven't been to Texas since I was little, Nana always cooks a big dinner every Juneteenth to celebrate. It's a time to reconnect with my roots and also eat really good fried fish, mac and cheese, and 7Up cake. I can't remember a time when I've missed Juneteenth dinner.

"Knowing your nana, there'll probably still be leftovers by the time you come home," Mom jokes. "You know what, I'll FaceTime you into the dinner so you can be there virtually."

"That sounds good!"

"Is there anything else that you want to talk about? Something's up. I can hear it in your voice."

I can picture her sitting at the table, eating an energy bar and drinking a big cup of coffee while doing her assignments for her college course.

"Well, I promised you that I wouldn't rock the boat while I was here, and I may have done that a bit. But in my defense, it's for a good reason."

"Is this because of Khadijah Ibrahim's death?"

I pause. "Yeah, how'd you know?"

"Your father called me and asked if I'd be okay with you going to the vigil, and I have to admit that I'm a bit apprehensive. Not because I don't think you can handle yourself, but because you're not very familiar with the area, and if anything were to happen, I'm not sure if you'd know what to do or where to go. I don't want you to be alone or lost during a worst-case scenario. You need adult supervision."

I tighten my grip around the phone. "I'm going with a friend who's been planning the vigil. I've been helping her out a bit, so I'm not going to be on my own."

Silence meets my words, and I chew the inside of my cheek.

"I'd feel more comfortable if you went with Tommy, Farah. Can you please ask him?"

I nod, even though she can't see me. As much as I want to be annoyed that she's springing this request on me the day of, after what happened last night, it's understandable that she'd want to make sure that I'm safe while at the vigil.

"I will ask, but I don't think he'll say yes."

"I think Tommy may surprise you," Mom says. "My shift starts in ten, but I'll talk to you later. I love you."

"I love you too, Mom. See you soon."

Once the call is disconnected I go to my text messages with Jamilah, fingers hovering over the screen. Staring at the blinking cursor, my mind goes blank. I can't not go to the vigil. If I don't go, I'm not doing all I can to stand up for Khadijah, for myself, and for some of the readers on the blog.

There's a knock on the door, and I look over my shoulder and say, "Come in."

Samson cracks the door open, and I gasp dramatically and gesture toward his outfit.

"Samson, you should've warned me that you were going to wear a Celtics jersey in my midst. Just when I thought we were really getting along."

He laughs and pats his jersey. "At least I'm not wearing a Clippers jersey, right?"

"You know what? You're not wrong," I say. "If you wore their jersey we might not be able to move past that."

He grins. "Got it. Dad said he wanted to talk to you downstairs."

"Sure, I'll head down with you," I say, standing up from the bed.

Tommy, Jess, and Ally all sit at the table, and Samson taps my shoulder as if to wish me good luck before he disappears to the basement to play video games.

"Good morning, Farah," Tommy says with a smile. "We'd love if you'd join us for this family convo."

I do have to ask Tommy if he'll come to the vigil with me, but this family convo probably isn't the right place for that. Especially not with Jess here. I start to open my mouth to politely decline, but Ally gives me a pleading look, and I sigh internally. I can't leave her to fend for herself. Or I guess I could, but then what kind of stepsister would I be? I sit down in the white chair, the plastic dipping underneath me.

"Sure. There's actually something I've been wanting to talk to you both about. I'd like to propose that Ally and I go to the vigil with you, Tommy," I say, throwing caution to the wind. "Khadijah's vigil is important to both of us, and while Jess's concern about safety is valid I think you going with us could help to mitigate that. We should all support Ally in her decision because some people never stand up for justice or it takes them until they're a bit older to do so. The fact that Ally wants to attend the vigil to support her friend and to help bring a bit of justice to Khadijah, who deserved so much more, is a really good thing."

Ally beams at me, and I give her a quick shoulder hug.

"That's actually what we wanted to talk to you about," Tommy says. "Jess and I wanted to let you both know that I'll be going to the vigil with you two today."

Ally's eyes widen. "So, I can go?"

Jess nods, but her expression is unreadable.

"Good talk, everyone," I say, starting to stand up.

"There was actually something else that Jess and I wanted to talk to you about, Farah," Tommy says, and I sit back down.

"Would you be comfortable watching Emma for a couple of hours?" Jess asks.

I look up from my bowl of frosted flakes. "I thought she was going with you to Ally's tennis match."

"She was, but she's still sleeping, and Samson has a last-minute basketball practice that I need to take him to since Tommy is taking Ally to tennis practice. Em had a rough night last night, and I really don't want to wake her. I called the babysitter, but she's busy."

"Sure, I can handle a two-year-old."

Tommy stands up with his empty plate, and it's only then that I notice his bright pink polo shirt and brown loafers. He looks like he stepped out of an '80s fashion magazine, but it works for him.

"You're sure you're okay with watching Emma?"

I nod, and Tommy and Jess leave the dining room to finish getting ready to leave.

What am I going to say? No? I knew as soon as the phone rang that this whole trip was a scam to sucker me into babysitting. I just knew it. But what I didn't expect was that the kids would grow on me so quickly, so I really don't mind spending time with Emma.

Ally comes back into the dining room and steals a strawberry off my plate, her tennis racket bag hitting me as she leans over. I push the plate toward her, and she grins.

"Thanks for sticking up for me today," Ally says.

"No problem, I'm pretty sure that's what older sisters do." I nudge her lightly. "I'm new to this though."

She laughs. "You're not too bad."

"Thanks, but I think part of that is because you're a pretty cool sister, Ally. Go out there and kick ass on the court. My bad, I meant butt."

She laughs. "I'll see you later."

Ally waves at me as she and Tommy leave, and once Jess and Samson leave in a couple of minutes it'll just be a sleeping toddler and me. Oh my. I finish my cereal and tiptoe upstairs. I see a sliver of Emma's room through the cracked door, spotting her mass of dark curls. The blanket moves up and down, so she must be breathing, which is good. I open the door a bit more and grab one of the baby monitor remote walkie-talkie things and head back downstairs, all while managing not to wake up Emma. Who knew I'd be so good at this?

I settle down on the couch, pull out my phone, and put the baby monitor next to me. Like the rest of the house, the living room looks like it came straight from one of those home design shows on cable that Mom likes to watch when she has free time. Everything feels meticulously picked out from the color scheme to the pattern of the rug to the placement of the pillows on the couch. I don't know how they live in this house without fearing that if they move one pillow, everything will be thrown out of whack. My phone rings with an incoming FaceTime call, and I grin when Riley's name pops up on the screen.

"Hey, Riley!"

"Farah! Hi!"

"Hi!"

"Why are you whispering?"

I stretch out on the couch. "My baby sister, Emma, is sleeping. I somehow ended up on babysitting duty for the morning."

"Oh, okay!" he says. "How are you? I miss talking to you."

"I've been busy. But I miss you too. A lot."

I knew going into the trip that I was going to miss him, but I wasn't sure if simply missing him would be enough. But after starting fresh with Tommy, speaking to Mom earlier about how being away doesn't mean that I don't still have her back, and coming to terms with the fact that I can't be with her for everything, I feel more confident about trying long-distance and giving our relationship that chance.

"A lot?" Riley asks, a playful glint in his eyes.

"Yeah, a lot."

He laughs. "How are Tommy and Jess?"

"They're fine. I—"

I almost drop the phone when the baby monitor starts flashing green lights, Emma's whimpers piercing the air. I jump up from the couch, like the fire alarm is going off and I have to save the house from burning down. Because that's how horrible it sounds when Emma starts crying.

"Oh, Emma's up, and she's probably hungry, which honestly same, but I should probably go check on her before she erupts. I miss you a lot, like a lot a lot, Riley. Talk again soon?"

"What kind of question is that? Of course we will."

He blows me a kiss and hangs up first.

"I'm coming," I say, taking the stairs two at a time.

I push her bedroom door open softly and walk in. Emma's room might be my favorite in the house. I love the lavender walls, the soft white accents, and the overall simplicity. It's the room that reminds me most of Mom's and my room.

"Hey, Em."

Emma sits up in her toddler bed, eyes wide and her hair disheveled.

"Em, you could've gotten out of the bed and played with your toys. You're two, this is the beginning of your independence, sweetie. Go out and crawl and explore the world."

She looks up at me, hugging her stuffed elephant.

"You don't want to say anything, hmm? It's too early for you? Need some food in that tummy?"

She grins, probably at the word *food*, and I reach down and pick her up. She giggles, wrapping her arms around my neck, and it's the cutest sound. I set her on my hip and head down to the kitchen.

"Cheerios!" Emma says, squishing her cheek against mine.

I set her down in her booster seat and buckle her in.

"As you wish."

I pour her a bowl and sit down next to her at the dining table. Emma pops a few Cheerios into her mouth and claps.

"Play! I wanna play."

I lean in to tell her to eat her food, and she taps my nose.

"Boop," I say, flicking hers gently.

"Stop it, Farah," she says, laughing.

The way she says my name, Fah-ah, is adorable. She's so warm, and she smells like baby powder. Every time she smiles I want to smile. She's a little ray of sunshine that I didn't even know I needed. And no one told me that toddlers are actually cute. I almost want to take her back home with me. Almost.

"New sissy!"

"Who?" I say, looking over my shoulder to amuse her.

She laughs, clapping her hands. "You! You new sissy."

My heart swells at the nickname, and I swoop her up in my arms and spin a little.

"Who taught you that?" I ask, not expecting an answer.

"I did."

I turn toward the door to see Jess carrying a pack of Gatorade that I'm assuming is for Samson's teammates.

"Oh, uh, cool."

Jess gives me a small smile. "Ally, Samson, and Emma have all enjoyed having you here."

I return her smile and try to hide my surprise. It'd make sense if Tommy was the one who taught Emma to call me "new sissy," but I didn't expect that from Jess. Maybe she doesn't mind having me around as much as I thought she did.

"You're a good sister, Farah." Jess kisses Emma's cheek. "You two have fun."

"Thank you," I say, hoisting Emma up on my hip.

If Jess sees me as a good sister, then maybe she does see me as part of this family. Because even though I didn't expect it, I've slowly started to feel like I am. Maybe it's from all the love I've gotten from my siblings or starting fresh with Tommy, but there's a sense of belonging that I didn't have when I first got here. I can joke with Samson, stand up for Ally, watch Emma, and sit down at the kitchen table without feeling like I'm intruding. Jess unexpectedly revealing that she taught Emma the nickname strangely showed me how much has changed these past few weeks. And I don't think I'm ready to give that up at the end of this week if I don't have to.

I hug Emma tighter. Maybe I don't have to take her with me to Inglethorne, I can just come back to Kirby. I don't have to choose one part of my life over the other because this too is my family. I can have both. I want both.

FINDING INFINITY IN THE GREAT UNKNOWN

It's hard to believe that June ends in about a week. Soon it'll be *You Truly Assumed*'s one-month anniversary! I stan.

Not going to lie, this post may be kind of a Debbie Downer, so fair warning. But I always want to be as transparent with you all as possible. A few days ago, Kat, Rose, and I talked about potentially shutting down the blog. I felt like turning the comments off was getting rid of what makes this space so special, but we could also no longer have conversations among ourselves without having to worry about receiving threatening comments. That's why we came to the decision to turn them off, even though that hurt. We hope in the future to be able to turn them back on, and I know in the meantime you all have been coming up with ways to stay connected to one another. Thank you again for sticking with us.

In all honesty, I felt like I was disappointing you all and Kat and Rose. I created *You Truly Assumed* to be a safe space, and it was starting to turn into anything but. I didn't want to bring pain to all of you when I was trying to create a space separate from that. Kat and Rose talked me out of shutting down *You Truly Assumed*, and I'm so glad they did. This blog has so much growing left to do, and there are so many more comment convos to be had. They'll be back.

You all have rallied around one another and created a community within *You Truly Assumed* that I never thought possible when I accidentally made my first post public. It's incredible.

I'm not sure when the comments are going to be back on. Hopefully as soon as the wave of really threatening comments passes. But I can promise that *You Truly Assumed* isn't going anywhere.

You all have taught me how to find infinity in the great unknown, which is a truly terrifying expanse. I'm a planner, a lover of checklists and pro-con lists. Before this summer, I didn't see much value in the random, but this community and that mistakenly public blog post changed that, and I'm so grateful for it. I never realized how easy it could be to let hate have the last word. To stop fighting and accept things as they are. But I wasn't raised to do that, and I don't think it's in my DNA to do so. Despite the lessening of my trust in the world, I don't want to silence my voice. I can't silence my voice. I have to keep speaking so that when other young Muslim women speak, their voices don't only echo in isolation. But their voices and their words move mountains, create waterfalls, mend hearts, and bring the world closer to what it could be.

We'll be back together having comment convos soon! This is just a bump in the road, but we're nowhere near the end.

Until next post (and the next, and the next, and the next),
~Bri

SABRIYA

ABINGTON, VIRGINIA

Out of the corner of my eye, I study Hayat as he drives, the silence ringing in my ears. Even the cherry-red paint on Shanice seems duller than usual. The air in the car feels heavy and somber. I remember the meal delivery rides being upbeat and light, and, like when Zakat doesn't use exclamation marks, I know something's got to be up.

"Hayat, you okay?"

"Yeah, yeah, I'm fine."

"You seem a bit quiet?"

He shakes his head. "I'm tired and nervous about the performance next week."

But he keeps biting his lip, and I've taken enough drives with him to know he's holding something in, even though I've been away for the past two days. Still, as much as I want him to open up, he gave me my space when I needed it, and it's only right that I do the same. I would like to see him smiling and happy, and it shocks me how much I want that. How much I've come to care.

I look out the window, squinting my eyes. Today's one of those perfect summer days. Low humidity, bright blue skies, and tons of sun. The type of day that makes me feel like anything's possible. The summer days that feel like road trips, ice cream, picnics, and first kisses.

Hayat chews on the inside of his cheek like it's gum, and I feel my resolve soften.

"You know you can tell me whatever, right?"

He looks at me and gives me a small smile. "Yeah, I know. Thank you."

"No need to thank me. That's what friends are for."

He meets my eyes, some sort of energy crackling between us, and I look away before I get lost in them. The urge to lean over the console and kiss him rushes through me so fast it's as if the buildup from these past three weeks is catching up with me. Not only is he gorgeous, but his heart and mind are beautiful. I want to not like him, but I like him so much that it's overwhelming.

I pull out my phone and go to *You Truly Assumed*, thankful for a distraction. A blank black screen appears, and when I hit Refresh, nothing changes. I hit Refresh over and over, my annoyance growing with each tap. Everything is gone. All of the words, all of the comics, all of the positive comments. All of the time and energy, gone. My hands start to shake as I text Zakat and Farah, asking them if *You Truly Assumed* is shut down for them too. I go to the Twitter account for *Bloggingly* to see if the platform for the hosting company is down, but there's nothing on their timeline that mentions such a problem. I wipe my face and hold in a bitter laugh.

The day I make the plan to go back to blogging is the same day the blog gets hacked. Go figure.

Don't cry, don't cry, don't cry, I chant inside my head, but I stop when I feel the first tears fall down my cheeks.

I press my palms to my eyes, but they keep coming. I try to sniffle as quietly as I can, but Hayat looks over.

"Bri?"

"I'm fine. I'm sorry. I'm fine."

"Bri," he says, his voice cracking, and I start to cry harder. Embarrassment surges through me, and I look away from him. Here I am crying up a storm in front of the guy I like. A mess, a complete mess.

He pulls over to the side of the road and puts the car in Park. My wet sniffles fill the silence in the car, and I wish I could sink into the ground.

"Hey, what's wrong?"

"The blog, *You Truly Assumed*, was hacked. The site is still there, but everything is gone. It's only a black screen."

"Oh, Bri, I'm so sorry."

I wipe my face. "Maybe it's a sign. I mean, this morning I decided I wanted to go back to blogging. It's only been like three hours since I made that decision, and look what happened." I let out a thick laugh, coated with unshed tears.

I feel another round of tears well up, and I let them bubble up and fall. I can't fight a waterfall. And I know that Hayat isn't going to judge me, even though I'm past the point of bending. I had finally started feeling like I was healing and putting myself back together, and now I'm breaking all over again. I can't keep up.

"Oh, Bri."

He reaches for me across the console, and I rest my head

on his shoulder. Hayat shivers when my nose brushes against his neck, his arms tightening a bit around me. I cry until my well of tears is dry. Until I feel both empty and full again.

My phone buzzes, and I pull away, shifting back to the center of my seat. I look down to see a text from Farah saying that she'll do her best to see if she can fix the blog and not to overstress or worry. I wish. I rub my eyes and cringe. They're sore and probably red and puffy from all the crying I've been doing recently. My face feels itchy from dried tears and mortification.

"Uh, sorry about soaking your shirt. And having a bit of a meltdown."

"You don't have to apologize." He squeezes my hand. "Sometimes you have to have a meltdown before you can feel better."

I sigh. "It feels like I've been doing a lot of melting down lately." I give him a small smile. "Farah said she's going to try to get *YTA* back up. But even though she's a tech genius queen, I don't feel like I can get my hopes up."

He nods.

"But if she doesn't get it back up, I'm still going to go back to blogging even if it's not right away and I have to start from scratch. Working on *YTA* is a part of me living my best life, and someone once told me that's one of the best things I can do in the face of hate."

He smiles. "That person sounds kinda smart."

"They are." I set my shoulders back. "And I'm going to finish up this last week of relief work because I made a commitment to the families."

Hayat puts the car in Drive, and we start back on our way to the next house. I wipe the last of my tears away and take a deep breath, my chest feeling lighter. I take another deep breath, and it feels like the air moves easier through my lungs because it isn't moving around a heavy weight. I look over at Hayat, and it hits me that I can trust him. That I do trust Hayat.

"Bri?"

"Yeah?"

"You're a pretty incredible person."

I squeeze his hand. "You're not too shabby yourself."

He smiles and flips his hand, palm up underneath mine, an open invitation. I weave my fingers through his, and he closes his fingers around mine.

I smile up at the sun, trying to tap into my inner joy. Trying not to let the world break me to the point where I can't tap into that feeling anymore. The brightness of the sky lifts my mood as I watch the clouds float past. It's one of those summer days that feels like dashed plans, salty tears, renewed resolve, and endless possibilities.

★ ★ ★ ★ ★

Dad looks up from where he sits on the couch as I close the front door behind me.

"How was volunteering?" Dad asks.

I shrug. "It was fine."

He pats the empty space on the couch next to him, and I sit down.

"I wanted to let you know that I reported Jonathan at work for his harassing behavior. Even though it occurred off the clock, he still represents the organization. The report is currently under review," Dad says.

Pressure lifts off my shoulders, and some of the tension I've been carrying fades away. A small part of me was worried that I'd disappoint Dad, but it turns out that worry was a product of my overthinking. Standing up hasn't always been the easiest decision to make, but it's always been the right one.

I press a kiss to his cheek. "That's really great to hear. Thank you for letting me know, Dad."

"Of course. I've always got your back."

Adrenaline rushes through me as I head upstairs to my room. I swap my floral blouse for an athletic tank top and my jeans for leggings before rolling out my yoga mat and taking a seat. I sit in the butterfly stretch on my bedroom floor and sign into *You Truly Assumed*'s Twitter account. Frustration and anger bubble in my stomach, and I sigh, starting a new tweet.

> Unfortunately, #YTA is down right now, as a result of being hacked. As some of you may know, #YTA was added to an alt-right site's list of "leftist" websites to take down.

> Hopefully @BlogginglyOfficial will be able to resolve the issue soon. Whether or not #YTA is restored, Kat, Rose, and I will continue to fight. #YTA may be down, but we aren't. We won't be silenced.

I let out a breath as I click on the tweet all button and the thread pops up. My finger hovers over the tweet icon as I wonder if I should do more. I found Mr. Smith's social media account handle, and I already know the handle of the department he works for. Tweeting at the department publicly might make his company take Dad's complaint more seriously and review Mr. Smith faster. Maybe it'll also make him realize the consequences of his actions. Or it may also go nowhere if the person running the department's account doesn't respond. But even if I don't get a response, tweeting may still draw attention, so it's worth a shot. If Mr. Smith wants to fight behind a screen, so can I.

@FederalBureauOfficial Hello, your employee @JohnD0e23 has been making Islamophobic comments on a divisive and hateful site, as well as targeting blogs and websites run by creators from marginalized communities. A screenshot of his comments has been attached below.

Before I can talk myself out of it, I upload the screenshot and press Tweet. It won't get us taken off the list or stop the comments from flooding in, but at least I get the satisfaction. My phone dings, and I look down to see a response to the thread. I sit up straighter, anticipation sparking in my chest. I jump up from my yoga mat and start pacing back and forth across my bedroom, leaving tracks in the carpet. I pause, my finger hovering over the notification bell before clicking on the icon.

@YouTrulyAssumed Hello! We are @TICC (The Intersections of Climate Change), and our blog was both on the same list and hacked earlier today. It is quite possible that this has happened to other blogs as well.

Before I can type out a reply, my phone dings again with a new reply from a blog whose name I recognize from the list that *You Truly Assumed* was put on.

@YouTrulyAssumed This has happened to our blog too! **@BlogginglyOfficial**, this needs to be addressed immediately!

My phone continues to ding, and I click on my first post in the thread to see that it already has fifty retweets, quote tweets, and comments combined. The frustration and anger slowly morphs into hope. This isn't over yet.

★ ★ ★ ★ ★

The air feels like it crackles, and sparks seem to light up my skin as I move next to Hayat. We do a series of back and forth movements, and we move as individuals but come together as one. He pulls me close, so close that our noses brush, and he mouths the lyrics as we separate. The feeling of weightlessness carries me to the end of the dance, and I melt into my final pose as the music fades to silence.

"Woo!" Aliyah yells. "You two look so good! You're going to kill it at dress rehearsal at the end of the week."

I wipe my forehead, sweat sticking to my skin.

"Remember, I really want faces. Stay expressive. And go hard at the beginning, but also conserve your energy so that you don't fade out by the end of the dance." She fans her face. "And oh my goodness, is it hot in here, or is it me?"

Hayat coughs, choking on his water, and I feel my cheeks flame. I glance at Hayat, and he's already looking at me.

"Alright, team, I've got to get to class. Don't forget all the notes I gave you! I think this dance is going to look so good at dress, and hopefully it'll get me into the advanced choreographing class." She gives us a final wave and leaves the studio.

"So…" I say slowly.

"That felt good," Hayat says.

I raise my eyebrows, and his eyes widen.

"I mean, doing the dance," he adds in a rush. "I felt like I knew what I was doing."

"That's always good."

Hayat fiddles with the zipper on his jacket. "Do you want to stop and get a bite to eat? If you're not busy."

"Yeah, why not? Let me get my stuff, and I'll meet you outside the studio."

"Sounds good," he says, leaving the studio.

"Oh my goodness," I squeal.

Is this a date, or are we only hanging out? Do I want this to be a date? Does he? A ton of questions ping around in my head as I change my shoes and throw everything else into my dance bag. I move to the front of the studio, and I feel like skipping even though my muscles are exhausted.

"Ready?" Hayat asks when I step outside.

"Ready."

We walk side by side to the fast-food place across the street, both of us lost in our own thoughts. The smell of salty French fries hits me as soon as I walk in.

"What's your fave shake flavor?" Hayat asks.

"Strawberry's usually my go-to."

Hayat nods as we step up to the register.

"Hi," Hayat says to the worker behind the cash register. "Can I please get two orders of medium fries, one small vanilla milkshake, and one small strawberry milkshake? That'll be all. Thank you!"

I pull out my wallet, but Hayat shakes his head.

"I can pay for it, unless you really want to."

"Oh, okay! Yeah, that's fine."

Hayat and I slide into a booth.

"You know, I would've guessed that strawberry was your favorite milkshake flavor."

"Why would you guess that?"

"I get strawberry vibes from you. Like, it's a classic flavor, and it's colorful, which means it pops. But it's also a little bit slept on, so it takes the right person to realize how good the flavor is."

"That's deep, Hayat. Poetic even."

Hayat laughs, and the sound makes me grin.

"Number 324!" an employee calls out, and Hayat goes up to get our food.

My phone buzzes against my hip, and I glance at it to make sure it isn't Mom.

"Oh my goodness."

"What?" Hayat asks. "Is it about the blog?"

He puts the tray on the table and sits back down on the side next to me, and I grab a handful of fries.

"No, but close. I tagged the department that Mr. Smith works for in a tweet about his comments on the *Free the Right* site. I included the screenshot too, because if I was going to serve tea I wanted to make sure that it was piping hot. The company responded to me! Let's see what they said."

I curl into Hayat's side, and he wraps an arm around my waist.

"Okay, his job said, 'Thank you for your post. Our department stands against acts of hate in all forms and is looking into the matter at hand. Appropriate action will be taken if deemed necessary.'" I clap. "It's not much, but it's more than I thought I was going to get, so I'll take it."

"I'm glad they responded to you. You deserve more, but this is a good sign." He dips a fry into his milkshake, and I make a face. "What? It's so good!"

"To each their own." I nudge his shoulder. "So what are you going to be up to for the rest of the summer?"

"I've received a few invitations to attend recruiting events for lacrosse from a few different colleges, so I'll mostly be working on lacrosse training and working on college apps."

"You're getting offers?"

"Not yet. It's more like colleges are saying, 'Hey, we're interested, and we'd like to see more.' That type of thing. Which is great but scary because it means people think I'll still be good when I'm cleared to play again next season."

"Hayat, that's so awesome." I munch on a fry. "We can be like one of those hype workout couples—" I gasp, and my cheeks start to warm as soon as the words fly out my mouth. "Um…"

There's an awkward pause, and I envision the seat swallowing me up and making me disappear.

"Knock knock?"

"Who's there?"

"Honeydew."

"Honeydew who?"

"Honeydew you want to go out on a date?"

I try to hold in my laughter, but it slips out and brushes away any awkwardness.

"Did you seriously ask me out with a knock-knock joke?"

He rubs the back of his neck and gives me a sheepish smile. "I guess I did."

I lace my fingers through his. "Well, yes, the answer is yes."

"And we can totally be one of those workout couples. Should we get matching outfits too?"

"Alright, bet, we definitely should."

I turn to steal a few of his fries, and my eyes lock with his. All of a sudden, it feels like all of the air has been sucked out of the restaurant. It's only him and me and the space between us.

"Hey, quick question."

"Yeah?" Hayat asks, his voice low and breathy.

"Can I kiss you?"

He nods. "Yes."

I lean forward, or maybe he does, and warmth and salt and vanilla flood my senses as his lips press against mine. He smiles against my lips, and I laugh, pulling away.

"What's so funny?" he asks.

I rest my head on his shoulder. "Nothing. I'm really happy."

"I'm happy to hear that. I was nervous about asking you out earlier. That's why I was probably acting a little weird in the car earlier."

I can't help but grin. "I make you nervous."

He rolls his eyes at my teasing. "Yes, but in a good way."

It hits me that this is the happiest I've felt all summer.

Both of our phones buzz at the same time, and I look at him, sort of confused. Hayat picks his up, and a couple of seconds later, he pumps a fist in the air.

"Mr. Smith has been kicked out of volunteering."

"You're serious?"

"Yes! You must've gotten the same email that I did from the principal. He's officially outta here."

"Well, we truly love to see it."

I lean over and dip one of my French fries in Hayat's vanilla shake, and my heart warms when he pushes it closer to me. Nothing about this month has gone to plan, and it definitely hasn't been perfect. But maybe perfection is actually overrated because, despite all of the bad things that have happened, there's also been a surprising amount of good—new hobbies, new friends, and a new sense of self-worth. I'm not perfect, but I'm growing, and right now that's enough.

ZAKAT

LULLWOOD, GEORGIA

Mama walks into my room, and I look up from my business textbook. My notes from the first reading are printed out and neatly paper-clipped together. I'm not looking forward to the class that much, but it's being offered at the Lullwood community center so Baba encouraged me to take it. The class starts next week, on the first, but it's only three days a week so hopefully it won't be that bad. My pencil slips from my fingers, clattering on the desk, as she appears next to me.

"Mama," I say, gesturing to the door.

She looks between the door and me before realization passes over her face. "Oh, I forgot to knock. I'll try to remember next time! But I came to tell you that Lucy is at the door and she asked to speak to you."

I raise my eyebrows, curiosity getting the better of my nerves. I wasn't expecting to hear from Lucy, especially after I confronted Asher.

"Oh, alright. That's strange," I say, getting up from my desk. "Thank you for letting me know."

I follow Mama downstairs, and Lucy looks over from where she stands near the front door. Apprehension raises goose bumps on my arms. After our conversation yesterday, I had no intention of talking to her ever again, so I have no idea what she wants to discuss.

I walk over, and Lucy gives me a tight smile.

"Hey, can I talk to you outside for a bit?" Lucy asks.

Mama gives me a questioning look, and I shoot her a smile that's hopefully reassuring.

"Sure," I say.

I open the front door, and we both step outside. The humidity hangs in the air, and the summer heat presses down on me.

"I came to tell you that I turned Asher in and he's admitted to being involved in the graffiti incident and what happened to the bookstore," Lucy says, her shoulders tensing. "I saw the footage from both events and recognized his necklace. What he did was wrong, and I'm sorry for not taking what you and Aafreen were saying more seriously. And I'm going to go see Aafreen and tell her the same thing right after this."

I take a small step back as her words slam into me. "Oh, wow."

Lucy drops her eyes from mine, and her cheeks flush, as if she's embarrassed. She seems exhausted from having to tell me this, but I can't figure out if she's looking for me to accept her apology. But I honestly didn't think she would turn Asher in, if she knew he was behind everything, so it feels like she's finally seeing what Aafreen and I were saying all along.

Lucy's apology does bring some sense of relief because now not only do I have answers, but so does Lullwood.

"I also found out that he was the one who sent that email to you through my account. I gave him my phone to show him your art on that blog you're a part of because I thought he'd think it was cool. He sent the email then without me knowing." She reaches into her backpack, and I gasp when she pulls out the "Book of Secrets." "And this belongs to you and your friends."

"Wow," I say again, still shocked. "Thank you. I know it must've been hard for you to turn him in."

"It was. I called my sister, and she told me that I should speak up when I know something's wrong, so I took her advice." She gives me a small smile. "I know this doesn't make up for anything and I still love Asher because he is family, but I will no longer willingly support him unless he changes."

"It's a step in the right direction," I say. "And I appreciate you taking it."

She nods. "My sister is healing faster than expected, so I'm going back home at the end of this week. I wish you all the best, really."

"I'm glad to hear that. And same to you, Lucy."

I step back in the house and clutch the book tightly to my chest. Lucy's changed, and even though this doesn't absolve her complicity, what she did by turning Asher in and returning the "Book of Secrets" can't be understated. Maybe this summer gave her the push to create her own path, but only time will tell. If there's one thing that I've learned from being a part of *You Truly Assumed*, it's that it takes bravery to say something when things are wrong, and today that's what Lucy did.

I walk back inside the house, and Mama comes over.

"Everything alright?"

"Yes. Lucy came to tell me that she turned Asher in because he was behind the school being graffitied."

"Wow," Mama says. "It's good that we now know who it was."

I text Aafreen as I head upstairs, giving her a heads-up that Lucy is coming to see her and a brief rundown of everything that just happened. Knowing Aafreen she'll pass on the news to everyone else in our grade if they or their parents don't already know. Word travels fast in Lullwood. I walk into my room and sit back down at my desk, wondering if Bri posted anything new on *You Truly Assumed* today. I know she's still making her mind up about the future of *You Truly Assumed*, but I'm glad she's not going to completely delete it. It's wild to think about how different my summer would've been had I not sent that email to Bri. I thought I was in for a quiet summer full of sameness and steadiness, and I got the exact opposite. But looking at it now, that's exactly what I needed.

I go to the *YTA* group chat since there are a few unread messages. My stomach drops and my mouth goes dry as I read the text from Bri saying that the blog has been shut down. I throw the textbook across the room, tears stinging my eyes. How can a month's worth of work suddenly disappear? I take deep breaths, trying to keep a meltdown at bay. I wish the world could let us be, simply be, sometimes.

The title of my next doodle pops into my head, and even though I have no idea what the sketch or doodle is going to look like yet, I hurry to type it into my notes for later inspiration.

The Art of Simply Trying to Be.

★ ★ ★ ★ ★

Baba and Mama chatter among themselves, and I cringe when my spoon scrapes against the plate. I need to talk to them about *You Truly Assumed* and going away for college, even if the conversation is going to be hard.

"Baba and Mama, there are a couple of things I wanted to talk to you both about if that's alright," I say, my voice shaking.

They look at each other, having a conversation with their eyes, before looking at me. Mama sets her utensils down and laces her fingers, her attention focused on me.

"Yes, Zakat, what is it, dear?"

"You both know that a few weeks ago I received a threat to my school email that was about *You Truly Assumed*," I say, the words I practiced in the mirror earlier flowing smoothly. "I found out that Asher sent it through Lucy's school email as a way to rattle me. Knowing that I'm not in any real danger now, I'd like to go back and keep blogging."

Baba and Mama share a look, and my eyes flit between the two of them, trying to gauge their reactions. Mama sighs, her shoulders dropping.

"*You Truly Assumed* has become a second home to me, and I never thought I would be able to find a home outside of Lullwood," I say, my voice thick with tears.

"Your mother and I have discussed that you have to adhere to our rules, Zakat, and if you ever disagree with those rules, we want you to come and talk to us so that we can have a conversation as a family on how to change them. But if you go behind our backs again, we'll have to take away your phone," Baba says.

I nod. I understand that even if my reasons were good, I still ignored their instructions in order to join *You Truly Assumed*.

"Your baba and I have talked, and this is clearly something that is important to you. So if blogging is what you want to do, we won't stop you," Mama says. "You are growing up, and you're almost an actual adult. Though I worry about you, I cannot control you. I know this blog must be special because you have never gone against us before, but I hope that doesn't become a pattern."

Tears leak down my cheeks, and I wipe them away. "It won't. I promise."

Their change in attitude makes all of the feelings from this month rise up. All the tension drains from my body, and I feel like a balloon that's letting out all of its air. I should've come to them sooner. They could've helped me navigate some of the stress. I take a deep breath, gearing myself up for what I'm about to say next.

"I know you both want me to consider in-state options for college more than I have been, and after what's happened this month I'll take that into consideration. But I'm still figuring out what I want my future to look like, and I'd like the space to do that. Howard is still my top choice."

Baba nods. "Your mama and I were the first in our families to go to college, you know, and just like our parents wanted the best for us, we want the best for you. As long as you apply to some in-state options, that is good. We will consider the financial aspect once you've gotten your acceptances and aid packages next year. If Howard is where you are meant to be, then that is where you'll be, Insha'Allah."

"We love you, Zakat," Mama says, her voice soft but fierce. "And we want you to be happy more than anything else."

I wave my hands in front of my face trying to fan away my tears. "You two are going to make me cry more."

"We've raised you the best that we could," Mama says. "And as much as I want to shield you from the world, I can't. I know you have to learn some things on your own. I believe you will excel at everything you put your heart and faith into."

I get out of my chair and hug both of them. "What did I do to deserve such amazing parents?"

"Allah must've thought you deserved to get a little lucky," Baba says, smoothing a hand over my curls.

"Thank you. I love you both." I smile so hard my face starts to hurt. "Can I please be excused? There's one more thing I have to handle. I'll come back down to clean up the kitchen."

"Go, go," Mama says, waving her hand.

"Thank you!"

I race upstairs to my room and grab my phone off the desk. I go to the *You Truly Assumed* group chat, a smile threatening to overtake my entire face. I can already feel my cheeks getting sore. I send a quick text to Bri and Farah, asking if both of them are available to Zoom right now. They both text back in the affirmative, and I get my laptop and sit down on the window bench. I feel like I won the lottery, which is weird but in a good way. Usually I'm happy with a hint of sadness or frustration, but I feel a happiness that isn't contaminated by anything else now, and I haven't had that in a long time.

Bri and Farah pop up on the screen, and I clap excitedly.

"I have a big question to ask both of you!"

Bri leans closer to her screen, and Farah raises her eyebrows.

"Would you two be okay if I returned to *You Truly Assumed* when it comes back up?"

"Would I be okay?" Bri asks, nearly laughing.

Farah makes a face. "Zakat, what kinda question is that?"

"I'd be beyond okay!" Bri yells. "I'd be ecstatic."

I laugh, happiness and relief spilling out.

"Well, it looks like you're both in luck because I'm back."

Farah punches her fists in the air. "Yay, yay, yay. The squad's back."

"Welcome home," Bri says.

I replay those last two words over and over, smiling because I know her words are true. *You Truly Assumed* does feel like home. It's a space where I can just be, like Lullwood. *You Truly Assumed* may not come back up, and I might end up at a college thousands of miles away from Lullwood, but I know now that even if some of the memories fade or people don't see my doodles anymore, both Lullwood and *You Truly Assumed* will always be a part of me that I carry wherever I go. They'll always be places I can return to. They'll always be home.

"I actually have something that I want to tell both of you," Bri says.

I stretch out, taking up all of the window bench. "Of course! What's up?"

"IwentonadatewithHayat."

"Can you say that again, but slower?" Farah asks with a teasing smile. "The lag, you know, kind of makes things choppy."

"I went on a date with Hayat," Bri says.

"Oh my gosh!" I squeal. "My ship has sailed! You've got to tell us all the details. I need the where, the when, and the what. Everything!"

Farah holds out a hand. "Before we get into those very necessary details, I need to know if I need to give him the 'don't hurt my friend or I'll throw hands' talk. Because I can and I will. It'll be on behalf of both Zakat and me. Just say the word."

Bri wipes her eyes. "You two are too much."

"You're stalling," I say in a singsong voice.

"Maybe." She grins. "But before I forget, I actually did have something else to tell you both. You know how yesterday I went on like a mini rant on *YTA*'s Twitter to explain why the blog is down, and the thread is getting a lot of attention and it seems to be resonating with a lot of people?"

"Oh, yeah!" Farah says. "I saw that."

"Yeah, a lot of the other blogs that were on the list also got hacked. They shared the thread and made their own, and it kind of snowballed from there. Last time I looked, the thread had about thirty thousand retweets."

My mouth drops open. "Wow."

"Is *Bloggingly* going to fix all of the blogs?" Farah asks.

"None of the blogs affected have heard anything back from them yet, but hopefully yes."

"So we're famous?" I ask. "Lowkey?"

Bri laughs. "We're whatever we want to be."

And in the moment, Zooming with two people I would've never met had I not taken a chance, and returning to something that helps me feel healed when it's so easy to feel broken, those words feel true.

FARAH

KIRBY, MASSACHUSETTS

I sit down at the desk in the guest room and open my laptop. The blog is one of the few tabs that I have bookmarked, and when I click on the link a blank page pops up. I sigh and close out of the tab since nothing has changed from when Bri told Zakat and me that the blog was down. It's hard not to think that maybe this all could've been avoided if I had suggested we get security software earlier, but I guess it's too late now to beat myself up about it. But if—or actually when—the blog gets back up, getting some sort of internet security software is going to be the first order of business.

"Farah, you have a delivery!" Tommy yells.

"Coming!" I say.

Surprise and excitement propel me down the stairs two at a time. It's probably not from Mom since I'm going to see her at the end of this week. Maybe it's a goodbye gift from Tommy and the family.

Tommy looks up as I walk into the living room.

"The delivery is near the front door," Tommy says.

"Great." I pause. "You work at Google, right?"

He nods. "Yep."

"Do you know anything about security programs? The blog that I'm a part of got hacked by some white supremacists, so it's in need of a pretty good security system."

"White supremacists?"

I make a face. "Yeah, it's a long story."

"I have time to listen, if you'd like."

I hesitate but then nod and take a seat next to him on the couch. I start going through the events, beginning with how Riley showed me the blog, covering how I agreed to manage the more techy aspects, and ending on how all the hateful comments ultimately led to the blog getting hacked.

"Wow, that's horrible," Tommy says after I finish filling him in.

"Yeah, but it's okay."

"No, Farah, it's not. I'm sorry that happened to you and your friends."

I pause at his tone, taking in the depth of his sincerity.

"Yeah, I am too. It really sucks to have everything just wiped away. I just really hope it gets restored soon."

"I have some software programs that I can recommend, and if you and the rest of your team are comfortable with it, I wouldn't mind covering the cost of the software."

I grin. "Really? Thank you, Tommy!"

"Of course."

I give him a quick side hug before heading toward the front door. A square cardboard box sits by the front door, and my eyes widen when I see the name of the sender. My heart warms, and the gesture alone makes me melt. Even though I'm seeing Riley at the end of this week, him sending me whatever is in the box is one of many signs that he really cares about me. And he cares for me out loud.

"Who's the package from?" Ally asks as she walks past me to the kitchen.

"My boyfriend," I say, the words sweet.

Ally heads over to me. "Ooh, open it, open it."

I laugh at her excitement. "Do you know where I can find a pair of scissors and a Sharpie?"

"Yeah, in the kitchen."

I pick up the box and follow Ally into the kitchen, and she opens a drawer and hands both items to me. I scribble over the address and then grab the scissors.

"Here's the moment of truth," I say to Ally.

I open the box and pull out an oversized black drawstring hoodie with a white rose stitched in the right corner.

"Omigosh, this is cute," I say.

Ally gives me a weird look when I sniff it, but the soft material smells like Riley. I pull out a smaller box and take off the lid to reveal three potted succulents.

"Those are pretty," Ally says.

I tip the box, and a folded note falls out.

My dearest Farah,
Sorry, sorry, I know that was corny. I saw both of these things when I was out and about, and they made me think of you. You're always "borrowing" my hoodies, so I thought I'd send you another, and the succulents can make the

guest room feel homier. I hope you like them, and I can't wait to see you when you get back. Enjoy the rest of your time with the fam!

"This guy," I say, folding up the note and putting it in my pocket.

Even though a small part of me is nervous about trying to do long-distance, this whole month has been about taking chances. From going on this trip to joining the blog to helping Jamilah with Khadijah's vigil. And I think—actually, I know—Riley is worth taking a chance on. He makes me happy, and my happiness is worth taking a chance on. I'm worth taking a chance on.

"I'm going to go FaceTime Riley," I say. "Would you like to meet him? He's already met Samson."

"You let Samson meet him before me?" Ally asks, feigning hurt. "But yeah, sure! He should meet Em too. I'll get her."

I grab my gifts and head back upstairs to the guest room. The space instantly brightens as I set the succulents down on the nightstand. Ally comes in with Emma, and we all crowd into the bed. Ally scoots closer to me on one side, and I pull Em into my lap. She reaches for my phone as I pull up Riley's number.

Riley's face pops up, his smile reaching through the screen. "Oh my goodness, long time no see. Ooh, I see we have company!"

Ally leans closer to the phone. "Hi, I'm Ally. I'm Farah's sister. You must be Riley. She's told us a lot about you."

I roll my eyes, grinning. "I wanted to say thank you for the gifts. I loved them. And I also thought that since you met

Samson, you should also meet my sisters. Ally's pretty cool, much cooler than me."

Riley chuckles. "Ally, you're wearing one of my old shirts."

"Farah said I could have it, so oopsies?" Ally says, giving me a curious look.

"I got the shirt from Riley, which I then gave to you. Totally fine."

"Took, she took it."

"Ignore him, he's joking."

There's a knock on the door, and I fight to keep my expression neutral.

"What's with all the chatter going on in here?" Jess asks, popping her head in.

"We're talking to Farah's boyfriend," Ally says.

"Oh, okay, you all have fun," Jess says, leaving the door open behind her.

"I'll get it," Ally says, climbing out of the bed.

The fact that she knows my greatest pet peeve says a lot about our relationship.

I lift up Em's hand and wave it. "And last but not least, this is Emma."

"Aw, she's adorable."

Ally sits back on the bed next to me. "So, are you another big sibling, like through association?"

"Absolutely," I say.

"Totally," Riley says.

"So you'll send me all of your old clothes? Or give them to Farah to give to me?"

Riley nods. "Anything I don't want and that Farah doesn't want is yours."

"Yes!" Ally says, pumping her fist in the air. "Who knew I'd get so lucky this summer?"

And as I kiss Em's cheek, I can't help but think the same thing.

★ ★ ★ ★ ★

I twist Mom's crescent moon and star ring around my finger. Earlier, when I was searching through my suitcase for what to wear to the vigil, I found the ring tucked beneath all the clothes. Mom must've sent it as her way of watching over me, and that thought alone gives me a bit of calm. I look out the window, the setting sun streaking the sky with deep oranges and light pinks. My heart thumps in my chest and my stomach churns, like it does when I'm about to take a test that I know I'm going to fail.

I look at Ally through the rearview mirror. "How are you feeling?"

"Okay, mostly. A little on edge."

Tommy nods. "I am as well, but the nerves should pass."

Tommy parks, and we join the stream of people walking toward the rec center. Ally walks next to me, and Tommy falls behind us. I zip my jacket up, the temperature dropping with the sun. Jamilah stands at the front of the growing crowd, next to a lady that looks like an older image of Khadijah. Khadijah's mom holds a sign that reads: "Peace," a word from a Merciful Lord [Quran 36:58].

"Thank you all for gathering here tonight to honor the life of Khadijah Ibrahim. Please make sure to grab a candle as we walk from the rec center to the mosque that Khadijah loved dearly."

Someone in front of me hands each of us a lit candle, the warmth from the flame fanning across my cheeks.

"Excuse me," a person behind me says. "Can you please light my candle?"

"Of course."

I touch the flame to the wick of their candle, and that person turns and does the same for the person behind them. A chain of lights grows as more candles become lit.

"That's so cool," Ally says next to me, watching more flames light the darkening sky.

Hope slowly untangles the nerves in my stomach, and I cup my hand around my candle to absorb the heat. We start moving forward, a collection of small lights creating a collective shine that illuminates the sky. I breathe in wonder and tranquility, only a passing car honk piercing the silence.

"I'm glad I came," Ally whispers.

I look out at the sea of lights in front of me, my candle and presence one drop in the growing wave moving forward.

"Me too."

SABRIYA

ABINGTON, VIRGINIA

I turn the volume up on my favorite reality TV show as I rest against my beanbag. I convinced Hayat to start watching the first season with me as our next date next week, and we're going to get takeout and watch crappy TV. It's going to be great. June has been a whirlwind, but it's coming to an end on a really great note. If this month was a turning combo, I may have lost my spotting during a couple of *pirouettes*, but I've definitely nailed the landing.

There's a knock on my door, and I pause my show.

"Hey, what's up?"

"You've got to see this," Nuri says, storming in. "It's about *You Truly Assumed*."

"What is it?"

Nuri hands me her phone. "Look, your thread went viral last night."

My eyes widen at the numbers below the first post in the

thread. Forty-five thousand retweets, twelve thousand quote tweets, and five hundred comments.

"How did this happen?" I ask.

Another spark of anticipation flares up in my chest, and I push it down. I can't get my hopes up about *You Truly Assumed* getting fixed, at least not anytime soon.

"Well, a lot of your followers retweeted and quote-tweeted talking about how awesome *YTA* is. And they tagged *Bloggingly* a lot too."

"We only have seven hundred followers though. I don't understand."

"Well, then the other blogs that were on that list, most of which also got hacked, reshared and requoted and made their own threads. Many accounts tagged your thread, and when their threads spread, so did yours."

I blink in shock. "Has *Bloggingly* responded?"

"No, not yet," Nuri says, sitting down on the floor next to my beanbag. "But there's more."

I scoot over, and she squeezes in next to me.

"There was even a small news article about the hackings. And a lot of activists shared your thread too."

"I can't believe this," I say, grabbing my phone off my drawer.

I open *You Truly Assumed*'s social media account to see two hundred new followers and so many notifications that it only says 50+ because the app stopped counting. I open *YTA*'s email account and gasp. An email from Raheema Hakim, one of the few but also most popular Black Muslim influencers, sits in the in-box. I follow her on Instagram, but so do about seventy-five thousand other people. An unread email from *Bloggingly* also sits in the in-box, and my heart starts to race. I click on the one from *Bloggingly*, and Nuri leans closer so she can see my phone.

"Yes, yes, yes!" I yell, jumping out of my chair. "We're back. We're fucking back!"

Nuri throws her arms around me, and I wipe away tears, all the emotions from this month, positive and negative, rising back up to the surface.

I click on the last unread email, the one from Raheema, a popular Black Muslim YouTuber and Instagrammer who's best known for her series where she breaks down current news topics while doing really stunning makeup looks. I've been following her forever.

> Dear Bri, Kat, and Rose:
> I'm reaching out to see if you would be interested in a collaboration that would include all of you being featured on my YouTube channel for a guest segment! I could interview you about advocacy and the role that teens have in creating change in today's digital age. It could also be a great opportunity to expand YTA's readership. Let me know what you think!
> All the best,
> Raheema

Nuri and I look at each other in shock.

"How did this happen?"

Nuri smiles. "Sis, I think you may have started a revolution."

ZAKAT

LULLWOOD, GEORGIA

I swing my legs as I sit on one of the benches that lines the smooth gravel path that winds through Lullwood, jamming to the music flowing through my headphones since only the trees are watching. My phone buzzes, snapping me out of my reverie, and I click on the text.

Bri: aksyejk YOU TRULY ASSUMED IS BACK UP!!!!!!!!!!!!

Elation rushes through me, and my hands shake as I pull up the blog.

"Oh my goodness."

There it is, *You Truly Assumed* in all its beauty. I hug my phone to my chest and skip down the path. It's back, we're back.

Me: WE BACK! WE BACK! WE BACK!

I put my arms out and spin, the woods blurring. I spin, and I spin, and I spin, taking in the dizziness. Because I now know that no matter how much the worlds spins, I can find my own orbit and my own stillness.

The masjid comes into view, the metal gate still up. I walk inside and remove my shoes, the feeling of home wrapping around me. I head to the Sunset Room, and Imam Farad smiles when she sees me.

"Zakat, it's nice to see you!"

I sink into an armchair. "Same here, Imam Farad."

"What can I do for you?"

"I had a quick note about the fence around the masjid. Would it be possible to consider getting rid of it? I completely understand why it was put up after the attack in DC, but I feel like Lullwood has come a long way since the beginning of the month. I don't want members of the community to feel like we have to dim ourselves because some people don't like our light."

"That's a good point, Zakat. Now that the person responsible for the incidents has been identified, Imam Bashir and I are planning to have a conversation with our security team about how we want to move forward."

"Sounds good. Thank you so much for listening."

"Of course." She smiles. "You've grown an incredible amount over this month, Zakat. You should be very proud of yourself."

I beam. "I am."

With Allah's grace, a lot of tears, my sketchbook, and Bri's and Farah's friendship, I made it through the anger, sadness, and fear. I couldn't be prouder of me.

★ ★ ★ ★ ★

I set my bowl of popcorn and box of candy on the night-stand next to my bed and pull up one of my favorite '90s rom-coms on my laptop. I snuggle deeper under my covers and prop my phone against my laptop.

"Okay, I'm ready," I say.

"Great. Okay, I'm sharing my screen now, so let me know if you all can't see the film," Bri says from a square next to the movie. "Today we'll relax, and tomorrow we'll work on answers for the questions for our first interview. We more than deserve a break."

"Big facts," Farah says, her square below Bri's on my screen.

You Truly Assumed movie night was Bri's idea. Every other week we're going to watch a movie together, and I get to choose the first one.

"Okay. One. Two. Three. Play."

I press Play, and the movie starts rolling.

"Yes, I love this movie," Bri says.

"I've never seen it," Farah says.

"What?" Bri and I both yell, and I almost knock over my bowl of popcorn.

"Then you're in for a life-changing experience," Bri says.

A wave of contentment washes over me as I laugh. Despite the hate comments and buckets of shed tears, I'm so glad I joined *You Truly Assumed*. Bri and Farah are such awesome people, and I'm happy that I get to call them my friends. Because even though *You Truly Assumed* is all about tapping into the power of one's voice and speaking out against hate, it's held together by friendship. That's what makes *You Truly Assumed* so special, and I hope it always keeps that spark.

FARAH

KIRBY, MASSACHUSETTS

The movie credits roll, and Bri blows a kiss while Zakat waves before both of them disappear from my screen. I pull out my earphones and disconnect from Zoom, elation filling my chest. I can't believe that the blog is really back. When I joined the Zoom for our planned movie night, Bri dropped it so casually that it took me a moment to fully register what she said. And then we were all screaming, and I'm surprised we didn't break my earphones. Now I know I need to check the *YTA* group chat more often.

I jump up off the bed, punching my fists in the air over and over. I type "You Truly Assumed blog" in the search engine bar and click on the first result that pops up. My eyes fill with tears as the pastel graphics appear on my phone, and I sniffle as I scroll through everything.

I sit down on my bed, wiping my cheeks. Everything—all the posts and images and graphics—is still here, and seeing the blog feels like returning home after a long trip away. We're back. Giddiness surges through me, warming me from the inside out, and I squeal. My hands shake as I switch to the phone app and dial Mom's number.

"Farah?"

"Mom, guess what, guess what, guess what!"

There's a soft rumbling noise in the background, like the sound of the coffeepot starting up, and I can see her perfectly sitting at the two-person dining room table scrolling through her phone to catch up on what she missed the night before. I wait for the familiar pang in my chest of being away from her, but it doesn't come as quickly.

"What happened?"

"Nothing bad! The blog is back up!"

"That's awesome, dear. I wish I could give you a hug right now. I'm so happy for you and your friends."

I pace back and forth across the bedroom, the soft carpet tickling my toes. "Don't worry, Mom, I can feel your hugs from here."

"I can't believe this month ends tomorrow. It seems like June zipped past."

"Don't remind me, Mom! That only means that school is getting closer."

Mom laughs, and I pocket the sound.

"How do you feel about leaving tomorrow?"

I sigh. "I'm actually a little sad, but only because I got a bit used to having siblings."

As much as I'm ready to be back home, I'm going to really miss Ally, Samson, and Emma. And even Tommy, to some degree. They made me like them enough that I'd actually consider coming back to visit. A lot.

"How was the vigil?"

"It was good. I'm glad that I was able to go."

Mom claps in the background. "That's a relief to hear. How do you feel?"

I pause, the question tumbling around in my head. Being surrounded by so many people who cared as much as I do and who have as much hope, if not more, was overwhelming in the best way possible.

"This sounds cheesy, but it's like someone superglued all the pieces I didn't know were broken back together. And now I'm going to come back to Inglethorne feeling whole."

June has been a whirlwind, but it taught me that I can belong to more than one place and not lose anything from the first. Inglethorne is always going to be my home, but now part of me belongs in Kirby too.

"I'm so glad that you were able to have this experience and that you called," Mom says. "It's always great to hear your voice. I love you."

"Love you too. I'll talk to you soon," I say.

I wait for her to hang up, the sting of the beep not as sharp as it was when I first got out here. I plug in my phone and then head downstairs. I follow Jess's hums to the kitchen, and she looks up at the sound of my footsteps.

I set my shoulders back. "Before I leave tomorrow, I wanted to thank you for letting me stay here this month. I know we didn't necessarily start off on the best note."

Jess rubs her hands against her apron, flour still coating her hands. "I'm very sorry about that. I knew that you previously didn't want to see Tommy, so when he told me that you were visiting less than a week before you arrived, I was worried about him. He cares about you a lot, and I didn't want to see him get hurt. But after talking to Ally about the vigil, I realized I wasn't coming from a place of understanding. Our family has been through a lot, and I didn't want Tommy or the kids to be disappointed because they were so excited for you to be here." She puts the cookies in the oven before turning back to face me, her expression open. "The kids and Tommy are pretty bummed that you're leaving, and I was thinking that the two of us could plan a surprise visit."

The apology feels genuine, and since I'm probably going to be spending more time with the family in the future, I don't see the harm in taking a chance and giving Jess a fresh start. Now that we're on the same page, I think we'll be able to really move forward and maybe even get to know each other.

I give her a small smile. "Yes, I'd be down."

"Great! And I should've said this when you first stepped into the door, but welcome to the family, Farah."

★ ★ ★ ★ ★

Raindrops splatter against my cheeks as I step outside the car. Tommy starts to open his car door, but I motion for him to stay in. If he gets out, he's going to make a scene, and then I'm going to feel more like the dreary gray skies above than I already do. Don't get me wrong, I'm ready to leave, but I didn't expect to be this bummed. I'm actually going to miss the kiddos, and even Tommy, more than I thought. They all somehow weaseled their way into a small sliver of my heart.

Tommy gets out of the car anyway and holds out his arms. I roll my eyes and hug him back.

"Don't be a stranger. You're welcome anytime. And even if you don't want to call me, please call your siblings. They're going to miss you."

"I'm going to miss them too." I pull back. "Thank you, Tommy."

"No, thank you, Farah. Thank you for giving your old man a chance."

I give him another quick hug.

"Text me when you land," Tommy says.

I tighten my grip on the handle of my suitcase. "I will."

"Bye, Farah," Ally and Samson yell, and Emma waves.

Jess gives me a small parting smile, and I return it. I might never be close with Jess, and I'm okay with that. But it's nice to leave with some semblance of understanding.

"Bye bye bye bye bye," Emma says.

"Come back to visit," Ally says, leaning out of the window.

"Yeah, you still have to come to one of my basketball games," Samson adds.

"I will," I say again over the traffic and the sounds of people saying their goodbyes.

I give one last wave and start heading toward the entrance of the airport. I look over my shoulder and see Tommy still standing there. He raises his hand, and I wave back. Then I turn and keep moving forward. This month wasn't what I expected it would be at all. It was far from perfect, but as I get in line to check in, I can't help but feel satisfied with how it ended up coming together.

Resting against my suitcase, I pull out my phone, the line

moving forward slower than Emma running after me when I took her Cheerios. I go to my photos, and I can't help but grin at the picture that Tommy took of Ally, Emma, and me yesterday. Of my sisters and me. It's the cutest thing ever, and I set it as my home screen photo.

My phone dings, and I look down to see a text from Bri, asking me if I'd be comfortable writing a section of the "we're back" post and, if not, it's no problem. At the beginning of the month, I would've laughed at the text. Me? Write? But even though I do a lot of behind-the-scenes stuff, and all of it's important, I know now that I can lead in front of the scenes too. I guess that means I'm onstage, but I'm okay with that because I'll be sharing the spotlight with Bri and Zakat. And I know that if I forget my lines, they've got my back.

So I inch forward and type back yes.

WE'RE BACK!!!

I thought this was going to be just another quiet summer full of ballet. I guess you can say that I truly assumed ;). This summer has moved at breakneck speed, and I can't believe it's already July. This past month has been full of new experiences, growth, and learning that sometimes the best moments of life are unplanned. Don't get me wrong, I still love my pro-con lists, but I've learned that going with my gut works too. Among the biggest takeaways from June are the friendships I've made. Working with Kat and Rose has taught me the value of taking chances. *YTA* wouldn't be *YTA* without the two of them.

I also think it's super cool to see how I've changed and how *YTA* has changed over the course of June by looking at the about page from then and now.

Then: Just a Black Muslim girl trying not to get caught up in the mix.

Now: Just a space for young Muslim women to simply be (and maybe sorta create change).

I couldn't be more excited about the future of *YTA*. And I can't wait to see all the wonderful posts you all submit *wink wink.* Here's to all the comment convos that have yet to be had. This journey is going to be incredible, Insha'Allah.

Until next post,
~Bri

Hi, Kat here:

At first, I was nervous about writing this because, seriously, you don't stop by *You Truly Assumed* for my words of wisdom. But if there's one thing I learned during the month of June, it's that there's so much value in expanding one's horizons. I've gained some of my closest friends, developed a more refined artistic voice, and become more comfortable with speaking for myself, even if it means ruffling a few feathers.

I've lived in an amazing tight-knit community for all of my life, and at times it felt impermeable to the harshness of the world. Though I knew hate existed, when I stepped digitally out of my community and began blogging on *You Truly Assumed* I wasn't prepared. Stepping out of my comfort zone and seeing so much hate hurt, and blogging started to feel like a roller coaster with really steep drops.

But a lot of people say life is just one big roller-coaster ride, and this month taught me that's true. But I'm all buckled in, and I've thrown my hands up. I hope you'll stick around—or get on board if you're new—for the wild ride. It's sure to be a good one!

Hi, hey, hello! It's Rose.

For those of you who don't know, I'm mostly responsible for making sure that everything on the blog looks nice and runs smoothly from a technological standpoint. When the blog got hacked, I was terrified. Despite my role in *YTA* being tech-related, I felt totally out of my element. There was nothing but darkness, on- and off-screen. But had none of us created light when we couldn't find it, we wouldn't be writing this post.

I guess what I'm trying to say is to take chances and to create the light when you can't find it. That's what *YTA* is built off of in a way. And also, you don't have to create the light alone. I don't think I would've gotten through this past month without Bri and Kat. They're truly amazing people.

Thank you, everyone, and I hope you continue to love and support *YTA*. Particularly since we're now open to submissions—but also just in general—I really want to end with this: don't be afraid to tell your story, in whatever form that takes for you. The world needs it.

* * * * *

ACKNOWLEDGMENTS

You Truly Assumed would not be out in the world without the generosity and support of so many people. To my wonderful agent, Kat Kerr, thank you so much for guiding me every step of the way and answering all of my questions at every turn. I'm grateful to be in partnership with you. To my editors, Natashya Wilson and Connolly Bottum, thank you for all of your work in helping to shape this book into the best possible version. To Gigi Lau and Alex Cabal, thank you for a cover direction and a cover design that are beyond my wildest dreams. I stare at the cover of *You Truly Assumed* at least once a day. Thank you to Bess Braswell, Brittany Mitchell, and the rest of the wonderful team at Inkyard Press.

To Adiba, thank you for believing in me and my story. I'm lucky to be able to call you a mentor and a friend.

Shout-out to the AMM Fam, especially round six. I'm glad that our paths crossed in such a wonderful way. Also, shout-out to the #MagicSprintingSquad for being my first writing community. You all's support, along with the writing sprints, helped so much when I was drafting this book. Aneeqah and Kris, thank you both for always having my back and motivating me to push on. Y'all are truly the best!

To my parents, thank you for always supporting me and giving me the space to follow my dreams. I know you both know way more about writing and publishing than you ever thought you would. And to my brothers, Murad, Kamal, and Jibril, I would not be who I am without you three.

So much of *You Truly Assumed* is about friendship, so to Hannah, Olivia, Helena, Gabrielle, Alyssa, Dasia, Madison, and Faith, I'm beyond glad to have you all and our friendships.

Thank you to literally anyone who's supported me or the book since I first started drafting it way back in 2017. It's been a journey and every kind word has helped me to get to this point.

To you, the reader, thank you for picking up *You Truly Assumed*. I hope you enjoyed the ride.

And lastly, to all the Black girls, especially Black Muslim girls, who've had people try to put them in one neat box, I see you and we're out here! *You Truly Assumed* is for you.